S

Mates

By

KA Moll

2015

Soul Mates © 2015 KA Moll
Triplicity Publishing, LLC

ISBN-13: 978-0996242943
ISBN-10: 0996242945

Printed in the United States of America
First Edition – 2015
Cover Design: Triplicity Publishing, LLC
Interior Design: Triplicity Publishing, LLC
Editor: Lauren Weiler - Triplicity Publishing, LLC

Acknowledgements

Soul Mates is special to me for so many reasons. You'd think the fact that it was my first novel would be the most important, but I'm not sure that it is. I think for me the most important reason is the heart of the story itself–that each of us has a person out there who makes us whole–each has a soul mate. I thank God for mine, each and every day.

My wife, Kay, has been so patient and supportive through this process of birthing a book. I couldn't have done it without her. She deserves so much more than what I'll ever have to give. She's my number one everything–my soul mate. *Amo te.*

I offer special thanks to my beta readers—Mary Alice, Paula, Cindy, Maureen, Jennifer, Valerie—and of course, Kay. Some of you, especially my wife, suffered through more than one of my early drafts. You helped this book become what it is today.

Last, but certainly not least, I offer thanks to my publisher; And to my editor, Lauren Weiler. Your insight and attention to detail were amazing.

<u>Dedication</u>

For Kay—my wife, my soul mate, and my very best friend.

Also by the Author

Coming to Terms

Prologue — More than a decade ago.

"Sex isn't everything you know," Zane yelled to Ashley as she made her way to the door.

Ashley paused to glare. "Maybe not, but I'm done. You're a sexually stunted freak and you know it."

Zane hurled her mug toward the counter as the door slammed. It hit the edge and smashed into a million tiny shards. Coffee splattered everywhere. Her blue dress shirt was ruined. Her stack of unopened mail was soaked. It was a mess—her life and the kitchen. She grabbed a towel, tossed the mail into the sink, and began to mop.

Ashley had been the most recent in her long string of short-term girlfriends. She, like the others, had managed to hit Zane's issues dead-on. Her words were said in anger, but they were accurate and hurtful. Zane was angry too, but not at Ashley. How could she be angry with someone for calling a spade a spade? In her heart, she knew what Ashley knew after only three dates that she had serious issues with intimacy, issues that she'd never had the courage to face. Loving girls was easy. Being a lesbian was hard. The technicalities had always fouled her up. She flopped into the overstuffed chair by the window, ran her fingers through her hair, and swatted the solitary tear that dared to trickle down her cheek.

Zane's life experience had quite simply crushed her. She stared out the window as her mind drifted to memories from long ago. The sweet smell of her mom's apple pie was such a contrast to the acidic burn of her words.

"You try too hard to be like the world," Nancy Winslow had said.

Zane could still see her mom's pinched lips and feel her glare.

"You'll never amount to anything if you walk that path," Nancy had said, "and you'll not walk that path in this God-fearing home."

Zane couldn't hush her mom's venom. It was as if her mind had a mind of its own, forcing her, day after day, to revisit the unimaginable. She dropped her head into her palms.

When the doorbell rang, Zane got up to answer. Thank God it was Drew. This was one of those times when she needed to talk with her very best friend. Drew was special, like no other friend she'd ever had. Friends since they were freshman, their friendship was one that had never been complicated by attraction, not even in the early days. And yet, they loved each other. Life after graduation on Sunday would never be the same. It was to be a time of new adventures and new beginnings, but Zane knew that what it really was, was a time for endings and goodbyes.

"I'm not going," Zane said softly.

Drew looked into her eyes. "I know. I figured as much when you didn't get any of the paperwork from UCLA. I was just waiting for you to tell me."

"It would've been a wasted effort," Zane said with a sigh. "Can you see me as a lawyer?" She shook her head. "I certainly can't."

"So what's your plan?" Drew asked.

"I don't know," Zane said. "I don't really have one, I guess. By the time I need one, I will."

"I know you will," Drew said. "You always do."

Drew had popped by in hopes that Zane would join her for dinner. Zane hadn't been herself lately and she was worried. She'd asked her about it, but Zane had let on like everything was okay. Drew knew that it wasn't. Going out for a burger was her best idea. At least that would get Zane out of her dark apartment.

"Not tonight," Zane said. "I've got too much to get done before finals." Her eyes broke away and then looked back. "I'll catch you before class tomorrow…okay?"

"Sure," Drew said, "tomorrow's good." She released a long, slow sigh. So much for getting Zane out into the sunshine. "It'll be okay, Zane. It will. You'll see." She paused, but Zane didn't respond. "You know how you are," she continued. "You fret, and then pass with all As. Just relax and try to cheer up."

"I will," Zane said. "See ya tomorrow, okay?"

"Yeah," Drew said, "tomorrow."

***

The antique clock ticked on the worn old mantle. It soothed Zane in a familiar sort of way. She looked up as the timepiece struck 11:00, leaned back in her over-stuffed chair, and took another sip of freshly brewed cinnamon-nutmeg coffee.

Zane had always been a person prone to distractions. No one had been surprised when her second grade teacher had pointed out the flaw. She was a daydreamer. Unfortunately, daydreaming didn't lend

3

KA Moll

itself well to study. This was especially true for Latin, a subject she'd hated in high school, and for no good reason at all, had taken in college. There was only so much of that beastly foreign language that she could tolerate in one sitting. She closed her textbook, picked up her cup of coffee, and headed for the garage.

The engine of the old Thunderbird convertible started with a rumble. Car lights flashed into the rearview mirror and Zane caught a glimpse of her chestnut hair as it whipped around her collar. She made a mental note to get a haircut. Zane cranked the volume and smooth jazz boomed through high-end speakers. It was a perfect night for a ride. She loved this car, not just because she was an eye catcher, but also because she was the very last gift from her dad. She'd been his baby from 1980 until the day he died. Now hers, Zane had discovered that the beautiful girl had a most extraordinary power. She silenced demons. Zane wondered if the car had provided the same service to her dad.

***

The trip to O'Hare was permeated by deafening silence. Both Zane and Drew were wrapped up in their own thoughts—the process of separation having already begun. Soon, they'd unload Drew's bags and check her in at the airport. She'd be gone. Her lifelong dream to produce documentary films was about to begin. Drew should have been ecstatic as she prepared to board that flight to LA. The UCLA graduate program in television and film was top notch and all she'd been able to talk about for months. She should have been ecstatic, but she wasn't. Instead, she was worried about Zane.

"You'd better stay in touch with me," Drew said. "I get that you need to get your head together, but don't you make me hunt you down someday." She moved into Zane's space. "Do you hear me?" Her eyes locked on— dead serious. "I'd better not have to move heaven and earth to find you."

"I hear you," Zane said. "Now go. You're gonna miss your flight." She choked and looked away as Drew walked up the ramp to board the airplane. "I'll miss you, my friend." A stream of tears left a taste of salt in her mouth.

***

Sarasota was a gorgeous 80 degrees and sunny with just enough clouds to cut the glare. It was perfect weather for the proudest day of Jaina Wakefield's life. A chill shivered through her body as she stepped onto the podium to accept her University of South Florida diploma. She didn't have what it took to use her degree in social work, but it had a purpose nevertheless. She'd earned it, and no one could ever take it away.

"Congratulations Ms. Wakefield," the dean said with a firm handshake, "and good luck."

Jaina looked into the audience, searching. Her gaze finally rested on the only pair of eyes that were there for her. She smiled. Miss Bonnie had come just as she'd promised. In a way, it surprised her. But in a way, it didn't.

Jaina had grown used to loss and disappointment in the course of her lifetime. It was just the way things had always worked out. Miss Bonnie was one of the very few people that she could rely on. She was there for her that day when her adoptive parents had thrown her away like a piece of garbage. She'd been there every time she'd needed her since.

Jaina's thoughts whipped back without warning to the day she became an orphan—the day she turned 11 years old. She remembered standing on the cold cement steps waiting for the door to open, clinging to the black plastic bag that held all of her earthly possessions. The demoralizing words of the heartless woman who'd thrown her away resonated in her mind.

"This'll be your new home," the cold-eyed woman had said. "You blew it with us, now don't blow it with these people."

The same shiver that traversed her body that day traversed it again.

***

Miss Bonnie was a soft-hearted African American woman. Born and raised in Florida, she'd had the urge to travel north for college. Jaina wasn't sure why, but she'd wanted her MSW to be from the University of Illinois. Miss Bonnie's first job as a social worker had been at the Loving Arms Group Home in Sarasota. It suited her, and she stayed until she retired.

She'd been the one to open the door that morning. She'd opened it, and without a moment's hesitation had opened her arms as well. Her hug had been the kind of hug a kid like Jaina could snuggle into, one like she hadn't experienced since she was three years old. Miss Bonnie had been there to comfort her on that awful day and was here to celebrate with her on this one. She was different than all the rest. She was trustworthy.

"You came," Jaina whispered into the crowd. She blinked back insistent tears. "You came."

Chapter One

Zane stared out her office window, deep in thought. There was just something about the autumn colors, crimson, gold, orange, and blue, that touched her soul. She loved this town, Champaign-Urbana, home of the Fighting Illini. It was a good fit, as good a fit as her hometown just a few miles south had been a bad one. In fact, this town, this town of her Alma Mater, was one of the few perfect fits that she had ever experienced in her life.

Her daydreaming had always been quite random. It usually occurred with little notice and could literally be about anything. Today, Zane was pondering beginnings, why for some they came so easy and for others, so hard. She'd always found beginning something new to be about as easy as pulling out a tooth with a pair of pliers while looking into the bathroom mirror. This morning, it was the beginning of this week's sermon that had brought the flaw to mind. Ten drafts, 10 wads of perfectly crumpled paper tossed expertly in the waste basket. It was Tuesday morning. Wednesday afternoon was her deadline. The first paragraph had yet to be written. She squinted and once again tried to rein in her mind.

***

Soul Mates

Twelve-hundred-twenty-five miles south of Champaign-Urbana, Jaina slept fitfully. Her strange and all too familiar nightmare had once again reared its ugly head, grabbing her by the throat and making her gasp. The grotesqueness of it all left her trembling—panicked. It shook her soul. She'd been trapped again, trapped in an all-too real, and yet unnatural, world of a night terror. Just Jaina and a talking cat—a talking cat who looked a whole lot like Fur Ball. Together, they'd clawed to escape, as they'd done the night before and the one before that. She awoke from the early evening unplanned nap to a racing pulse, a body dripping with sweat, and an unshakeable feeling that she had to find her brother as quickly as she could. Jaina lunged forward in her chair as Fur Ball went flying off her lap. He turned to hiss. She tried to pet him and apologized.

Jaina had settled into her Lazy Boy for a minute—one minute to rest after a long day on her feet. She'd planned to get right back up knowing that her cat wasn't a patient feline. He needed, no, he wanted his dinner within minutes of the time she got home from work. Maybe all cats were like that. She wasn't sure. Unfortunately, this evening she'd fallen asleep, something that she didn't dare do lately without risking a heart attack. The recent nightmares had left her sleep deprived, almost crazy. She didn't know what to do. She wanted to tell someone, but there was no one to tell. She had her cat, her job at the deli, and that was all. She felt scared and vulnerable—alone. It was no surprise that her thoughts turned to Miss Bonnie. They always did when she had a problem that she couldn't fix on her own. She looked up her number and dialed.

It didn't matter how many months passed between their contact. It didn't matter whether they saw each other in person or called. Miss Bonnie and Jaina could always pick right up where they left off. When the bell rang, Jaina set down her tea and ran to the door. She knew a hug would be waiting for her on the other side.

"Oh, my God," Jaina exclaimed. "You look good!" She shook her head. "Wow! How much weight have you lost?"

Miss Bonnie twirled. "Ninety-five pounds." She grinned with pride. "Just 70 to go." "Now, you on the other hand, don't look too good at all."

Jaina smiled a thin smile. "No, I'm not. You always could tack me to the wall."

"Yep," Miss Bonnie said with another hug. "Like a pro."

***

Long term commitments, whether to a job or another person, were never in Jaina's comfort zone. That's how a person got hurt and she'd already experienced enough hurt for a lifetime. Miss Bonnie was pretty much her only exception. She'd hung on over the years, even when Jaina had tried her hardest to shake loose. She'd proven herself to be worthy of at least a certain amount of risk.

Jaina ran. Miss Bonnie waited—time, after time, after time. Curfew violations and juvenile arrests always met with a stern look, but never abandonment. God knows Jaina did everything in her power when she was a teen to push people away, but Miss Bonnie had stuck with her. If Jaina was being honest with herself, she'd admit she'd grown to love the older woman. She'd grown to love Miss Bonnie like the mom she'd never really known. But she couldn't be that honest, not with herself, and not with her friend. It was too risky.

Miss Bonnie reached into her flowered purse, that is, if something that big could actually be called a purse. It was really more like an overnight bag that she always carried with her. It was her own personal, albeit quite eccentric, fashion statement.

"You looking for the kitchen sink in there?" Jaina asked with a chuckle.

"No. Now you hush girl," Miss Bonnie scolded. "I'm looking for your birthday present." She kept rummaging. "I know it's in here somewhere."

Jaina tried to catch the emotion lodged in her throat. "You never forget...do you." She took a sip of tea and looked out the window.

Miss Bonnie shook her head. "Nope, never do. It's an important day." She met Jaina's gaze and smiled. "It's the day we met and the day you were born, a very important day indeed." She continued digging with a look of pure determination on her face. "Ah, here it is." She pulled out a wrapped box. "Happy 36th birthday, sweetie."

Jaina took the small box, then gave it a few playful shakes. "What'd you get me?"

Miss Bonnie gave Jaina the "I shouldn't have to tell you this" look. "If I told you, it would spoil the fun of the surprise." She took a sip of sweet tea. "Go ahead girl, open it."

Jaina untied the strand of ribbon, tore the wrapping, and opened the tiny box. It contained a shiny gold locket with a sparkling star. She pulled it's clasp to look inside. Never in a million years would she have done it had she known it would hold the last portrait of her family. Never would she have made the choice to be pummeled by memories from her childhood.

Jaina bolted. She ran full tilt through the yard, came back in the side door of the garage, and dropped in the driver's seat of her Echo. Tears trickled down her cheeks as she opened the locket for a second time. This time, the images whisked her back to happy days, to moments she hadn't thought about in years; snuggling with her mom on the old porch swing; going to church as a family; playing in the park with her brother. Jimmy— God, she loved him so much. Jaina had no more than smiled when the pleasant images were ripped away and replaced by painful ones. It was the story of her life.

***

Miss Bonnie leaned back and took a sip of sweet tea. Jaina had run before she'd had a chance to tell her just how special that little locket was. This wasn't the first time that Jaina's feelings had terrified her enough to run, and it wouldn't be the last.

Jaina came back through the door within the hour. Her eyes looked so sad. They never failed to break Miss Bonnie's heart. Out of all the kids she'd worked with over the years, Jaina was the only one she loved like her very own child. Every time she gazed into those eyes, she just wanted to make things better. It'd been like that from the start.

"Mmm...you make the best sweet tea," Miss Bonnie said with another sip. "You cook in that sugar to make it taste really good." She picked up the paperback that Jaina had obviously been reading. "Intriguing ..." She looked up. "I didn't know you were interested in dream interpretation."

Jaina scowled, then sighed. "I wasn't...until recently." She got up and headed for the kitchen, then returned with a plate full of sugar-free Oreos. "I'm sorry about earlier."

"You have nothing to be sorry about," Miss Bonnie said as she reached for a cookie. She took a bite as her gaze drifted out the window. Her voice was soft. "That locket's very old." She paused. "It was one of my mama's favorites." A tender smile crossed her face. "Mama always did love her lockets. I have 'em all now that she's gone—all except that one." Her eyes returned to Jaina. "I wanted you to have it." Miss Bonnie looked down and mindlessly began to pet Fur Ball. "It was just a coincidence that I ran across those old pictures. I wouldn't have had I not had to clean out my desk when I retired. Fate, I guess. But when I found 'em, I knew exactly where they belonged."

***

Jaina screamed bloody murder. She lay gasping as Fur Ball jumped off the bed. He hissed on his way out. Not again! Even after she'd followed all of Miss Bonnie's suggestions, including the one that involved warm milk. She'd consumed a full glass of that nasty liquid for nothing. She peeled loose of her drenched sheets, reached for the phone, and dialed.

***

They met for dinner at their favorite restaurant. Once the meal was finished, both leaned back to suck in air. Somehow that always seemed to make a little extra room for digestion.

The too-friendly waitress paused beside their table…again…to top off their drinks. "Are you sure I can't tempt you two with dessert?"

"Nope," Jaina said. "One of us is on a diet." She broke eye contact with the waitress. Finally the cute redhead got the hint and moved along.

Miss Bonnie just shook her head. "So this is my second call in one week. Normally, I get two in a year. If I'm lucky, I get a third on my birthday." She pursed her lips and pinched her brow. "Why don't you just go on and tell me what's really bothering you."

Jaina gave her the look. "Okay …" She sucked in a breath, the kind you suck in when you know you're going to swim underwater. "I'm having these weird dreams and they're driving me crazy. There…that's it." She looked pleadingly into the pair of eyes that she hoped held answers. "Now please, tell me what I need to do to make them stop, and don't even think about suggesting warm milk. That didn't work."

Miss Bonnie leaned back. Her expression became pensive. "Hmm…dreams are funny things. They can be a little weird sometimes. They'll twist your reality to something that's a bit unreal. It's unreal, but you believe 'em anyway. You believe 'em, because in that moment you're in 'em." Her eyes met Jaina's. "I think your subconscious is trying to talk to you, sweetie. If you want my opinion, I think you probably ought to listen."

Jaina *was* listening. The nightmares and ongoing sleep deprivation had definitely gotten her undivided attention. She took another breath and described the nightmares the best she could. She saved the most disturbing part until last for no particular reason. It was just the way she was wired. When Jaina mentioned Jimmy, she could tell that Miss Bonnie knew they'd touched on the heart of the problem.

Miss Bonnie gazed out the window and back. She was gathering her thoughts. "I've always believed that life was a series of connections, all interwoven like a fabric. Blood connections are the strongest." She shook her head. "You can feel them sometimes, even when you don't know their source. I think you've been feeling one of those connections in your dreams, one that's really powerful." She lifted her shoulders in an *I don't know*. "Maybe your brother's in trouble, maybe he's not. Maybe he needs help, maybe he doesn't." Her eyes locked with Jaina's. "Maybe it's you who has the need. Maybe it's a need that you haven't been able to acknowledge. Whatever it is, I think you need to explore it."

Jaina's brain was on overload. She felt like a deer must feel when it gets caught in the headlights. She had much to think about. Thank goodness Miss Bonnie knew her well enough to suggest they call it a night.

"See you tomorrow," Jaina called out as she dropped into the Echo.

"I'll be ready." Miss Bonnie said. "Bring your appetite."

***

Take a shower. Dress in a pair of comfy pajamas. Do the crossword. Watch the nine o'clock news. Go to bed. Sleep without nightmares. That was Jaina's plan for the rest of her evening. She shed her clothes and stepped under the hot spray.

Tomorrow would be a busy day. Fridays always were, both at work and in the social arena. People got paid on Fridays. Jaina played on Fridays. Fridays were for getting drunk, sleeping with a stranger, and then getting on her way before the woman knew her too well. Fridays were about working hard and playing harder. They always had been and probably always would be.

Jaina lulled herself to sleep with thoughts of her last Friday out—two weeks ago. She'd spent almost that entire evening wooing a gorgeous blonde at her favorite tiki bar near Siesta Key, kind of a cute place with straw accents and brightly painted walls. Behind the building, white beach and water stretched for what seemed like miles. She loved that place, loved the salty breeze, and loved that it was always full of hot women. Some lesbians, some not. All tourists who would head back to whoever and wherever once their Florida vacation was over. She was free to be who she was, a sexy stop along the way. It was her perfect sexual hunting ground.

The blonde had begged her to stay. They usually did, but Jaina didn't cave. It wasn't her style. Hot sex— one way—was all she ever wanted. She laid it all out upfront in a verbal contract. That way there were no surprises when it was over—no expectations—no hurt feelings. She had rules, simple rules designed to protect herself. The most important one was to never bring a woman to her home. That way, Jaina could always leave when she wanted. She could leave when she was done.

That night, Jaina slept like she hadn't slept in what seemed like ages. She'd slept nightmare free and couldn't help but wonder what had made the difference. It wasn't warm milk because she hadn't had any.

***

Miss Bonnie had given a lot more thought to Jaina's situation by the time the Echo chugged into her driveway. Jaina's dilemma about whether to embark on a search for Jimmy was a tough one, but she had to make the decision on her own. All Miss Bonnie could do was provide her with information so that her decision would be well informed. She may have retired, but she still had the skill and experience of a seasoned social worker. Tonight, she'd share all she knew of Jaina's adoption and how she might go about a search for her bio-family. She hoped that what she had to offer would be enough.

Much of what Miss Bonnie ended up sharing was new to Jaina. It was information she'd never been able to listen to before. This time she seemed to absorb it like a sponge. She listened intently as Miss Bonnie shared the reasons behind her adoptive parents' move from Illinois to Florida, asked questions about the group home that had facilitated her adoption, and even took notes about the church with which the agency had been affiliated.

Each adoptee approaches the topic of his or her own adoption in their own way. Some speak freely about the fact that they were adopted and some don't. Some long to connect with their bio-family and some never do. Miss Bonnie watched as Jaina assimilated each new piece of information, fully expecting her to bolt for the door at any moment. She didn't.

Miss Bonnie lifted herself up from the rocker and stepped behind Jaina's chair. She began to rub her shoulders. "You doing okay with all of this?"

Jaina cracked a slight smile. "Yeah, I think so." She looked up into her friend's brown eyes. "To be honest, I'm blown away. It's a lot to take in all at once."

"It is, child," Miss Bonnie said. "And there's no hurry, no hurry at all. You take it at your own pace. Search, if and when you want." She sat back down and began to rock. If Jaina decided to do this, she'd be in Illinois searching all by herself. She'd need all the nuts and bolts of the process. Miss Bonnie ticked through her list to be sure that she hadn't left something out.

"So," Jaina asked, "if I want to, I can contact the adoption registry and give them permission to release my name and contact information to my mom and brother? And my dad too?" Jaina looked down, then back up. "Even though he was never part of our family?" She took a breath and released it slowly. "But that's only if they want it, right?"

"That's right, child. Any or all of 'em might already be signed up. You won't know until you try. If they are, you'll be able to get in contact with each other easy." Miss Bonnie had gone onto the Illinois website to print off the necessary forms. She handed them to Jaina. "Here, just in case."

Jaina's eyes widened. "Wow, there's a lot to this." She picked up the first of several forms. "I might as well get started."

Chapter Two

Zane heard footsteps in the hall. She tilted her head and tried to figure out whose they were. They seemed vaguely familiar, but weren't ones she immediately recognized.

"Trouble getting your thoughts together?" a familiar voice asked.

Zane looked up and her mouth dropped open.

"Some things never change," Drew said as she leaned just inside the door. Her grin was about as wide as the entrance. "Always did choose a pencil over a computer."

Zane bound toward her friend. "I can't believe it." They shook hands and hugged. "It's so good to see you again." Their gaze held on. "It's been way too long."

"That it has," Drew said, "and I had one heck of a time finding you." She shook her head. "Should've known you'd never leave this place." She stepped back to take a closer look. "And just look at you. Who'd have thought?"

Zane peered into her old friend's eyes, then out the window. "Yeah, who'd have thought?"

Curious how there are just some people that you click with, people who are so in sync with you that years can pass, even a decade, and you pick right up where you left off. Zane knew it would be like that if she ever saw Drew again. It was.

"I thought I told you not to make me hunt you down," Drew scolded.

Zane looked down then back up to meet her eye. "Yeah, I know…and I'm sorry. I was just so mixed up back then." She smiled the thinnest smile. "I still am, but hopefully not quite as much."

"I know," Drew said, "and it's alright." She straightened her friend's pastoral collar with pride. "I'm waiting for you to tell me how all this came about."

Zane grinned. "I'll tell you over dinner. How about 6:00?"

Drew nodded. "You're on!"

***

A soft knock called their attention to the door. The stylish older woman popped her head inside. In less than a second, her body followed.

"Oh, I'm sorry," the woman said. "Forgive me, Pastor. I didn't know you had someone in your office with you."

"That's okay," Zane said with a warm smile. You just provided me with a perfect opportunity to make introductions."

Irene McGillis was an organized and efficient church secretary. She was a perfect fit for Zane. Without her, Zane knew she would never get anything done. She was one of those people who just naturally used every minute wisely. She met Zane's gaze, a reminder that it was time for her to get back on task.

"I have a young lady on hold," Irene said. "She insists she speak with you immediately." Irene shook her head. "I explained to her that you were in the process of writing your sermon. At that particular moment, I thought you were. I told her you'd prefer to call her back." She pursed her lips. "The woman simply will not take no for an answer." She pinched her brow into a frown. "It has something to do with the adoption service we used to have in the rear wing."

"Thanks," Zane said. "I'll take her call in a minute."

Irene cocked her head and again met Zane's eye. "And don't forget…I need your sermon by noon tomorrow."

Zane nodded. "And you shall have it." She winked and flashed a grin.

Irene winked back, then scampered to her desk.

"Well, I'd better let you get back to work," Drew said. "It appears you have a deadline."

"She keeps me on track," Zane said with a chuckle as she scribbled down directions to the parsonage. They shook hands. Both held on for an extra moment.

"Drew," Zane called out as her friend stepped just outside the door.

Drew paused and turned around.

"It really is good to see you again," Zane said.

Drew nodded. "Yeah, for me too."

***

The parsonage was a delightful old Victorian near downtown Champaign. It had been lovingly cared for by

Zane's congregation since 1875. Back then, its location had been closer to the church building. The congregation still kept her as their parsonage even though she was now on the other side of town. She was a special house, a sight to behold, and a show place for the older neighborhood in which she stood. The painted lady was another perfect fit for Zane. At 6:00 sharp a silver Lamborghini Roadster rolled into her driveway.

"You certainly are full of surprises," Zane called out as she stepped onto the front porch. "Boy, will my neighbors ever be keeping an eye on me tonight." She chuckled. "And I don't even want to think about what the talk will be on Sunday morning."

Drew climbed the steps and pressed the button on her key chain. The locks clicked and the horn sounded. "I couldn't afford it on my own. It's way more than half Stacey's." She raised her eyebrow. "One of our toys."

"Oh yeah, some toy," Zane said. "Man, you've really done well for yourself." She looked again at the fancy car parked in her driveway. "And I believe we need to take that out for a spin later on."

Zane had followed her friend's career over the years. She knew that Drew had produced a couple IMAX documentaries and figured that she was financially pretty well off. As she stepped back inside, Zane realized that she'd underestimated just how well off she was.

Drew paused next to the old porch swing before she followed. It was so different here, like visiting another world. She inhaled a deep breath of crisp, clean air. Her pulse slowed and her stress level bottomed out.

"Ah…this is the life," Drew said as she sucked in another deep breath. "I'd almost forgotten what real fresh air smelled like. We've got the chemically, not-soenhanced version back home. You're one lucky dog, Zane Winslow." She stepped inside the door and once again paused to look around. "Wow, this is gorgeous." A grin stretched wide across her mouth. "Stacey's gonna love this place." She sniffed. "Are you cooking? Oh, my God, you are." Her eyes widened in shock. "When did that start?"

***

Zane had left her office early that afternoon. She wanted to be sure she had enough time to make a grocery store run, chop the vegetables, and get dinner in the oven—all of which were accomplished ahead of schedule. She loved to cook, loved gourmet food, and loved to entertain. It didn't matter whether it was for one or 20, she loved it just the same. It was hard for her to believe that some never took the time to prepare a fine meal just because they lived alone. She looked up from the stove and grinned. "Chicken cordon bleu with prosciutto wrapped asparagus." She raised her eyebrows a couple times. "I thought I'd show off."

Drew leaned inside the doorway to watch the final steps of meal preparation. Their talk was mostly meaningful, but sometimes not. It felt easy to be together again, like they'd never been apart. "You'll like Stacey." Her smile seemed faraway, maybe with her wife. "She completes me like I never thought another person could." When Drew looked back her eyes were moist.

Zane met her gaze. "I used to dream of having someone. You know that." She shook her head and looked deep into the sauce that she was stirring on the stove. "I don't anymore. It's best to not hope for things that aren't ever going to be a reality." Again, she shook her head. "Nothing's really changed, you know."

"Hey, don't give up," Drew said. "Someday you're gonna find her. You'll find the right woman where you least expect—just like I found Stacey."

Zane smiled a half-hearted smile. "Yeah…I'm sure I will."

***

They reminisced, hardly noticing the decade that had passed. Many things had changed, but many things hadn't. The talk was fast, furious, and non-stop. Drew wasn't surprised that Zane's call to the ministry had occurred just days after their graduation from college. She also wasn't surprised when Zane admitted to the severe bout of depression that she'd suspected all along. The only thing that really surprised her involved the Thunderbird; That Zane believed she had a spirit of her own, like an angel sent by God; That the car had been responsible for Zane's call to the ministry and possibly for saving her life.

Zane knew that her belief was somewhat unorthodox. She'd just never been able to come up with a more reasonable explanation for the circumstances of that night—for the direct route the Thunderbird had taken to Pastor Kate. She'd helped Zane through a dark moment many moons before—maybe the darkest of her life. Zane had thought about her and wondered if talking with her once again might help, but she didn't know where she was. Zane remembered mindlessly driving through campustown. There'd been nowhere to park. Then, a car pulled out. She'd turned off the engine and looked up.

Pastor Kate had been standing in the doorway of her ONA church. It had to be divine intervention. It had to be God's hand driving the car. They'd talked for hours, talked until Zane had no more words. It was in the silence that followed that she heard God's call.

Drew shivered as she listened to Zane's story. "I should've stayed," she said softly. "I knew you were depressed when I left. I shouldn't have gone."

"It was as it was supposed to be. God's will," Zane said as she met Drew's gaze. She stood and began to stack the dishes. "So, you never did say how you found me."

"I called your mom," Drew said in a matter-of-fact tone. "I remembered that she lived just south of here so I got her number from information and called." She grinned, obviously proud of her accomplishment. "She gave me directions and I showed up at your door."

Zane felt the blood drain from her face. She sucked in a breath. Her mouth hung open. "She knows I'm here?" She sucked in another. "Oh dear God, she knows where I am?" And a few more quick breaths. "She knows what I do…Oh, God…"

Drew reached over and laid her hand on Zane's shoulder. "Take it easy. I think she's worked through whatever it was that you two had going on. She seemed fine. She misses you."

Zane jumped up from the table. She grabbed the stack of dishes and dashed to the kitchen. "I'll be back." Once out of sight, she collapsed against the counter, frozen as images from that awful day flashed through her mind.

Zane recalled walking down the stairway, setting down her suitcase, and looking around. She didn't know for sure how long she'd stood there, but it was a long time. All she knew was that it was long enough to soak in a lifetime's worth of home. Her mom's final words roared from the past, assaulting her eardrums.

"If you leave here tonight," her mom had screamed, "don't ever think you're coming home."

Zane remembered turning and slowly walking toward the door.

She heard her mom's scream again as if she were beside her. "Zane," she'd cried out, "your father will be heartbroken if you leave."

The screen door snapped shut in her mind. The stairs squeaked under her weight. Zane remembered thinking that it was probably the last time she'd hear their sound.

Chapter Three

The old steps creaked, as they had the day Zane left home at 17 and as they had the day of her dad's funeral. The old steps creaked. They always had. Zane's heart thumped wildly as she climbed them toward the front door of her childhood home. Her adrenaline pumped. She was primed and ready to flee at the first hint of danger. It'd been years since she'd climbed these steps and years since she'd seen Nancy Winslow. A week ago, the thought of standing on this porch wouldn't have even crossed her mind. Now, as she raised her finger to the doorbell, Zane contemplated how it had come to be, that today was the day she'd chosen to re-establish contact with her mom. Within a few moments the door opened.

"Hello Zane," Nancy said. Her greeting was as if she'd been expecting to see her daughter standing at the door, but she hadn't. Zane's decision to visit had been made on the spur of the moment.

"Hello, Mom." Zane's voice cracked.

"Well, are you going to come in or just stand there?" Nancy nudged the door open a little wider.

Zane stepped inside.

"I just took an apple pie out of the oven," Nancy announced. "Do you want a piece?"

The experience was surreal. It was as if Zane stopped by every day, like a person might stop into a coffee shop on their way home from work. She'd not spoken to her mom since the day of her dad's funeral. Zane considered how many years had passed. She'd been a junior in college. You'd have to go back further than that, to the day she'd left home, for a conversation that wasn't superficial and meaningless. Today, after all these years, there was no *welcome home*, no *I've missed you*, and not even a *what are you doing here? Get off my porch*. Just, "Do you want a piece of pie?"

"Yeah," Zane answered. "A piece of pie would be good." She made her way to the seat that used to be hers. The slice was waiting. As she ate, Zane tried to recall if she'd ever seen her mom smile, if she'd ever seen her…happy. She didn't think that she had.

Nancy had nothing of importance to say nor to ask during their time of pie sharing. It was as if the visit was just routine, like they'd never been apart. Not a routine like families who love each other fall into a routine, but more like a "nothing interesting has occurred since I last saw you" routine. There was no mention of that day—that day that everything changed. It was as if it had been the most typical of days, and yet they both knew that it wasn't. It was a horrid, life-changing day that Zane was unable to forget regardless of how hard she tried. It was a day that she wished her mom had cared enough about to mention.

Zane recollected coming home from school later than usual and terribly upset. She'd tried to tell her mom about what had happened. Nancy didn't care, wouldn't listen. She'd just continued frying her chicken. She didn't even look up when her daughter began to choke back sobs. Her mom hadn't pulled her nose out of that pan until Zane blurted out that it had happened because she was gay. Then, Nancy was all about it.

Eat pie. Talk about all things that don't matter—weather, gas prices, and the price of corn. Say goodbye. Zane walked down the creaky steps and slid under the wheel of the old Thunderbird. For an instant, she had the strangest feeling that her dad slid in beside her.

***

It had been a week since Jaina had spoken with the pastor and just over a week since she'd mailed the form. Still, her mind was totally preoccupied. She tried not to care what information came back from Illinois, but she did, and she couldn't stop thinking about it. In a last ditch effort to distract herself, she headed for her favorite recreational spot, the tiki bar on Siesta Key. It was the one place she could relax and be herself.

Jaina loved women. She had an uncanny sense of what they wanted. It was like her special talent—a gift. She knew how to make women come harder than they'd ever come before, knew how to leave them gasping.

"Mmm…you're so good," the redhead said as she made efforts to reciprocate. "Come on, baby. Let me take care of you too."

"No way," Jaina said as she pushed away the woman's hand. "That's not how it's gonna go. I told you the rules when we started. I do all the touching." She pushed the woman down. "Lay back, I'll do you again before I leave."

Not wanting to be touched wasn't about feeling embarrassed. Jaina knew she looked good—long blonde hair, sky blue eyes, and tight jeans. There was no doubt that hot women found her attractive. It also wasn't that she didn't feel desire or enjoy an orgasm. No, she felt desire alright, and who doesn't enjoy an orgasm? It was simply that she didn't care to be touched. Being touched by another woman was too risky—too personal.

***

Jaina had called Miss Bonnie within minutes of receiving the long-awaited envelope. Her friend had thrown on her clothes and hurried across town.

"I wonder how come she didn't keep us," Jaina asked softly. She looked up with those eyes.

Miss Bonnie pulled her into her tightest hug. "I'm sure she wanted to, child. She probably just hit some kind of rough patch. We all hit rough patches from time to time in our lives."

They sifted through the thick packet of information together. It was full of clues, but few answers. Jaina had hoped for more—about her mom, about her brother, and about who she'd been before her family had shattered. She was disappointed.

"Maybe you need to take a trip to Illinois," Miss Bonnie suggested, "do some digging on your own. I could stay here and take care of Fur Ball."

"I don't know," Jaina said with an uncertain tone. "You really think I should go? I wouldn't even know where to begin."

Miss Bonnie hugged Jaina again. "You'd know, sweetie. If it were me, I'd begin by calling on that pastor. Maybe by now she's looked through those old records she told you about." Miss Bonnie nodded, satisfied with her suggestions. "Yep, that's where I'd start."

Jaina leaned back in her chair. "Huh…maybe I should." She smiled. "It's worth thinking about, anyway."

***

Jaina awoke that next Friday filled with anticipation and nausea. She'd already packed her bags the night before. She was ready to go as soon as she worked through a few second thoughts. She got dressed, tossed her bags over her shoulders, and lugged them to the car.

Miss Bonnie followed. "Looks like you're all loaded." She stepped outside. "And you've got room to spare."

"Yep," Jaina said. "Luggage is easier to stack than garbage bags." Their eyes met. "Sorry…you didn't deserve that. I'm just in a mood."

"You don't need to be sorry." Miss Bonnie said. "It's one of the many ways the foster care system failed you. It's the system that needs to be sorry." She opened her arms for a goodbye hug. "Now drive safely and call me when you get there…and don't worry about Fur Ball, he'll be fine." She held out several large bills. "Here…just a little extra so that I don't have to worry about you."

Jaina grinned. "Thanks, you're the best…I'll call."

***

The private Boeing business jet taxied down the non-commercial O'Hare runway toward the terminal gate. Zane stood at the window beside a most eager and animated Drew. She was glad she'd taken the day off to be with her friend.

"That's her jet," Drew said. "See it? It's parked right over there." She pointed. "Do you see it? It should just be a few more minutes now." She stopped moving for a moment to make eye contact. "I think you'll like her." Her attention gravitated back toward the airplane. "We should be able to see her any minute now. Just watch the ramp." She moved an inch closer to Zane and the window. "Are you watching?"

Zane shook her head and chuckled. "Yeah, I'm watching." She raised an eyebrow. "I've never seen you like this." She chuckled again. "You are so funny."

Shoulder to shoulder, they watched the staff of uniformed personnel scurry about the airplane until finally Drew's moment arrived. The door opened, the ramp went down, and Stacey stepped gracefully across the threshold. She stood for a moment, acclimating to her new surroundings, then navigated the stairs and came their way.

"She's beautiful," Zane said. "Really something."

"Yeah," Drew agreed. "She is, isn't she?"

The terminal door burst open.

"Well now," Stacey boomed, "aren't you two the most handsome pair I've seen for a while." Without another word, she handed Zane her toy poodle and fell into Drew's arms. The terminal was crowded. People bustled around, but it didn't matter. It was as if the two were alone in their bedroom. Stacey stood on her tiptoes with her arms around her wife's neck. Both were lost in the tenderness of a welcome home kiss.

Zane looked away. To not, felt like an intrusion. She'd never envisioned her best friend pairing off with a woman like Stacey, but she could tell that what they had together was perfect. Stacey was 15 years older than Drew, but her radiance was that of a much younger woman. Her brown hair was long and flowing. Her dress clung intimately to her curves. They were a complete contrast in both appearance and style. A striking couple. Eventually, they came up for air.

Stacey came over and gently touched Zane's cheek. "Drew's spoken of you for years. She's missed you, you know."

Regret filled Zane's heart and eyes. "And I missed her."

"You are quite dashing. Photos don't do you justice, darling." She stepped a little closer, close enough for Zane to get a whiff of her very expensive perfume. "And those eyes." She held Zane's cheek in her gloved palm. "They're like indigo kaleidoscopes." Stacey winked and then resumed a more appropriate distance. "I'll bet the ladies in your congregation just love you."

Zane blushed and looked to Drew.

By that point, Drew was laughing so hard that she could barely breathe. "I meant to warn you about that." She raised an eyebrow. "My wife likes to play. React, my friend, and you're a goner."

The warning had been given too late. Stacey had already smelled blood in the water. "If I'm really good, maybe later you'll show me your collar." She batted her long eyelashes. "Would you do that for me, darling?"

Drew roared in laughter beside her wife.

Zane turned even redder and sighed. "I simply don't know how to respond."

Stacey kissed Zane's cheek. "You are so sweet. I can see why Drew adores you."

Zane shook her head as she extended her elbow. "Come, Ms. Shanning. With Drew's permission, I'll escort you to the car."

Stacey flashed a perfect smile and took hold. "I can already see that we are destined to become the best of friends."

***

Drew bubbled with constant chatter on the ride back to the parsonage. She was so excited to have Stacey with her again and equally excited that two of the most important people in her life had finally met. She simply could not stop talking. There was so much that she wanted Zane and Stacey to know about each other. She told of Stacey's successful film career with such pride and love that it squeezed Zane's heart. She shared stories of their life together; how they'd met filming different films, but on the same location; how it had been love at first sight. They'd been together for years, but hadn't married until the fall of Proposition 8. When Drew ran out of Stacey stories, she told Zane's for the remainder of the trip home. It was utterly exhausting.

Zane wasn't surprised when Drew and Stacey marched straight upstairs to unpack and settle into the guestroom. She knew what they needed most was a few minutes alone to unwind. Actually, she needed a few minutes too, a few minutes of peace and quiet. She built a crackling fire and sat down on the nearby stool. It wasn't long before her friends gravitated back down to join her.

Their conversation was easy and light-hearted. Mostly, they talked about the parsonage.

Once the conversation had worn down to a nub, the three stretched and headed upstairs. Zane made her way up the winding staircase and down the hall a bit slower that night. Even with company, the house felt empty. It'd been years since she'd felt so alone. Zane shut her bedroom door and did what she'd done every night since she was a small child. She dropped to her knees beside her bed in prayer.

Chapter Four

It seemed like it took forever to get out of Florida. Advertising billboards, scrub grass, and a scattering of palm trees were all Jaina saw for mile after mile after mile. By nightfall, she was climbing and coasting through the Tennessee Mountains. Finally, in the wee hours of the morning, Jaina rolled into the Land of Lincoln, still hours out of Champaign. She was beat, but had to keep going. She was too excited to stop. The Echo chugged into town just as the sun emerged over the horizon. Both Jaina and her car were about out of gas, but the trip was over. The search could begin, but noon would be soon enough. She located her motel with little effort and collapsed into bed.

When Jaina re-opened her eyes, her day felt full of promise—a very rare occurrence. She hadn't always been a "glass half-empty" person, but as the years had passed, the more "glass half-empty" she'd become. She stepped out and into the frosty air just as a brisk wind whipped from the north. It knifed straight through her lightweight jacket. The experience awakened something deep within her soul. This was a place new, and yet strangely familiar. It was a place that rocked the center of her core. Jaina slid under the wheel of her Echo. The vinyl felt strangely cold. She shivered as she flipped the switch to turn on the heater. The air smelled warmed. The smell was new, and yet strangely familiar.

Armed with a map of the city, Jaina set off to discover this new place, this place where she was born. She'd circled all the locations that she wanted to visit with a bright red pen and checked them off one by one. None jogged her memory and she was afraid her trip had been a waste of time. She unfolded the map with a sigh and headed for the next location. It was her last chance. In a few blocks, what she'd been looking for came into view.

Jaina toed the accelerator down to the floor, then whipped into the nearest parking space. The experience was unreal. How often does a person get to step into a dreamscape? After a few minutes and a dozen deep breaths, she got out and made her way across the park toward the tallest tree. She leaned back against her old friend's trunk, then slid down to sit in the crunchy leaves. Jaina closed her eyes as memories of her family in this park floated through.This had been a place they'd spent considerable time. She scanned the row of nearby houses and wondered if they'd lived close by. She wondered if her mom…or Jimmy…still did.

Jaina got up and pushed the squeaky swing. Then, she grabbed its chain. The swing halted and she settled into its seat. A nostalgic smile crept across her face. Jimmy had been the best big brother. He'd pushed her for hours on end…*higher, Jimmy, higher.* God, he'd been a handsome boy—sandy hair, tall and lean. By now, he'd probably grown to be a fine looking man. She ran her fingers down the worn-slick slide, pausing as an unfamiliar calm oozed in. Safe. How long had it been? Maybe not since she was three.

***

Butterflies fluttered in Jaina's stomach as she pulled into the church parking lot. She cut the engine, got out, and walked up the sidewalk toward the door—*Faith United, An Open and Affirming Congregation.* The door opened automatically, then snapped shut. An arrow pointed toward the church office. She made her way down the hallway and stepped inside.

"Good morning," the well-dressed older lady chirped. "How can I help you?"

"I spoke with you guys a couple weeks ago," Jaina said. "Is your pastor in?" She introduced herself and explained that she'd just arrived from Sarasota.

The woman moved a little closer and touched Jaina's arm. "No, I'm sorry, she's not. Pastor Zane usually doesn't keep Saturday hours." She shook her head. "Actually, I don't either. I just came in this morning to play catch up." She smiled. "I'm so glad I did. Otherwise, I wouldn't have been here when you arrived." She touched Jaina again. "We had no idea that you planned to make the trip to Illinois." Her smile widened. "Pastor Zane will be so pleased to speak with you in person." Irene invited Jaina to attend worship since Zane wouldn't have office hours until Monday.

Jaina choked. "Uh…okay…well I'll either see her tomorrow or on Monday then." She backed her way toward the door. "I'm actually pretty tired from the trip so it'll probably be Monday." She smiled, thanked the kind woman for her help, and bolted.

Irene followed her to the parking lot. "Good day, Ms. Wakefield."

***

Zane bounced past Drew and Stacey as she came through the kitchen. "Good morning. I hope you both slept well." She grinned and raised an eyebrow. "I'm not even going to inquire as to what time you got to sleep."

Drew's eyes met Stacey's and they exchanged a knowing smile.

"Worship's at 10:00," Zane said with deliberate eye contact. "I was hoping you'd join me." She nodded to Stacey. "I'll wear my collar."

"Oh my," Stacey said with a laugh, "in that case, darling...."

"We wouldn't miss it for the world," Drew said. She took her wife by the arm. "Come on, let's get out of Zane's way." They moseyed into the parlor to await their breakfast.

***

"Man," Drew exclaimed, "Zane certainly is bubbling with the spirit this morning." She shook her head. "It's good to see her happy, though."

"It is," Stacey said softly, "but the sadness never really leaves those beautiful blue eyes." She leaned in to kiss Drew's lips. "I think we remind her that she's alone."

"Yeah," Drew said, "I think we do."

***

The old clock chimed it's ninth time as Zane leaned back in her chair. She was dressed in her robe and had her sermon notes ready on the pulpit. There was plenty of time left for a daydream. She looked out her office window and watched as the autumn breeze swept a carpet of colorful leaves across the church grounds. The breeze swept her thoughts with them. This morning, Drew and Stacey were on her mind. It felt good to have them in her home. She thought about them as a couple. They were so in love. Drew had managed to find her soul mate. Zane's heart was happy for her, yet her soul cried. So lonely. The breeze swirled again. Colorful leaves and thoughts twirled in a different direction. She felt a yearning deep inside, one she hadn't felt in years. It was an ache to have someone in her bed, someone who was mated to her soul. It was the first time in forever that she allowed herself to consider…the possibility.

***

Jaina slept well, then rolled out of bed early. She was actually planning to attend the worship service that morning, a decision as surprising as her decision to come to Champaign by herself. God, how long had it been since she'd stepped inside a church? Years. She considered and reconsidered her decision as she rummaged through her clothes trying to piece together a decent outfit. She found one and slipped it on.

Terror didn't actually smack Jaina down until she drove into the church parking lot. It had been almost empty yesterday. Today it was full. She panicked and couldn't force herself to go inside. What was she scared of? Not being accepted? For some reason, this place—a church—seemed like the true beginning of her search. What if she found her brother? What if she found her mom? Would they be glad to see her? Would they welcome her home? What if she wasn't good enough? What if they didn't accept her? What if they were just like all the rest? Too many "what ifs." Jaina couldn't deal with it. She kept rolling—left without going in—left without saying a word.

***

Drew and Stacey were not church-going people. In fact, none of their LA friends were. Their attendance this morning was for one reason and one reason only, to see and hear Zane preach. They'd timed their arrival within moments of the start of the service, not wanting to be there a minute longer than they had to. The pipe organ rang out as they slid into their chosen pew, one just in front of the pulpit.

"She looks good up there," Drew whispered. "In a robe and everything."

Stacey patted her wife's thigh and smiled. "Yeah…she does. You can tell that this is where she belongs."

"Yeah," Drew said, "you can. Zane has finally found her ever-elusive fit."

When the service ended, the congregation lined up to shake their pastor's hand. Zane took time with each and every one. A warm gaze into their eyes, a handshake, and an "I'm so glad you came." She loved these people and there was no doubt that they loved her in return.

***

Jaina awoke rested and hungry after her second consecutive night of uninterrupted sleep. It must be the motel bed. She showered, dressed, and headed for the pancake house down the road from Faith United. The sexy brunette poured her coffee and took her order. After what seemed like forever, she delivered Jaina's blueberry pancakes.

"Coffee refill?" the woman asked as she purposely brushed her thigh against Jaina.

Jaina shook her head as she scooted over. "No thanks."

The waitress hung around, quite flirty. Jaina wasn't interested. Not this morning. She had more important things to think about than bedding someone. She just wanted to eat her breakfast in peace.

Eventually, the waitress got the hint and moved along to her other tables. She circled back when Jaina stood to leave. "I'm Emma," she said as she handed Jaina a slip of paper. "See you around maybe?"

Jaina opened the note, then held Emma's gaze. "Yeah, maybe you will." She slipped the phone number into her back pocket. "Thanks."

***

Jaina's anxiety increased the closer she got to Faith United. By the time she got there, she was a nervous wreck. She hated meeting new people. They always got too personal and didn't have enough sense to keep their distance. She'd prepared herself for the worst, expecting to spend the morning with a judgmental and very straight woman pastor. Pastor Winslow had sounded nice enough on the phone, but phone voices could be deceiving. This wouldn't be fun, but it would be worth it if she came away with information that could lead her to her brother. The automatic door hissed open. She took a breath, stepped inside, and looked down at what she thought must be the largest rainbow welcome mat in the world.

Irene came out of nowhere. "It's good to see you again." She smiled the kindest smile. "Please, make yourself comfortable. I'll go get Pastor Zane."

Jaina rummaged through the stack of magazines, selected one, and sat down. She'd barely had a chance to look at the cover when the most striking dark-haired woman strode into the room.

"Good morning," Zane said as she extended her hand. "It's good to meet you in person."

Jaina's attention wasn't on their conversation. It was on the pastor's swagger and on the most intense blue eyes she'd ever seen.

Zane tipped her head and raised an eyebrow. "Ms. Wakefield?"

Jaina startled to attention. "Oh…sorry," she said with a nervous chuckle. "My concentration wandered off there for a moment…yeah, it's good to meet you too."

Zane smiled. "You're miles away from home and beginning a search for family you haven't seen since you were a small child. I'm sure you've got a lot on your mind."

Jaina nodded. "Yeah, I do. I have to admit, it's all a bit overwhelming."

Zane gazed warmly into her eyes. "Just let me know how I can help."

Jaina looked up, almost surprised. "Thanks…I will."

"Sleeping any better since we last spoke?" Zane asked.

Jaina furrowed her brow. "Uh…what? Oh…that. Rough one night, then better the next. The last couple nights have been pretty good." Her defenses dropped and she smiled. "Thanks for asking. I can't believe you remembered. It's been two weeks since we spoke."

Zane shook her head. "I can't either." She grinned. "I guess it struck me as important."

They talked for hours. Gazes lingered longer with time. Jaina's search for family was the main topic, but they spoke of other things as well.

"So you know," Zane said, "we no longer operate the group home. In fact, we haven't been in the business of adoption for years. I'll head up to the attic this afternoon before I go home. I know those old records are up there somewhere. It's just a matter of finding them."

"Sorry to cause you extra trouble," Jaina said.

Zane grinned. "It's no trouble at all. Actually, it's my pleasure."

***

Periodically, Irene would peek into the room. She had a feeling and just couldn't keep herself away. It wasn't that she was nosey, it was that she cared. There was an ease that Zane had with Jaina, an ease that she'd never seen her have before…especially with an attractive woman. Irene was hopeful that that ease might lead somewhere. She was fond of Zane, cared about her as a person as well as a pastor. It broke her heart to see her walk alone. A person needed another person to share their life with, as she had shared hers with Bob. God rest his soul. Irene was a firm believer in the power of prayer and had she ever been praying. Today, she had a feeling that she might be witnessing God's answer.

***

Zane watched as the old compact car drove away. She watched long after it was well out of sight. She didn't realize that Irene had stepped up beside her.

"She's nice, isn't she Pastor?" Irene said softly. "Seems sad though. Don't you think?" She smiled. "I hope you'll be able to help her."

Zane heard Irene speaking, but hadn't gotten around to a response.

"Pastor?" Irene nudged her arm. "Are you listening to me?"

Zane shook herself back to awareness. "Oh…yeah. Sorry." She met Irene's eye. "Truthfully, I wasn't." She smiled, slightly embarrassed. "Can you say it again?"

"That's okay," Irene said. "I'm sure you have a lot on your mind."

***

Zane headed for the attic the moment she was back inside. She climbed the old narrow staircase two steps at a time. They creaked and she made a mental note to get them repaired. At the top, she peeked inside the body-hugging doorway and was struck by the strong musty odor of the pitch-black room.

"Ugh," Zane muttered as she ran her hand along the wall, searching for the light switch that she knew had to be there…somewhere. Her fingers tangled unexpectedly in a giant sticky web. She squealed an octave higher than should've been humanly possible and scrambled to escape its hold. She wasn't sure exactly what might be lurking, but whatever it was, she was sure it would be large, have eight hairy legs, and teeth that were long and sharp. She stopped breathing until the lights were on.

Zane glanced over her shoulder and down the stairs. With any luck, Irene hadn't witnessed her meltdown. Satisfied that she hadn't, Zane took a couple more steps forward. The filing cabinets were in the corner. Thank goodness she'd found them straight off. Zane moved closer to get a better look, but the boxes were piled two-high on every cabinet. She'd be searching in this disgusting room for hours.

Chapter Five

Dinner was served late, but no one seemed to care. It had been a busy day for all. The conversation at the table was light-hearted, engaging, and fun. The three friends talked about their day's activities and their plans for tomorrow. Drew couldn't help but notice that Zane had a twinkle in her eye that evening, one she hadn't seen for the longest time.

"Oh, man," Drew said as she forked a piece of beef Wellington. "How do you do this? You work all day, grocery shop, and serve food like this for dinner."

Zane grinned. "I don't know. It's easy. I guess it's just something I enjoy doing."

Drew told of their visit to campus that morning and shared that she'd purchased an extra ticket to homecoming. She claimed she didn't know why. Zane had insisted that she didn't have a use for it, but by the time they called it a night, it was in her back pocket. The trio and hopefully a fourth would make a day of it on Saturday. They'd attend the football game, eat junk food, and take a walk around the quad. Whether or not the Fighting Illini prevailed…and they probably wouldn't…it would be a good time.

***

Spending time, sharing, and enjoying each other's company had become the routine. It was a routine that lifted Zane's spirits and she dreaded that the good times would be ending all too soon. In a matter of just days, Stacey would fly back to Miami, the location of her next film shoot; Drew would head for Chicago to resume production on her most recent project; and worst of all, Jaina would return to Florida. Crazy, right? She barely knew her, and yet…. The only bright spot was that Drew loved Chicago's Cenespace Filming Studios and expected that there would be many more filming projects at that location in her future.

"So…should we carry on with our tradition in front of the fire?" Zane asked. "It's vanilla custard."

"Just a small one for me, darling," Stacey said, "I have got to get back on my food plan before I outgrow that bikini they paid so much for. My agent will simply die if the project loses money because I ate too many sweet treats while I was in Illinois."

Drew began to pout. "I'd almost put the fact that you're heading back in a couple days out of mind. Now it's front and center again. Thanks."

Stacey planted a sympathetic kiss on her wife's lips. "I'll try to make it up to you tonight." Her ornery smile returned as she met Zane's eye. "You'll forgive us if we're a bit noisy, won't you darling? It'll be our last chance for a little while."

By this point, Zane had enough experience with Stacey to know to keep her reaction to herself. She smiled, but said nothing. Zane was a bit out of sorts anyway. Instead of responding, she got up and headed for the kitchen.

"What's going on?" Drew asked softly as she followed Zane into the room. "You've been acting weird off and on all evening." She laid her hand on her friend's shoulder. "One minute you're all pumped up and happy and the next minute you look like you killed a pretty little yellow bird."

"Nothing's wrong," Zane said as her gaze fell to the counter. "I'm fine."

"Uh-huh," Drew said. "Sure you are. Where have I heard that before?" She stepped a little closer and met Zane's eye. "Is it that we're leaving? Because you know we're coming back for Thanksgiving, right?"

"I know," Zane said. Her voice trailed off to nowhere. "It's not just that."

Drew met her friend's gaze. "Aw…Zane. You haven't."

***

Drew and Stacey headed upstairs shortly after dessert was finished. Zane stayed downstairs awhile longer. When the fire had burned to only embers, she headed upstairs too. She undressed and stepped into the shower. The steaming hot water pounded into her muscles. It felt good and she tried to relax. Unfortunately, the variety of sexual sounds coming through the wall from the next room made that virtually impossible. She finally gave up, stepped out of the shower, and crawled into bed. The love-making in the next room had given her a headache.

Zane propped a couple pillows against the headboard, flopped onto her back, and cracked open her new book, *Techniques of Pastoral Counseling*. She gave up after reading the same introductory paragraph for fifth time. It wasn't that the book was boring, it was that her concentration had been clouded by arousal. Against her will, her mind filled with Jaina—her tight jeans, her long blonde hair, and her sky blue eyes.

***

They spent their mornings in the church library pouring over Jaina's adoption records. Afternoons were spent strolling down the dilapidated halls of the old group home. Jaina had walked these halls as a small child. She'd walked them during the long days that followed being taken away from her mom. Her eyes teemed with tears as she revisited those terrifying and heartbreaking times, yet she trudged on. The little girl who'd lost so much had grown up to be an incredibly strong and beautiful woman.

Zane's feelings for Jaina had grown stronger with each passing day. If behavior was any indicator, Jaina felt the same way about her. Hands brushed lightly as they walked. Eyes caressed swells and curves. Gazes lingered. It was a slippery downhill slope and Zane could feel herself losing her footing. She knew she should back away, but couldn't. She couldn't because this routine, this time they spent together had become...everything.

"I won't be here tomorrow," Zane said. "It's Saturday."

Jaina smiled a thin smile. As had become the norm, their gazes lingered. "Yeah, Irene told me. That's okay. We both know I have plenty that I can work on at the motel. In fact, most of what I have left to do can be finished up after I get back home." She pursed her lips. "It won't be long before I'll be on my way."

Zane sucked in a breath. It was now or never. "Uh…there's something else…something I want to ask you...uh…" She fumbled for the words. Finally, she found them. "I've got an extra ticket to homecoming tomorrow. I was wondering if you'd like to go…with me, I mean."

Jaina froze. She didn't answer. She didn't move. She didn't do anything.

"It's okay if you don't want to," Zane said. "I just thought I'd ask."

"Sure, I'll go," Jaina said almost inaudibly. "Miss Bonnie would love it if I saw her old team play."

Zane swallowed—hard. Jaina had accepted her invitation. In a way, she'd expected that she would. But in a way, she hadn't. "Uh…okay then…uh…how about I pick you up at nine?"

"Nine's good," Jaina croaked. "I'll see you then." She spun, jumped into her car, and sped away. She had the look of someone about to throw up.

Zane knew the problem well. In fact, it was pure luck that her own queasy stomach made it all the way out back to the Thunderbird. She dropped into the driver's seat and crumpled forward, laying her sweaty brow against the creamy leather steering wheel. She'd done it, done what she hadn't done since college. She'd asked a girl out. Zane tried to convince herself that it wasn't really a date, but she knew in her heart that it was.

***

The Thunderbird rumbled into the La Quinta parking lot. Washed and waxed, she sparkled. Top down and shiny, the old girl looked good. Zane looked good too. Both were spit and polished for the occasion. It took forever for Zane to open the door and get out. In fact, she sat there long enough that she almost made herself late. She sat, fretted, and sat some more. Finally, she mustered the courage.

Zane got out, walked inside, and knocked on the door. She knocked, but Jaina didn't answer. She knocked again and called out her name. Again, there was no answer. The door didn't open and she didn't hear a sound. She was disgusted with herself. If she hadn't wasted so much time sitting, she wouldn't have been late. Zane was sure she must've gotten mixed up on the room number and headed for the front desk to inquire.

"I'm sorry," the motel clerk said, "Ms. Wakefield checked out quite early this morning...no, no note was left. I am very sorry."

Zane caught her breath. She'd been blindsided. A fist had come out of nowhere and rammed into her stomach. It knocked the wind right out of her.

The clerk laid his hand on her shoulder. "Can I help you to your car?"

Zane shook her head. "No, thanks. I'll be fine." She made her way back to the Thunderbird and laid her head on the steering wheel. This felt so much worse than it it ever had before.

***

Drew was standing at the front door when the Thunderbird pulled into the driveway. She'd been watching, mostly because she was anxious to get on their way, but also to get her first look at Jaina. It was 9:30 and with no parking pass, she feared they wouldn't find a place to park the car. She glanced over to Stacey. "Zane doesn't have anyone with her." She furrowed her brow. "I wonder why not."

Stacey got up to look for herself.

They watched as Zane slowly got out of the car and made her way up the sidewalk.

"Something's wrong," Stacey said softly.

"I know," Drew said as she moved to meet her friend at the door. "Hey there. Did Jaina decide not to come?"

Zane walked right past Drew and into the kitchen. "I guess so."

Drew followed her. "How come?"

Zane dropped her keys on the table and her butt in the chair. "It appears she decided it was time to head back to Florida. I really don't know."

"Aw, Zane. I'm so sorry," Drew said. "Are you okay?"

"I guess I have to be, don't I," Zane said. "She's gone." She clenched her jaw. "It's not like it's never happened before, right?"

Drew stepped behind the chair to rub the back of her friend's neck. "I'm so sorry."

"Yeah," Zane said, "me too."

Drew squeezed Zane's shoulder. "You know…if you don't feel like going today…"

Zane stood and picked up her keys. "I do. Come on. Get Stacey and let's go."

***

Miss Bonnie startled awake when the front door opened. It squeaked and then clicked shut. She glanced at the clock on the nightstand—a wee hour of the morning—and listened to determine if the sounds in the house were familiar. They were. She got up and poked her head around the corner. "How come you're back so soon? It hasn't even been two full weeks." She pursed her lips. "Did you drive all night again?"

"Yep," Jaina said. "I sure did." She hefted up her bags and walked back to her bedroom.

Miss Bonnie followed. She'd been concerned that there might be some kind of problem when Jaina hadn't called the day before. Now she was absolutely certain that there was. Getting her to talk about it would be the tricky part. "Well, I'm just glad you made it home without falling asleep at the wheel." She shook her head in an exaggerated manner. Then, she pursed her lips. "Too bad I'll have to miss that movie though." Her voice trailed off.

Jaina looked up with a crinkled brow. "Huh?"

Miss Bonnie continued on, playing her part. "Oh, it's nothing. Don't worry about it…just a movie I was going to watch on HBO tomorrow night."

"Uh…well that's stupid," Jaina said. "You don't have to go just because I came home early. You can stay all week if you want."

Miss Bonnie smiled. She was pleased that she hadn't lost her touch. "Well now, aren't you just too sweet for words?"

Chapter Six

Drew absentmindedly turned the pages of the Sunday paper, not absorbing one solitary word. Her mind was elsewhere, lost in thought and worry. In just a few hours Stacey would board her jet and be gone...again. Weeks would pass before they'd see each other. She swallowed the lump in her throat. God, she missed her wife already. Their careers had become the dictators of their lives. Long absences had become the norm of their marriage. Drew felt an ache in her chest as she longed for the good old days when their relationship was their number one priority.

"I'll miss you too," Stacey whispered as she slipped her arms around Drew from behind. She must have sensed her wife's melancholy.

Drew met her gaze. "I know you will." She swallowed hard and then began to cry.

"Come here baby," Stacey said softly. She took Drew by the hand and tugged her toward the parlor.

They settled onto the sofa and Drew melted into her arms—nuzzling, kissing, caressing.

Stacey slipped her thigh between Drew's legs. "We've got time before Zane gets home from church." She applied just enough pressure to just the right spot.

Drew responded like she always did. There was never a problem with her libido. It always burned hot.

KA Moll

"I love you," Stacey whispered.

Drew manipulated the second button on her wife's blouse. "Mmm...and I love you too."

***

Out of the blue, the front door swung open and Zane stepped inside. "Where is everybody?" She cocked her head and listened to the unusual noises that were emanating from the parlor—a crash, a bark, a scream, and an "ouch." Before she'd figured out what was going on, Drew, Stacey, and the poodle tumbled out the door and into the foyer.

"Uh...hello," Drew stammered. "You're home early, aren't you?"

Stacey scrambled to adjust her clothing.

"Why yes, I guess I am." Zane shook her head and smiled. "I can leave and come back later if that would help."

Drew didn't catch the humor. Her melancholy had returned. "No, we're out of time anyway." She caught her wife's gaze. "Aren't we, Stacey?"

***

Drew pressed her palms and laid her forehead against the reinforced glass. She watched silently as an airplane took off from the nearest runway. Before long, Stacey's plane would taxi up to the gate. "You'd think after all this time I'd get used to doing this, but I don't." She turned to look at her wife.

Soul Mates

Stacey was about to respond, when one of a multitude of her adoring fans interrupted for an autograph. This life they led had gotten old.

The guy left and Drew resumed their conversation. "I don't know how much longer this is going to work for me." Tears once again welled up in her eyes.

Stacey kissed Drew's temple. "Don't worry, we'll figure something out. Our marriage is what's most important."

***

Zane heard the Lamborghini pull back into the driveway. "In the garage," she called out. "I'm just about finished." She continued polishing the rear fender of the Thunderbird, expecting that Drew would join her in the garage, but she didn't. She dropped her rag into the bucket, washed her hands, and went inside. Drew was sitting at the kitchen table with a cup of coffee. Zane poured another and sat down.

"It looks to me like it'd be really hard," Zane said softly, "to love someone who has to be far away so much of the time."

"It is," Drew said, "but each time we seem to make it through." She looked over to meet Zane's eye. "But I don't know for how much longer." She took a slug of hot coffee. "How about you? You doing okay?"

Zane shook her head. "Not so much." She tried to summon more words, but they wouldn't come.

"You know," Drew said, "it might help if you talked about it."

"To talk, I have to drive." Zane forced a thin smile. "Want to go for a ride later on?"

Drew patted her on the back. "Sure I do."

***

"So what movie are we watching?" Jaina asked as she dipped her hand into the bowl of buttered popcorn.

"Hum…I'm not sure I remember the title," Miss Bonnie stammered. She snatched the guide from the coffee table. "Let me check to be sure." She ran her finger down the page. "Ah, here it is…uh…*Boardwalk Empire*."

Jaina made a face. "That's not a movie, it's a series. It must be in its fourth season by now." She shook her head. "I didn't know you liked that kind of show. It's pretty bloody."

"Well, the preview looked good," Miss Bonnie said, "and I was gonna watch it."

"Okay," Jaina said. "Let's watch it then." It didn't really matter. No show would be good enough to hold her attention tonight. Her mind was elsewhere. As it turned out, neither watched much. They mostly ate popcorn.

"See," Jaina said after the show was over. "I told you it was bloody." She switched the TV off.

"And I should've listened to you," Miss Bonnie said with a scowl. "I had my eyes shut through almost all of it." She shook her head. "I don't see how people watch all that gore."

Jaina didn't respond. Her thoughts had already returned to Illinois.

***

Miss Bonnie was trying her best to be patient. She was trying to let Jaina share in her own time, but she looked so troubled, so vulnerable that she could barely stand to let it all play out. Finally, Jaina leaned back and began to talk—about the town, the church, the adoption record, the tidbits she'd discovered about her family, her rekindled childhood memories—and the pastor. The details that weren't shared spoke volumes.

As Miss Bonnie listened, she came to realize the significance of what had occurred during the time that Jaina had been gone. She also came to recognize the significance of the pastor. Jaina had reached a turning point in her life, one that she'd almost given up hope of her ever reaching. Miss Bonnie was almost certain that it would shake the very foundation upon which Jaina stood. She rocked and considered what she could do to help.

***

Drew had a good idea of what was troubling Zane. After all, she did know her pretty well. She knew of her ongoing struggle to deal with some kind of demon from her childhood. She knew of her longing to have someone of her own. She knew that her past relationships had all been short-lived and she knew why. Tonight, she knew that it had all come together to form Zane's perfect storm. It had come together because of one woman— Jaina Wakefield.

The top was up, the heater was on, and the old Thunderbird rumbled south. It was the perfect direction for this conversation and it didn't take long before it all poured out.

"I don't know what to do," Zane said. "I think about her all the time. I feel her in the pit of my stomach. I love her." She glanced over to Drew. "Jaina's gone and I miss her so much. How can that be?"

Drew didn't have an immediate response. She'd never seen her friend quite like this before. Stacey would know what to say, but as usual, she was on the other side of the country.

"I don't have the answer," Drew said softly, "but you do. In your heart, you know exactly what your next step needs to be." She took a breath and gathered her thoughts. "What I do know is that everything is easier when a person is your soul mate. What's hard becomes simple with the person who makes you whole." She paused, thinking about her wife. "I've known you for a long time, seen you through a lot of breakups. I've never seen you get as shook as you are right now." She touched Zane's arm. "I think Jaina might be your soul mate. So…my only advice is to take a deep breath, square your shoulders, and do what you need to do."

***

Zane awoke before the crack of dawn that next morning. Sleep hadn't come easy, but it had come easier than the night before. She dressed and tiptoed out of her bedroom. Drew snored softly as she crept past her door.

With a donut in hand, Zane headed for the office. The sun had just peeked over the horizon when she pulled into the parking lot. Faith United should be quiet today since Irene had taken the day off. Zane planned to roll the phone calls over to the answering service so that she could complete her entire week's work. It was a lofty goal, but doable if she could remain on task.

***

Zane settled into her chair—paper in front of her, pencil in hand, and the Bible on the corner of her desk. She pulled her blinds and prepared to write. After only a couple hours, her sermon was almost finished. She looked up when she heard footsteps approaching. Her visitor was the queen of all her distractions.

"Hello, Mom," Zane said. She reached up to rub the back of her neck. "I wasn't expecting you."

"I was in the neighborhood," Nancy said crisply. "I knew I'd never be invited, just thought I'd stop by." She pursed her lips. "I wanted to see this church of yours for myself." She looked around. "No secretary, huh?"

Zane sucked in a breath. "Today's her day off."

"You didn't have much to say the other day," Nancy said as her eyes narrowed.

Zane knew more was coming.

"You thought I didn't know you were in town," Nancy continued, "but I did. I read the article in the paper when you were called by this church. That was three years ago." She shook her head. "You never called, never stopped by. I figured you weren't interested, so I left you alone."

Zane looked out the window and then back to her mom. "I didn't think I was welcome." For a moment, she thought her mom was going to cry. That would've been so unlike her.

"Those words were said long ago." Nancy's voice trailed off.

"They were," Zane said. She shifted the position of the items on her desk, back-and-forth, and then looked up. "And I remember them as if you said them yesterday."

Nancy fidgeted and she looked away. "Looks like we have weather blowing in. I'd better get on back to the farm." She stood, picked up her purse, and headed for the door. "You are welcome." She glanced back over her shoulder. "Stop by if you want."

"Bye mom," Zane said softly.

Zane heard the front door latch and sighed. She picked up her pencil. It was a struggle, but she finally got back in the groove and became productive. By the end of the day, she couldn't have been more pleased with all she'd accomplished. Her sermon was written and the service was planned. She'd even found a moment to call the handywoman about the stairs to the attic. It had been a good day in spite of her mom's visit. Zane couldn't help but notice that since Jaina, she was better able to focus on the things that really mattered.

Chapter Seven

Irene arrived early that Tuesday. She'd enjoyed her shopping trip with her daughter, but was glad to get back to work. This was the place that she felt the most needed. She poured a cup of coffee and scurried to her desk.

A note was taped to the center of her monitor—quite out of the ordinary. It probably meant Pastor Zane needed something first thing this morning. She plucked it off to read.

A Note from Your Pastor
Good Morning Irene,
I hope you had a pleasant day with your daughter.
Next Sunday's sermon and service order are attached.
I'll be off the next few days. You can expect me to call mid-week to check in, but I won't see you until Sunday morning.
Have a blessed week.
Pastor Zane

***

The parsonage lights had switched on well before daybreak that morning. It had been early, but almost not early enough for Zane to make her flight.

"Thanks for the lift," she said. "I hated to leave the Thunderbird in an airport parking lot for a week. I know they have security cameras, but I'd worry about her anyway."

"I know. It's no problem," Drew said. "It's not like I wasn't headed for Chicago anyway." She held Zane's gaze. "No matter how it all turns out, I want you to know that I couldn't be any more proud of you than I am right now."

Zane smiled. "Thanks...I wouldn't be doing this if you hadn't given me a nudge. You always did know just what to say."

Drew pulled Zane in for a goodbye hug. "That's what friends are for."

Zane met her gaze. "So, you are coming back for Thanksgiving, right?"

Drew nodded. "Absolutely! We wouldn't miss it for the world."

***

"Attention, please. This is the last boarding call for flight 4171, Chicago nonstop to Sarasota-Bradenton International Airport..."

Zane's carry-on luggage flopped wildly as she broke into a full-tilt run. She hadn't allowed enough time to get through security. It'd been years since her last flight. She'd heard how much more difficult the airport process was, but hadn't dreamed it would take as long as it did. Zane was gasping by the time she held out her ticket to board. She located her seat, slid her bag into the above compartment, and waited for the passenger on the aisle to allow her access. The cramped quarters seemed to be missing considerable leg room. She shifted around and tried to get as comfortable as she could. The airplane lifted off and Shytown faded into the distance. She was on her way and amazingly calm.

***

Jaina hadn't been herself since she'd returned home. It wasn't just that she was moody or anything, because Jaina wouldn't have been Jaina without a mood swing or two. It was that she wouldn't eat. Jaina always ate, but she wouldn't eat. She had Miss Bonnie worried.

"I've got crispy bacon and hot cakes on the griddle," Miss Bonnie said. "Used to be your favorite."

"Thanks, but I don't think so." Jaina's dull eyes met those of her friend. "I'm not really hungry."

"And you weren't hungry yesterday either," Miss Bonnie said with a frown. "Have you decided to starve yourself to death? That's a really slow way to go." She raised an eyebrow and cracked a smile. "Come on, sweetie. Sit and have breakfast with me."

Jaina shook her head. "Okay, but just a little." She made a sick face. "My stomach's been off the last few days."

"Uh-huh," Miss Bonnie said. "You know, it might help if you talked about it." She patted Jaina's arm. "I know something's wrong and I'm almost certain that it has something to do with that pastor."

Jaina leaned over the arm of her chair to stare out the window. A tough expression washed across her face.

It was an expression that Miss Bonnie had seen many times before. "I had to leave." Jaina's lower lip began to quiver. "I just had to."

Miss Bonnie had been Jaina's sole source of comfort for years. She pulled her close.

Jaina sniffled, then talked. The handsome pastor with the deep blue eyes had done what no one had ever done before. She'd broken through Jaina's wall of defenses and stolen her heart.

"It feels like someone's ripping it right out of my chest," Jaina whimpered. "I want to run, but I don't know where to go."

Miss Bonnie smiled a tender smile. "She sounds really special, your pastor. I think maybe you've fallen in love." She rubbed Jaina's back in circles. It used to calm her down.

"I can't deal with this." Jaina looked up with teary eyes. "Zane just won't get out of my head." She closed her eyes. "What am I gonna do? I knew I shouldn't have waited so long to leave Illinois...thank God I'm off this week."

***

Irene answered the phone. She was convinced that God was answering her prayers by the bucket-full. "No, I'm sorry...Pastor Zane is out of town for a few days. Is there something I can help you with? Her mother? Well, my goodness. It's so nice to talk with our dear pastor's mother. She's invited for Sunday dinner? Oh my, she'll be so pleased ..."

***

Jaina had just finished putting away a week's worth of clean laundry. As she shut the top drawer of her dresser, she caught a glimpse of an unfamiliar red car pulling into her driveway. She moved closer to the window. The door opened and the woman got out. Jaina's heart began to race. Tears welled up in her eyes. She didn't know what to do. Eventually, she did what came naturally. She ran.

***

Miss Bonnie groaned as she lifted herself out of the rocker. Jaina must not have heard the bell. "I'll get it," she called out. She opened the door.

"Good morning, Ma'am," the sharply dressed woman said with a tilt of her head and a raise of her eyebrow. I'm looking for Ms. Wakefield. Is she home?"

"Speechless" was usually not a word used to describe Miss Bonnie, but at this moment, it was. She stood searching for a word. "Hello."

The woman shifted the bouquet of roses from her right hand to her left. "Ma'am?"

Miss Bonnie found her voice. "You wouldn't happen to be from Illinois, would you?"

The woman grinned. "My goodness, does it show?"

"No," Miss Bonnie chuckled, "but circumstances gave me a strong suspicion."

"Zane Winslow, Ma'am. I'm a pastor in Champaign. Jaina and I recently worked together on a project."

KA Moll

Miss Bonnie nodded. She couldn't help but smile. "Uh-huh, I know who you are. It's nice to finally put a face with a name. I must say I've heard a lot about you." She held open the door and Zane stepped inside. "Boy will Jaina be surprised. I'll go get her."

Zane watched Miss Bonnie disappear down the hall. She listened to her call out for Jaina. After several minutes had passed, she was certain that Miss Bonnie would come back empty handed. "So let me be sure I have this straight…" She ran her fingers through her hair. "You just saw Jaina a few minutes ago in her bedroom. Now you check and she's nowhere to be found." Zane furrowed her brow. "Since I'm parked in the driveway, I'm guessing she hasn't gone far." She raised an eyebrow. "If you don't mind, I believe I'll just wait her out." She sat back down.

Miss Bonnie shook her head. "I think you got to know my Jaina pretty well while she was in Champaign." She chuckled. "Make yourself comfortable. I'll go take another look around." She headed promptly for the garage.

***

"I thought I might find you here," Miss Bonnie said as she leaned into the driver's window. "I know I don't need to tell you that you have a visitor."

"God…what is she doing here?" Jaina caught back a sob. "And what am I gonna do?"

Miss Bonnie locked gazes and provided a bit of tough love. "Well…since it appears your pastor has decided to wait you out…I think when you're ready, you'll probably need to come back inside." She shook her

68

head and smiled a loving smile. "You know you want to." She turned off the garage light and left.

Jaina sat in the dark for several minutes before slipping back inside.

Zane looked up as she came through the door. "Hello…" Her eyes were so kind. "I missed you." Her words lingered.

Jaina responded with her eyes.

"Here," Zane said. "These are for you." She held out the beautiful bouquet of roses.

Their gazes locked.

"You came all this way without calling first," Jaina said. "What if I hadn't been home? It would've been a long trip to make for nothing." She raised an eyebrow.

Zane raised one in response. "I had to. I couldn't take a chance with something this important."

Jaina swallowed. "What is *this*?" she asked softly.

Zane's eyes began to twinkle. "Why, *this* my dear is *you* being courted."

Against her will, Jaina's lower lip began to tremble. She fought back tears. What in the world had gotten into her?

***

Zane opened her arms and pulled Jaina close. They kissed—a first kiss, sweet and tender. The evening was much like the kiss—sweet, tender, really nice. Zane left feeling better than she'd felt in literally forever, but she was nervous. The hardest part was yet to come. Jaina needed to know what she was getting into. She needed to know that the woman who wanted to date her was damaged goods.

Zane unlocked the door of her motel room and stepped inside. She turned on a couple lamps and flopped back on the bed. The day had gone well, but what was she going to do when this budding relationship ended up just like all the rest? After all, that was the most likely outcome. She picked up the remote and began to mindlessly flip through the channels. Zane paused on a comedy as she tried to push tomorrow out of mind.

Chapter Eight

Zane hung the blue pinstriped shirt back on the hanger. She slipped on the yellow one, tucked it into her navy trousers, and fastened her belt. She stepped over to check her reflection again. This time, she nodded to her mirror image. The fourth outfit had passed inspection. It was a good thing too, because she was due to pick Jaina up at 9:00. If she left right now, she'd make it on time. One last check in the mirror, a splash of cologne, and she was out the door.

***

Miss Bonnie watched as Jaina fluttered about the duplex that morning. One outfit came off a hanger as another went back on—time after time after time. In between, Jaina looked out the window to see if Zane had pulled into the driveway. Miss Bonnie lost count of how many times Jaina touched up her make up, but it was a lot.

"My goodness," Miss Bonnie said. "Settle down, girl. You're making me tired just watching you." She patted the seat beside her on the couch. "Come here for a minute. Sit. Tell me about your plans for the day, your plans for lunch."

Jaina fluttered over and sat down. "I'm gonna see if she wants to go to our favorite, that is, if she likes seafood. If she doesn't..." Jaina's eyes widened. "I don't have a plan. Oh, my God, what if she doesn't?"

"They serve other things too," Miss Bonnie said. "Either way, you should be fine." She rubbed Jaina's back. "You need to breathe and settle down."

"I'm so nervous," Jaina said. "I don't know what's gotten into me." She hopped back up to check the window and sat back down. "I'm a mess."

Miss Bonnie rubbed her back again. "You can do this. It's hard because you're not used to it. You're just not used to allowing yourself to feel. But sweetie, those feelings are the good part, kind of like the filling is the good part of the key lime pie."

A car door shut. Jaina jumped up and ran outside. Miss Bonnie shook her head and smiled.

***

Sometimes a day just feels perfect. That's the way this one was for Zane. She felt good. For no apparent reason, her nerves had calmed. She was with Jaina and they were sightseeing in what she was certain was the most beautiful place in the world. It was all new, exciting, and wonderful.

Zane looked across and winked. "You're a beautiful woman."

Jaina blushed and smiled. "Thanks...you don't look so bad yourself." She shook her head and then lightened the subject. "I can't believe you've never been to Florida. Thirty-six years old and you've never been here. Not once? How can that be? Everyone goes to Florida. It's what families do on vacation."

Zane tipped her head down to look over her sunglasses. "Not my family. We didn't go on vacations. We were a nose-down, on task, farm family. No messing around for us. Our vacations were Sunday afternoon rides in the country."

Jaina's eyes widened and again she shook her head. "You've got to be kidding. No way!" She raised an eyebrow. "You are so not 'farm-like'."

Zane laughed. "Huh. I guess I didn't turn out right." Her smile revealed a dimple.

"I think you turned out just fine," Jaina said. "In fact, I wouldn't change a thing."

Zane met her gaze as she turned the corner. "Oh I think there'd be some things you'd change."

"I don't think so." Jaina smiled. "So you really do like seafood, right? You're not just saying that because you think this is where I want to eat?"

"No," Zane said, "I wouldn't do that." Her eyes briefly left the road and locked on. "I'll never lie to you, not even about the little things. You can count on it."

"Good," Jaina said. "I'll never lie to you either."

They fell silent as they traversed the last few miles to the restaurant. Zane watched the road while Jaina watched the scenery.

Jaina noticed an older man leaning over the railing of a tall bridge. Risky. She watched him drop his trap into the water—it was crab season. Perhaps some things, some people, were worth a certain amount of personal risk. Seagulls squawked overhead as she looked over to Zane. She smiled and their conversation resumed where it had left off.

***

They slid into a booth that overlooked the Manatee River. Large gators swam below in clear view. Zane was awestruck. "I'll bet this would've been a fun place to grow up."

Jaina poked at her salad.

"So was it," Zane asked, "fun?"

When Jaina didn't respond, she backed off. "I'm sorry," Zane said. "Sometimes I get too personal. Forgive me."

Jaina looked up and met her gaze. "It's not that you got too personal. It's me—me and all my baggage."

Zane reached across the table to hold Jaina's hand. "Don't worry about it. I come with a bucket load of baggage myself." She smiled and shook her head. "Just wait, you'll see."

***

The afternoon was filled with sightseeing. They visited the Classic Car Museum, the Ringling History of the Circus Museum, and the Marie Selby Botanical Gardens. Jaina wanted to take Zane to a variety of places to give her a feel for Sarasota. She even took her to the deli where she worked.

"Here it is," Jaina said. "I'm not sure how much longer I'll be here, but I wanted to show it to you anyway." She swept her hair back into a ponytail out of habit. "I've got a little money saved up. It might be time for a change."

Zane pulled into a parking spot.

"You want to go in?" Jaina asked in disbelief. She raised an eyebrow. "It's just a regular ol' deli. The highlight…we'll give you a taste of our Boar's Head meat and cheese."

Zane stared back at Jaina with an equal measure of disbelief. "Of course I want to go in. I want to know you. I want to see the place you spend your days."

***

Jaina usually went out of her way to avoid the route past Loving Arms. The place never failed to awaken intense and conflicting emotions. It represented abandonment and yet it also represented safety and love. Who knows what possessed her to tell Zane to turn left instead of right, but she did. As they approached the group home, Jaina willed herself not to look. Though she tried to refrain, she still looked. Then, she fell silent.

Zane's brow creased in concern. "Are you okay?"

Jaina worked to dismiss her feelings. "Yeah, I'm okay." She smiled a thin smile. "There's a lot you don't know about me."

Zane smiled back. "There's a lot we don't know about each other. Luckily, we've got all the time in the world."

***

Jaina rummaged through her purse as the red convertible rolled into her driveway. Finally, she located her house key. "Want to come in?"

"Sure I do," Zane said with a grin. "I just flew across the country to spend time with you…and I don't fly. Of course I want to come in."

Jaina unlocked the front door. "Sometimes you say the nicest things."

The aroma of spicy chili took Zane's breath away. "Mmm, does that ever smell good!"

A voice boomed from the kitchen. "Want some?" Miss Bonnie asked. "I made plenty."

Zane grinned. "You bet I do."

***

The big cat stretched his hind leg across Zane's lap onto Jaina's.

Zane stroked him. "I think he likes this arrangement." She met Jaina's eye. "I do too." Then, her attention turned to Miss Bonnie. "So tell me, how'd you two meet?"

Jaina sucked in a breath. Everyone in the room must have heard her.

Miss Bonnie was at a loss for words.

"I'm sorry," Zane said. "I keep doing that. Please forgive me."

"It's okay," Jaina said. "It's just my baggage again."

When Zane thought it was time for her to leave, Jaina followed her to the door. "You don't have to go." She tiptoed up to put her arms around Zane's neck.

Zane lowered down to kiss her. "Yes I do."

Jaina fingered Zane's collar and twirled her hair between her fingers. "Whatever you say." She smiled. "I had a good time today."

"Yeah," Zane said softly. "Me too." God, this felt so good. What was she going to do when she lost her? Zane opened the door. "Sleep well. I'll see you tomorrow." She cocked her head and caught Jaina's eye. "No running this time, okay?"

"Okay." Jaina nodded and smiled. "No running."

***

Jimmy, now Jim, sat in the antique rocker in front of his picture window, as he'd done yesterday and the day before. His hands were moist with perspiration. The small bottle of narcotics rested in his palm. Funny, he'd never really considered that life could change in an instant until recently. He could hardly believe a month had passed. Still, he expected to hear her voice calling him to breakfast. The high chair sat in its usual place. It was unoccupied, yet he still expected to hear the happy squeals of his only child. Jim couldn't bear to move it—the chair. It served as a constant reminder of what had been. Just one month ago—31 days come three past eight—the phone rang and life as he knew it ended. Jim stared out the window. The neighbor lady was in her robe. She picked up her newspaper and went back inside. In the distance, he could see the park where he'd played ball as a child. He looked down to his watch, two past eight, and back to the small bottle. He unscrewed the cap, emptied the contents into his sweaty palm, and swallowed.

***

KA Moll

Zane rolled over and rubbed the sleep from her eyes. The digital clock on the nightstand gleamed two minutes past nine, two minutes past eight back home. Her first thoughts were of Jaina. She was probably up by now. Zane swung her legs over the side of the bed and padded in her boxers to the bathroom.

***

Breakfast had been eaten. The dishes were done. Jaina was dressed and ready to go. She checked her watch—two minutes past nine. Zane would be there to pick her up in less than an hour. Anticipation surged in the pit of her stomach. Yesterday had been so much fun, more fun than she could remember having in a very long time. Today should be fun, too. They'd go to the Tampa Zoo, the Mote Aquarium, and then head back home for dinner. She popped in to check her make-up one last time. The car door slammed. Jaina dropped her eyeliner and ran.

***

Zane finger-combed her hair as she checked her reflection in the driver's mirror one last time. When she looked up, Jaina was watching her from the door. She'd stepped out in what had to be the world's skimpiest pair of shorts. Zane sucked in a breath. Soon, Jaina would have expectations of her. She sucked in another. She'd expect and Zane would fail. That's the way the story always ended.

A small Gecko scampered across the sidewalk as Zane stepped onto the porch. "I love those little guys."

She bent down to watch the amphibian scurry into the rock garden.

"Oh yeah," Jaina said, "they're everywhere—dried crispy in the dryer, dead between your sheets, smashed just inside the door." She crinkled her nose and shook her head. "They're loveable, alright." Then she rose up to kiss Zane good morning. "I'll grab my purse and be ready to go."

Chapter Nine

It was another beautiful day in Florida. They drove with the top down, warm breeze whipping through their hair. The pair laughed and played as if they didn't have a care in the world. Jaina couldn't remember ever enjoying the sights as much as she did that day, not even when she'd first moved here as a small child. Today had been like seeing Florida for the first time through Zane's eyes. By the time they pulled into her driveway late that afternoon, Jaina felt like she'd just come off a whirlwind tour.

They found a note on the door. Jaina peeled the tape and removed it.

It was in Miss Bonnie's handwriting. "Gone to the store."

Jaina raised an eyebrow. "Well, how about that. We have the house to ourselves."

Zane lost her color as they stepped inside the door.

Jaina noticed, but didn't say a word. They made their way through the living room, but Zane stopped dead in her tracks before they reached the hall.

Jaina reached up to brush away a wrinkle from Zane's shirt.

Zane flinched. Fear.

The front door opened as Jaina tiptoed up to kiss her.

Zane released the breath she'd been holding as she backed away. Jaina noticed her color had returned.

"Hello," Miss Bonnie called out. She lumbered in with two bags of groceries. "Is anybody home?"

Zane and Jaina stepped around the corner.

Jaina sighed. "Yeah, we're home."

Miss Bonnie bumped the door shut with her butt. "I hope I didn't interrupt anything."

"No," Zane said, "nothing at all. Here…let me take those for you." She grabbed the bags and headed for the kitchen.

Jaina watched, puzzled by the change in Zane's demeanor.

***

The phone rang and Miss Bonnie answered. She was about to hang up, thinking it was a telemarketer. Thank goodness she figured out the call was for Zane.

Zane crinkled her brow. "Who'd be calling me here? No one knows where I am."

Miss Bonnie shrugged her shoulders in an *I don't know* as she handed her the phone. "A woman. I think she said her name was Irene."

Zane reached into her breast pocket for paper and a pen. Her expression changed and her color drained as she listened to the caller.

Miss Bonnie wondered what had happened. The woman had sounded upset. Now Zane was.

"Oh no," Zane said. She shut her eyes, but re-opened them to take notes. In a few minutes, she hung up the phone. Then, she just stood staring out the window, not saying a word.

Miss Bonnie wondered if something terrible had happened to someone she loved.

***

Zane headed for the kitchen once she'd regained her composure. She stood inside the door until Jaina looked up. She'd been dicing tomatoes for their salad. Jaina smiled, but as she met Zane's troubled gaze, the smile faded. "What's wrong?"

"There's something I need to talk with you about," Zane said tenderly. "Come sit with me for a moment."

Jaina pinched her brow. "Okay..." She laid her paring knife on the cutting board and followed.

"Irene just called," Zane said. "She took a call this morning from a social worker at the hospital." Zane looked into Jaina's eyes. "They found a letter written to you by your brother." She explained that it had mentioned Jaina's adoption through Faith United. "The social worker didn't know how to reach you, so she called us."

Jaina's mouth fell open and her eyes widened. "Oh, my God! Jimmy wrote me a letter?"

Zane took another deep breath. "He did." Her voice got softer. "About a month ago, he lost his wife and baby daughter in a tragic car crash." She squeezed Jaina's hand. "This morning, he tried to kill himself with an overdose of narcotics."

The blue eyes held onto each other.

"It was a suicide note...addressed to you."

"Oh, my God…" Jaina clamped her hand over her mouth. Her tears began to fall.

Zane pulled Jaina close and she laid her head on her shoulder. "He's alive, but in intensive care. The doctors are hopeful that he'll recover."

***

Jaina's search for Jimmy was over. She knew exactly where he was. She knew she could lose him in a split-second. "If I hadn't waited so long…."

Zane kissed Jaina's forehead. She ran her fingers through her hair. "None of this is your fault. There's nothing that you could have said or done that would have changed this outcome." She kissed her again. "All that you can do now is be there for him when he wakes up."

Miss Bonnie probably knew Jaina better than any other person in the world—been there through it all. She knew her as a troubled youth and she knew her as the woman she'd become. Jaina had always looked to her when there was a problem, until this moment when she didn't look to her at all. In the blink of an eye, Zane had become what she had always been—Jaina's anchor in a storm.

***

Zane booked an earlier flight home. Jaina booked the seat next to her. Miss Bonnie, and of course Fur Ball, followed in the Echo.

To say Jaina was a mess by the time they arrived at the airport would have been an understatement. She was worried and angry about absolutely everything. "I would've quit if they hadn't given me the time off. No way I'd let a job get in the way of me going to see my brother in the hospital."

Zane squeezed her hand. She made sure her voice was calm. "It's good that it all worked out." She placed their carry-on bags on the table to be checked by the security officer.

Jaina snarled at the inconvenience. Her grumbling was non-stop. She didn't quiet until she fell asleep in her seat on the airplane.

In contrast, Zane was the picture of cooperation and calmness. On the inside, though, she was as anxious as a cat in a swimming pool. She prayed most of the way back to Champaign, then thanked God again when the wheels of the airplane finally touched ground.

***

Zane carried their luggage into the parsonage. She put Jaina's in the bedroom down the hall from her own. They'd argued over whether she should stay at the parsonage or at a motel. Zane won. Jaina's plan was to stay at the hospital as long as she was needed. It simply made no sense for her to get a motel room. The guest room in the parsonage was the most prudent choice.

Jaina took a few minutes to look around before heading upstairs to take a shower and change clothes. Zane could tell that she liked her place, but mostly, she could tell that she was anxious to get to the hospital. Tired or not, that's where they needed to go.

Zane showered and changed clothes, all black with a white clerical collar. She was still raking through her damp hair as she came down the stairway. Jaina had already showered and dressed. She was sitting on the sofa with her bag on her lap. She was ready to go.

***

Jaina watched Zane make her way toward the parlor. Her pulse quickened. The woman, the white against the black, was breathtaking.

Zane smiled as she came through the door. "I have a couple members of my congregation on the ICU. They should be fairly near your brother. I hope it's alright that I dressed to visit them as well."

"Of course it is," Jaina said.

Zane smiled. "Good, then we should be ready to go."

The Thunderbird rumbled across town and into the multi-floor parking garage. After a thorough search, Zane finally found a space on the farthest end of the last row on the fifth floor. A full garage meant that many were recovering from illness…or not. As they made their way across the huge medical campus, Zane bowed her head in silent prayer for all.

***

It had been 32 years since Jaina had seen her older brother. The last time was the day their adoptions became final. Jimmy had been adopted by a kind-eyed older couple, Jaina, by a cold-eyed career couple. She liked the kind-eyed older couple better. If only they could have taken her too, things might have been different.

For the cold-eyed career couple, status was most important. Nothing mattered more than the amount you earned and what other people thought of you. They'd been embarrassed by Jaina from the moment she'd moved into their home. At first, they'd just been embarrassed that they weren't able to have children and had to adopt. As time went on, they became embarrassed by Jaina herself. No amount of polishing or beating could smooth her rough edges. No one would've ever guessed her to be the cold-eyed couple's biological child.

Jaina recalled that last visit as if it had just occurred. She remembered following the cold-eyed couple out of the social services building. She remembered the lecture as they walked toward their late model car. She was never to speak of her mother or brother again. The word "adoption" was never to be used in their home. Jaina had been directed to forget about her mother and her big brother, but she didn't. She never did what the cold-eyed couple told her to do.

That word, that horrid word, "adoption," was never spoken in the cold-eyed couple's home. It was never spoken until that day they loaded Jaina and all her belongings into the back of their SUV and drove to the lower end of town. They'd returned her like a piece of defective merchandise. On that day, the cold-eyed couple had no problem saying the word "adoption" at all. Jaina could still hear them explaining how it all just hadn't worked out, referring to her as if she was nothing to them at all.

"The child is not a good fit," the cold-eyed woman had said, "and we'd like to return her."

The cold-eyed couple had made sure that Jaina lost track of Jimmy and her mom. They'd taken great care to assure that she had no one. For a lifetime, Jaina didn't know where they were, only that they were out

Soul Mates

there somewhere. Now, she knew exactly where her brother was. He was just around the corner. Jaina took a deep breath as she walked beside Zane through the large double doors. Today, she was in charge. Today, she would choose to reestablish a connection that the cold-eyed couple had tried so hard to destroy.

***

The nurse's station was a flurry of activity. They waited. Jaina paced the entire time. Finally, the nurse took a moment. Jim was more alert and doing better and they were given permission to visit him.

They crossed the open ICU circle and stopped just outside room number four. Jaina looked over her shoulder before going inside. "Please don't leave me." She held Zane's gaze. "I don't think I can do this alone."

"You can, but you don't need to worry," Zane said with a tender smile, "because I'm not going anywhere."

Jaina peered through the doorway. The sandy-haired man lay quiet under the white sheet that covered his body. He seemed so small, so frail. Beeps and other machine noises resonated. It was a sterile space that smelled of antiseptic. She stood there, frozen in the doorway.

Zane waited a couple moments, then gave her a gentle nudge. "Go on, you can do this."

The nudge was all Jaina needed. "Hey there," she whispered as she moved close to her brother's bed. "Long time no see." She bent over and brushed a strand of hair the color of her own from his eyes.

Jim struggled to become aware. His voice was weak and barely audible. "Hi."

"Hi," Jaina whispered with a tender smile. "It's me…Jaina."

Jim's breathing became labored. Then, he choked. "I never thought I'd see you again." He gasped another breath. "You're beautiful." Jim's eyes shut, exhausted. His few words had robbed him of his strength. He needed to rest.

Jaina quietly backed away from his bed. She was relieved to find that not only was her brother still alive, but he was probably going to be okay. What Jim needed now was rest.

She turned around expecting Zane to be right behind her, but she was gone. Jaina found her around the corner, sitting in a hardback chair, her head dropped back against the wall. She looked either sick or in pain. Zane opened her eyes as Jaina dropped to her knees beside her.

"What's wrong?" Jaina asked. Her voice was full of concern.

"I don't know." Zane said she didn't, but she did. She said she'd never lie to Jaina, but she did that too. It was for her own good. "Something just came over me." Zane sucked in a breath and then another. "I've got to get out of here."

Jaina cocked her head. She didn't know why, but she wasn't convinced that she was getting the whole story. "Okay, you go for awhile. Try to shake off whatever this is and feel better." She reached up to brush a lock of hair from Zane's eyes.

Zane's eyes widened and she pulled away as if she'd been burned.

Jaina startled, then backed off in tears.

Zane jumped up, ran through the double doors, and into the elevator. On the ride down to the ground floor she prayed and kept her focus on her breathing. The doors whooshed open and she sprinted toward the parking garage and up the five flights of stairs. She reached the Thunderbird in time to jump in and lean back out to vomit. Zane wiped her mouth, brushed the tears that, by this point, were tumbling down her face, and started the engine.

Chapter Ten

Tears streamed down Jaina's cheeks too. One tissue after another wiped them away. The nurse who popped in to check Jim's vitals must have noticed because she met Jaina's gaze with a caring smile.

"He's doing much better, you know," the nurse said. "The first 24 hours are the most critical after an overdose. He's stable now and improving with each passing hour. That's really good."

"Thanks for taking such good care of him," Jaina said as she leaned back in the chair. Her tears had slowed, but her thoughts were still revolving around Zane's behavior. It hadn't made any sense. She'd reacted as if she'd been burned. It was puzzling. She'd been fine just 10 minutes earlier. Then the pieces came together. Zane hadn't reacted to her, she'd reacted to something else—something that must have just occurred. Jaina's anger turned inward. She was angry with herself for the way she'd reacted. She was also afraid because Zane's reaction suggested that something was terribly wrong.

Jim stirred and opened his eyes. He looked over at Jaina. "I'm glad you came. I'm better now that I have you here…not so alone." His eyes drifted shut again, but he struggled to open them. "I want you to go…rest…come back later. I'm gonna be okay."

"I'm so happy that you're better," Jaina said. She bent over to kiss Jim's forehead. "I'm glad to have you back in my life. You sleep, I'll check on you later."

Jim closed his eyes as Jaina headed for the nurse's station to tell them she was leaving. Then, she bolted through the double doors. She jumped into the elevator and ran to where they'd parked the car.

Zane was gone.

***

Zane hadn't meant for things to turn out this way again. She'd tried her best, but it wasn't good enough. She hadn't meant to react that way, hadn't meant to hurt Jaina, hadn't meant to drive her away. She hadn't meant for any of those things to happen, they just did. That's the problem with damaged people—the damage gets in the way. They do things that they don't mean to do.

Zane willed the Thunderbird to work her magic, but tonight she couldn't. There's just so much an old car can do. Jaina would be gone just like all the others. The problem was she wasn't really like them. She was different. Out of nowhere, Jaina had become the love of Zane's life and she couldn't imagine going on after losing her.

***

Jaina flipped her cellphone open and dialed. She took a deep breath and tried her best to not sound upset. On the third ring, Irene answered. "Sorry to bother you at home, but I didn't know who else to call."

"That's quite alright," Irene said. "Is something wrong?"

Jaina didn't feel she could be totally honest. "Zane and I got our wires crossed. Now, I'm stuck at the hospital without a ride back to the parsonage and she's not answering her phone. I was hoping you could pick me up and maybe let me in?"

Jaina made her way back to the circle drive. Irene would be there soon.

***

Jaina curled up on the end of the sofa and waited for Zane to get home. The antique clock struck 11:00 when she heard her car door slam. Within moments, her key turned the lock in the door. By the time it opened, Jaina was in the foyer waiting. She lifted up to slip her arms around Zane's neck.

"I'm so sorry," Jaina said. "I put my own baggage in front of being there for you." She kissed her cheek. "You needed me, but I didn't come through. I promise, next time I'll do better." She brushed a lock of Zane's damp hair to the side. "I don't know what happened today or what's wrong for that matter, but I do know that whatever it is, we can get through it."

Zane slipped off her jacket. "How's your brother?"

"He's better," Jaina said. She met Zane's gaze. "Do you want to talk about what happened?"

Zane shook her head. "I can't…I just can't…not now, anyway. I've got problems, Jaina. I don't think you'll want me when you know what they are." She touched Jaina's cheek. "You deserve so much better than me, and you don't have to stay. I'll take you to a motel if you want." Her voice was full of pain and exhaustion.

Jaina backed off. The conversation could wait until Zane felt better. "I'm staying. The subject is closed. Come on, how about we hit the sack. I'm tired. You're tired. We can talk in the morning."

Zane exhaled and her face relaxed. "Good plan. Anything you need?"

Jaina rose up to kiss her goodnight. "Just you. You're all I need."

Zane's eyes widened and she didn't breathe.

Jaina noticed. She yawned with exaggerated yawning sounds and stretched. "I'm beat. I'll see you in the morning, okay?"

Zane smiled, relieved again. "Yeah, that'd be good."

***

Zane dropped straight into agitated sleep the moment her head hit the pillow, tossing and turning as nightmarish images flashed through her mind. Each one had the same ending. She'd lose the beautiful blonde with the gorgeous light-blue eyes and jolted awake under the woman's disgusted gaze. Zane would wake, drenched in sweat, time after time after time. She'd struggle to get back to sleep, only to re-experience the nightmare. Finally, she gave up and went downstairs.

It was the middle of the night and quite an unusual occurrence. Zane stood in the center of the kitchen in her boxers. She stood there praying and considering options—milk or hot chocolate? She never really did decide.

Zane had fallen in love with Jaina and *HE* complicated everything. A sob escaped her lips. It caught her by surprise, as did the comforting arms that slipped through the darkness. They turned her around and pulled her close. Her knees buckled. She slid down the cabinet to cry. Jaina slid down beside her. She held and stroked her until sunrise.

***

"Hey there," Jaina said softly when Zane opened her eyes. She'd fallen asleep on Jaina's shoulder.

"I'm sorry," Zane said as she straightened her body. She looked away and then got up.

Jaina had barely moved a muscle for hours. She hadn't wanted to wake Zane. She groaned as she rolled to her knees and then pulled herself up to a standing position. She walked over to join Zane at the table.

Zane sat staring and unresponsive.

Jaina wasn't sure she'd even noticed that she sat down. She reached over and gave Zane's chin a gentle nudge. "Hey you." She kissed her on her lips. "There's nothing you need to be sorry about." The beautiful sparkle was gone from her eyes. "You want to talk about it?"

Zane swallowed. "I can't." She looked up. "At least, I don't think so."

Jaina pursed her lips and nodded. "Okay…we'll talk later. I think what we need now is coffee and breakfast." She raised an eyebrow. "I believe someone promised me scrambled eggs."

Zane forced a half-hearted smile. "Scrambled eggs, coming right up."

"Good," Jaina said. "Because I'm starved."

***

Jaina stayed at the kitchen table through her fourth cup of coffee. She'd been relieved when Zane had finally gone upstairs to take a shower. Jaina needed a few minutes alone to gather her thoughts. She needed to figure things out.

The morning had been full of tension and was mentally exhausting. Miss Bonnie would've known what to do, but she wasn't here…yet. As if her silent plea had been heard, the doorbell rang, and she scurried to answer.

"I thought you might get in this morning," Jaina said as she squeezed Miss Bonnie into a hug. She held the door open. "Man, am I ever glad to see you. Come in."

***

Miss Bonnie grinned. "My goodness girl, now that's what I call a welcome. It almost makes that life-threatening trek across the country worthwhile. Crazy drivers!" She cocked her head as her expression became more serious. "Something happen with Jimmy?" Jaina's eyes always told the story. Something was wrong.

Jaina shook her head. "No, he's actually doing much better. They're supposed to transfer him out of the ICU and over to the psych unit today. He's still a threat to himself and won't be able to have visitors for a couple days." She smiled. "But at least he's okay."

"That's wonderful news," Miss Bonnie said. "He's going to be alright and he's getting the help that he needs."

"Yeah," Jaina said. "That's as good as we could've hoped for."

"So what's wrong then?"

"I don't know how you do that." Jaina shook her head then met her gaze. "We'll talk later…when we have time alone."

Chapter Eleven

Zane loved the parsonage. It was such a beautiful house and so full of history, a perfect fit, an old fashioned home for an old fashioned soul. People who visited always wanted the full tour. Most who toured fell in love with the house. Miss Bonnie was no exception.

"I'll show you around," Jaina said, "but Zane's really the one who knows the history."

"I'll take your tour now," Miss Bonnie said, "and Zane's later."

Jaina shook her head and smiled. "Okay, as long as you understand that on my tour, you get the somewhat accurate broad strokes." She had learned quite a bit about the house and the era during which it was built, but by no means did she know it all.

Jaina walked Miss Bonnie through each room and down the hallways. She pointed out all that she knew of the irreplaceable decor—the original and perfectly restored elegant chandeliers, the ceramic fireplaces in pink, cream, green, and gold, and the circular stairway that was itself a breathtaking piece of carved art.

"Okay, so these are the bedrooms," Jaina said. "Zane's down the hall in the master and I'm in here. You'll be in there." She pointed to the room next to her own. "How about I go on down to get your luggage? I'm sure you're anxious to unpack and get settled in." She patted her friend on her shoulder. "After that drive, you have to be exhausted."

"I can get a motel," Miss Bonnie said. "I don't want to impose."

"Nonsense," Jaina said, "we want you to stay with us."

Miss Bonnie acquiesced. "So you're in this one…huh." She pointed down the hall toward the master bedroom. "And not in that one?" She raised an eyebrow. "That's so…unlike you."

Jaina couldn't help but smile. "Yeah," she said, "it is." She shook her head. "We'll talk later."

***

The master bedroom door opened and Zane stepped out. She was still raking her fingers through her hair as she came down the hall. She looked to Miss Bonnie and smiled a half-hearted smile. "Good to see you made it safely. I see Jaina's giving you the tour." She walked on by, down the stairs, and out the front door.

Jaina locked eyes with Miss Bonnie as she released a slow sigh. "Come on, let's go get your luggage from the car." When it had all been carried upstairs, she couldn't help but comment. "You sure brought a lot of stuff. I didn't know you were such a heavy traveler."

Miss Bonnie looked a little sheepish. "It's possible that I may have accidently brought a few of your things too…just in case you needed them." She braced for Jaina's hot temper to fly.

Instead, Jaina threw her arms around her neck, hugged her, and kissed her cheek. "Thank you. I was worried, afraid I'd be doing non-stop laundry."

Miss Bonnie shook her head. She'd looked away and Jaina had become a new woman. "You're welcome, sweetie. Anytime."

***

Jaina could see Zane struggling, but didn't know what to do. Zane had pulled away from her and as hard as she tried, she couldn't seem to close the distance between them. When Jaina touched, Zane flinched. When her eyes lingered, Zane's darted away. She'd pulled away, but Jaina could sense that what she wanted most was to be close. The beautiful sparkle that had once twinkled in her eyes was gone, replaced by a dull, dying ember. Jaina could pinpoint exactly when the unwanted transformation had occurred, she just couldn't figure out what had triggered it. She was desperate for a chance to brainstorm the situation with Miss Bonnie. Unfortunately, they had difficulty getting a moment alone. Finally the opportunity presented itself.

"I'll be back in time to fix dinner," Zane called out. She was off to meet the furnace repairman at the church. They heard the screen door shut behind her and the rumble of her Thunderbird as it backed out of the driveway. Finally, they had some time alone.

***

The floodgate opened. Jaina couldn't stop talking. She felt guilty about sharing what had happened at the hospital and about Zane's breakdown during the night. She felt guilty, but she had to do what she had to do in order to help her. Something was terribly wrong and she needed assistance in figuring out what it was. Who better to go to than Miss Bonnie?

"Come on now," Jaina said. "I'm counting on you to know what to do."

Miss Bonnie leaned back in her chair as she often did when she considered something carefully. "Hmm…it's difficult to know exactly what to do when you don't know what triggered the change in behavior. I do have some thoughts that may be helpful." She met Jaina's gaze. "First, I don't believe in coincidence. Since Zane's affect changed within minutes of the time you entered your brother's hospital room, I'd say that we can be fairly certain that he has something to do with what you're seeing. I know you'd thought it might be jealousy, but I don't think so. Zane hadn't even seen the two of you interact at that point. She simply looked into the room and reacted. There was no time for her to get jealous."

"I don't understand how this could have anything to do with Jimmy. I'd just seen him for the first time in 32 years." Jaina sighed and then looked up. "Unless…Zane knew him from somewhere else."

"That's exactly what I'm thinking," Miss Bonnie said. "See, you can do this."

Zane's reaction had not only been extreme, but instantaneous. Something significant had to have triggered that radical change in mood and behavior. Jaina was worried, but felt better knowing that Miss Bonnie was there and that she had her support.

"Zane's special, like you are," Miss Bonnie said. "She'll be worth your effort. You mark my words."

Jaina shook her head and smiled. "Oh, my effort is just beginning." She exhaled. "I'm frustrated, though, because I can't get her to talk about what's bothering her."

Miss Bonnie leaned forward in her chair. She cocked her head and they locked eyes. "And do you think that you were easy to get to talk, back when we first met?" She raised an eyebrow. "I don't think so." And chuckled out loud. "Why, I've been working on getting you to talk for years. It takes patience and firm nudges. Try it. It worked with you and it might just work with Zane."

***

The front door opened and Zane stepped inside. She immediately looked for Jaina and then broke eye contact. "I started dinner before I left. It shouldn't take too long to get it on the table—chicken kiev, baked potatoes, and corn pudding." She darted to the kitchen.

Miss Bonnie leaned over to whisper in Jaina's ear. "She cooks like that when she's short on time." She winked. "You just let me know if you change your mind about putting in that extra effort, because this straight woman might want to reconsider her options."

Jaina swatted her friend with the newspaper.

***

The parlor was the most romantic room in the house—fire crackling in the fireplace, comfy sofa, and soft lighting. It was a perfect place to make love. Jaina was glad that Miss Bonnie had gone to bed early. She scooted close and palmed Zane's thigh.

Zane stiffened, scooted. Then, she stood.

Jaina sighed audibly. "Zane…we need to talk about this."

"I think I'll head on up to bed," Zane said. "It's been a long day. I'm tired. See you in the morning, okay?" She headed for the stairway without even a kiss goodnight. "Eggs and toast for breakfast," she called out as she climbed around the first turn of the spiral staircase.

Jaina dropped her head over the back of the sofa and looked up at the ceiling. Her mind was clicking through her options. She wasn't known for being long on patience, but she'd been trying. She'd been trying to be patient with Zane, but her tiny bit of tolerance was all gone.

Jaina sucked in a breath and marched upstairs. She came to a halt just outside the closed master bedroom door. "Zane Winslow. I've had just about enough of this. You open this door or I swear I'll count to five and come in uninvited. Dressed or not. I mean it." The door didn't open. She stood there, mustering the courage to follow through. "One. Come on, open the door. We need to talk." She pressed her ear against the door. No movement. "Two. Open it, Zane…or I'm coming in." Jaina stepped back, frowned, and stared down the obstacle. She pursed her lips. "Three. I'm running out of patience, Zane. You'd better open this door." Jaina was out of patience, but was she really going to follow through? Yes, she was. "Four. Alright, that's it. I'm coming in." She dropped her palm over the knob. "Five…" The door opened.

Zane stood in the entrance wearing red plaid boxers, a white T-shirt, and an expression of total disbelief.

Jaina stood in the hallway. Her expression was stern, but loving.

"Feisty," Zane said. "I like it."

Jaina thought for just a moment that the beautiful twinkle had returned to Zane's eyes. She watched Zane swallow. It was gone.

"I don't know if I can summon the strength to do what you're asking me to do," Zane said. "I know I need to and I really do want to. I'm just not sure I can."

"Whatever it is that's troubling you," Jaina said softly, "we'll face it together."

Zane began to sweat. "I've fallen in love with you." Her breathing became more rapid. "And I'm afraid that if I do this, you won't want me anymore." Tears pooled in the corners of her eyes. "I'm afraid that in the end, you'll regret…"

Jaina stepped forward to touch her, but then reconsidered. "Nonsense. There's no way that's ever going to happen." Their gazes locked and then she smiled. "I'll never regret…us."

Zane took a breath. "I think we need to go for a drive. It'll be easier for me if I'm behind the wheel of the Thunderbird." She rubbed her eyes. Then, she looked away. "I need to stare at the road."

"Okay," Jaina said. "We'll do this however you want."

"Once you know the details…" Zane tried to catch a wave of emotion. "I'm pretty sure you won't want me after tonight." She looked deeply into Jaina's eyes. "I want you to know that I'll understand if you decide to walk away."

Jaina pierced Zane with her glare. "I believe you underestimate me." She spun back into the hallway. "It's

chilly, Pastor. You might want to put on some pants."
She headed for the stairs.

Jaina felt different these days—stronger and more
confident. She was sure that it was because of Zane. The
woman had changed her somehow. She'd made her
whole. Jaina knew deep within her heart that together,
they could get through anything.

Chapter Twelve

Zane tugged on her faded jeans and a long-sleeved t-shirt. She knew that what she was about to do would be difficult, probably the most difficult thing she'd ever done in her life. The only close second was burying her dad. This would be difficult, but she had to do it. A bandage had covered her wound for over 19 years. It was time she found the courage to rip it off. It was time, but ripping it off would be painful. She squared her shoulders, stood up straight, and looked in the mirror. "It's time to face your fears."

***

Jaina was waiting at the bottom of the stairs. They slipped on jackets and stepped out into the cold evening air.

Jaina bolted for the car. "Brrrr." God, how long was it going to take to adjust to this frigid climate?

Zane walked around and did the same. She looked over and smiled a thin smile. "The heater is on. You should be warm in a minute."

Jaina couldn't stop shivering. "Good, because I'm freezing my tail off."

***

The Thunderbird knew the route well. She was used to heading south to silence demons. Tonight would be different, though. Tonight, her job was to wake them up. By the time her rubber hit the four-lane, Jaina's teeth had stopped chattering and she was toasty warm.

Zane squeezed the steering wheel with both hands as her demon whispered in her ear. "You know you have nothing to offer her, but don't worry...she'll be gone soon."

Zane shivered and pushed the demon back into the recesses of her mind. She set the cruise control to 65, leaned back in the seat, and leapt into her nightmares. She trusted and loved the woman who sat beside her, trusted her enough to brave the pain, to face her fears. With a prayer for strength, she began.

"It was the last week before graduation," she said softly. "All the teams were having parties or whatever, our swim team too. The water was nice that day, nice, you know, like the chemicals and temperature were perfect. It had been a good season and we were feeling good...I was feeling good. The water was unbelievable." She glanced to Jaina with a sad, thin smile. "I was a good swimmer. That was the last time I swam."

Zane fell silent, drifting in her thoughts, and then resumed. "Our swim party wasn't just for our team. People could bring their friends, whoever, you know. I didn't bring anyone. Didn't have a boyfriend." She looked over and shook her head. "I was never into boys that way and I couldn't bring a girl. People already had their ideas." She sighed. "I didn't fit, never did, as far back as I can remember." She drifted again. "I went to the party. At that point, I thought they were my friends. Man, was I ever stupid back then."

Jaina was quiet. She was sure that she knew where Zane's story was headed. Jaina needed to be strong and hold herself together. She was already fighting back tears.

Zane's eyes went up to check the rearview mirror. She slowly returned her gaze to the road. It was like a hypnotic trance or something. She continued on in a steady monotone, kind of eerie. "It was my week to put away the pool equipment. We took turns, you know, and it was my week. The coach headed back to his office to wait for me to finish up. I put everything away and then headed back to the locker room to change clothes. It was dark. Everyone was gone. At least, I thought they were." She shook her head. "Man, I was so stupid."

Jaina swallowed nausea. She swallowed again and tried to push it down. This was like a horror movie. She wanted to turn it off, wanted to change channels, but couldn't. She took a deep breath and willed herself to push through. If Zane could do it, she could too.

"I took off my swimsuit and got into the shower. The water was cold, colder than the pool. I remember having goosebumps. Shivering. That's a funny thing to remember, but I do." Her eyes widened. "He grabbed me from behind and drug me into the towel room. It was so dark. I screamed but no one came. There were five of them, some from my class, some already out of school. God, I screamed and screamed. No one came." Zane shivered, but the car was toasty warm.

Jaina struggled to hold herself together. God, why had she forced Zane to do this? "You can stop, baby."

She wanted to touch Zane, but didn't. "You can stop…I understand."

It was like Zane hadn't heard a word she said. She continued in the monotone. "I screamed. I couldn't understand why no one came to help." Her gaze locked even tighter to the road and she gripped indentations into the steering wheel. "It was to teach me a lesson because I was gay. Everybody took a turn. I scrubbed and scrubbed for weeks. I just couldn't feel clean."

"You can stop, baby. It's okay," Jaina said. "You don't need to keep going."

Zane looked over as Jaina began to cry. "It was bad, Jaina. Really bad. I screamed and screamed and screamed."

Jaina put her hand over her mouth and swallowed hard. She reached over to touch Zane, but once again reconsidered.

Zane clenched her jaw. "They held me down and had their way. I heard them laughing as they left, laughing about getting kinky with the queer." She shook her head. "I thought I'd never stop shivering. I put my clothes on and walked home. I didn't stop crying for days."

Tears ran steadily down both their cheeks.

Zane looked over for a moment to hold onto Jaina's gaze. "I walked home that night. I climbed our creaky stairs." She shook her head. "I can't stand stairs that creak. I went into the kitchen where my mom was. I just didn't want to be alone. She was frying chicken. She always made the best chicken. I don't know why, but I just blurted out that I was gay. I told her the boys hurt me to teach me a lesson. I told her I was scared. Man, was I ever stupid back then. I was so stupid. She looked at me with such disgust. My mom said I probably needed the lesson to help me change my sinful ways. She said she was ashamed to call me her daughter." Zane's expression turned dead serious. "My God didn't sanction what they did to me. That was their own free will." She swallowed as she brushed away tears. "I left home that night and never went back, not until the day of my dad's funeral." She looked over once again to Jaina. "I've never told anyone about any of this before. You're the first. I just couldn't bring myself to say the words. Since that night…" her voice choked. "I've never been able to be with a woman and I probably never will. My life was ruined. They were bullies and they destroyed me."

Zane pulled over to the side of the road and turned off the engine. Her deep blue eyes locked on the lighter ones beside her. "There's more." She pursed her lips. "This is the part where I'm absolutely sure that I'll lose you." She looked forward as she spoke. "Your brother Jim was one of the ringleaders."

Zane checked her mirrors and pulled back into traffic. "I'll take you back home now. If you want to get your things and go somewhere else, I'll take you wherever you want to go." She drove with her gaze fixed on the road. Zane couldn't look to Jaina, not yet. She needed time to recover, time to prepare for the loss, which most certainly would come.

***

Jaina stared out the passenger window, still trying to absorb the horrors that had led to where they were at this moment in time. She'd spent virtually her entire life feeling angry and sorry for herself. Her baggage had been her all-consuming and driving force. It had prevented her from experiencing the splendor of life. Now, in a split-second of clarity, as she struggled to grasp what had been done to Zane, Jaina realized that she'd actually been the lucky one. In that one clarifying moment, all the randomness came together and she realized a much larger force had been at work in their lives. She did what she didn't often do. She thanked God.

Chapter Thirteen

Miss Bonnie was still awake when Zane walked down the hallway. When the master bedroom door clicked shut, she rolled out of bed. She smiled as she scurried downstairs. She'd been hoping for an opportunity to talk with Jaina.

Jaina heard Miss Bonnie coming. She was so predictable. "Hey there," she said as her friend poked her head around the corner. "Couldn't sleep?"

Miss Bonnie chuckled. "Oh my, yes. I've been sleeping like a log for hours."

"Uh-huh," Jaina said. She knew Miss Bonnie wouldn't have slept a wink until they were back home and she knew they were safe.

"Why, I just wake up about this time of night, have ever since I went through the change. I thought maybe I'd fix me a warm drink, settle myself back down to sleep."

"Uh-huh…whatever you say," Jaina raised an eyebrow and gave her a hug. "You don't fool me one bit." She smiled. "How about I fix you a cup of hot tea?"

"Want to have a cup with me?" Miss Bonnie asked hopefully. "Maybe we could chat for a little while."

Jaina shook her head. "Sorry to disappoint you, but I think I need to head on upstairs to be with Zane." She was only in the kitchen to get Fur Ball his dinner.

"Something happen this evening?" Miss Bonnie asked. "It's hard to miss those swollen eyes."

Jaina smiled a thin smile. "I'm okay." She set a steaming cup of apple-spice tea on the kitchen table. "Goodnight. I'll see you in the morning."

Miss Bonnie took a sip and held her gaze. "Goodnight, sweetie."

***

Jaina made her way up the stairs—slower than usual. She'd come to a decision. She flopped her bag open on her bed and dug until she found her silk nightgown. It had gotten buried. The tricky part was about to begin. She tossed the nightie over her arm and padded down the hall.

***

Zane heard the squeak of the shower door in the guest bathroom. It had to be Jaina. She was upstairs. The water turned on. Now, she was naked in the shower. Zane lay back on her bed and counted the spins of the ceiling fan. She knew that sleep wouldn't make an appearance for hours, not after the evening she'd had. It had been an evening of intense emotions all swirled together— including relief. Finally, after all these years, she'd managed to summon enough courage to re-experience the nightmare—out loud. She knew it was because of Jaina. She'd made all the difference in her world.

Soul Mates

Zane didn't hear her bedroom door open. Maybe without realizing it she'd fallen asleep. Or maybe she'd just been lost in thought. It was more likely though that the person sneaking in had been super quiet. Zane hadn't realized that she wasn't alone until she felt a warm body on the other side of the bed. She swallowed, closed her eyes, and began to pray.

"Hi," Jaina said softly from the far side of the bed.

Zane released the breath she'd been holding. "Hi."

Jaina turned to her side so that she could look into Zane's eyes. She couldn't help but also look at her body. Even in those plaid purple and green boxers, she looked amazing. She swallowed hard as she felt the familiar ping of desire. Jaina took a deep breath and tried to center her thoughts. She knew that this moment, these moments, might be the most critical of their lives together. What she said and how she said it could make all the difference in the world.

"I'm not sure I know the right place to begin so I'll just start," Jaina said with a soft smile. "Like you, beginnings have always come hard for me. I want to say some things." She brushed the back of her hand against Zane's cheek. "And I want you to lay quietly and listen."

Panic was swirling in Zane's beautiful blue eyes by that point. She choked an almost inaudible, "okay."

"Okay then…" Jaina smiled another tender smile and held her gaze. "I'm sorry for so many things right now." She thumbed away a tear. "Mostly, I guess I'm sorry that I put you through this tonight. I'm sorry that I forced you to relive that nightmare." She closed her eyes as she exhaled. "And I'm so very, very sorry that they hurt you." Jaina paused to catch her breath and regain her composure. "And, God forgive me, I am so angry. I am so angry…that I could kill them." She looked over and held Zane's gaze.

***

Zane was struggling to hold it together, but it was a lost cause. She simply couldn't stop her tears—not since Jaina. More had fallen this week than she had permitted to fall in her entire lifetime. This woman had effortlessly reached deep inside and made her feel, feel with such intensity that it seemed she couldn't breathe.

"You're not alone," Jaina said. "I want you to know that you're not alone anymore. I'm right here and I'm going to stay right here." She nudged Zane to meet her gaze. "Please don't be afraid of me. I won't hurt you. I'll never hurt you, Zane." She caught back a soft sob. "In fact, I think I can help you if you'll let me." Jaina raised up to fluff her pillow then lay back down. "Now, I'm going to sleep right here tonight. Don't worry, I'm not gonna touch you… just be here. Okay?"

Zane tried to smile. "Okay."

Jaina reached over to turn off the light. "I love you, sweetheart."

"I love you too," Zane said as a flood of tears broke free.

***

Miss Bonnie poked through the kitchen cabinets on a search for needed utensils. It was 11:00 a.m. She was starved half to death. She wasn't exactly trying to be quiet and wouldn't have been a bit surprised if her banging woke up Jaina and Zane.

***

Zane opened her eyes and glanced to the other side of the bed. Jaina was awake. She stretched and yawned. "Good morning."

Ah," Jaina said, "so much better. I like the sparkle." She smiled. "Hey there." She stretched and sniffed the air. "Do you smell bacon?" She sat up to check the clock. "Oh…it's late."

"Uh-huh," Zane said. "I believe we've forced our guest to fend for herself this morning."

"And I'm sure that's exactly what she did," Jaina said. "No way would she wait this long for breakfast." She chuckled. "And if I know Miss Bonnie, she fixed our breakfast too."

Zane lifted an eyebrow. "Well…what are we waiting for then? Let's go eat."

***

After breakfast, Zane headed upstairs to dress for the office. She needed to look over her sermon one more time. Since she'd only be there for a couple of hours, casual would be fine.

Jaina evidently heard Zane's footsteps as she came back down the stairway. She was heading straight for the door. "Aren't you forgetting something?" she called out just as Zane's hand touched the door knob.

Zane backtracked toward the kitchen with a sheepish smile on her face. She stepped behind Jaina and planted a tender kiss on the back of her neck. "Oh yeah, I definitely am…something pretty important."

115

Jaina tipped her head back and allowed their lips to meet.

Zane kissed her, and then was ready to be on her way. "I'll see you in a couple hours."

***

Miss Bonnie raised an eyebrow the moment the front door clicked shut. "Hmm…your pastor sure is walking with a bit more spring in her step this morning. I hope that means you two finally worked things out." She grinned. "I couldn't help but notice where *you* slept last night."

Jaina sighed. "It was a tough night, but we got through it."

Miss Bonnie got up to get the pot. "How about we pour another cup of coffee and you can tell me all about it."

Jaina shook her head. "I trust you, you know I do, but I think I have to handle this on my own."

Miss Bonnie's eyes narrowed with concern. "Things are better though, right?"

"Yeah, I think so," Jaina said.

Miss Bonnie smiled. She respected that some things were meant to be private between couples. The fact that Jaina had chosen not to share the details didn't bother her at all. "You've grown so much." She shook her head. "Sometimes I can hardly believe that you were once that defensive 11-year-old kid who stomped through our door so many years ago."

Jaina couldn't help but laugh at the memory. "Me too."

Although Jaina had made the decision to handle things with Zane on her own, she knew that she still needed Miss Bonnie's guidance. She was worried that she might be out of her depth. After all, it had been years since she'd practiced social work, and that practice hadn't continued one day beyond her internship.

Jaina had walked away that day, not because she hadn't done well, but because it simply hadn't been a good fit. She'd mastered the skills but couldn't deal with the personal nature of the profession. Now, she found herself in a bind. She knew a social worker couldn't hope to be objective when she was working with someone she loved, and yet Zane refused to talk with anyone else. Jaina didn't see any other option but to go forward and try to help her heal.

Miss Bonnie didn't either. "You can do this. You've been trained, just like me. Actually, from what I heard, you were quite good. But regardless of how good a social worker you are, it's hard to use your clinical skills effectively with someone you love. Be sure to ask for help if you need it."

"I will," Jaina said. "You can count on it."

***

It was a quiet meal that evening except for the ping of the China cups as they kissed their saucers. They were three hungry people. They also were preoccupied with their own thoughts. When the plates were clean, Zane got up and began to clear the table.

"Thank you for a wonderful dinner," Miss Bonnie said. "Your food was delicious."

"You're welcome," Zane said with a smile. "I'm glad you liked it." She stacked the plates. "Just sit and enjoy each other's company. I'll clear the table."

Miss Bonnie turned to Jaina. "So, did you talk to Jimmy today?" She sensed something was up.

Jaina swallowed. Her jaw tightened and she pursed her lips. "No, I didn't have a chance." She stood to gather up the remaining dirty dishes. "I'd better help Zane with these. I'll be right back."

Miss Bonnie leaned back in her chair and considered this most recent and very interesting development. She was still lost in her thoughts when a mouth-watering plate of lemon tiramisu appeared before her. She looked up with a grin. "Why thank you, Zane."

The atmosphere of lightheartedness returned to the room. The dessert was sinfully good. The conversation was easy and entertaining. Toward the end of the evening, Zane invited Jaina and Miss Bonnie to join her for church that next morning. They accepted without a moment's hesitation.

Eventually, Miss Bonnie began to stretch and yawn. She excused herself and headed up to bed. As she pulled on her purple and red flannel pajama bottoms, she looked forward to the next day. It held the promise of being quite interesting.

***

Jaina helped Zane unload the dishwasher. Before long, they too decided to call it a night. As she reached the top of the stairs, she turned in to her own bedroom to get her night clothes. Zane walked right on down the hallway. Jaina exhaled a sigh when the master bedroom door clicked shut. She shook her head, grabbed up her bag, and dropped it on the bed to dig out her skimpiest nightgown. Her head was still shaking as she marched down the hallway and into the bathroom.

Jaina had been thinking a lot about what had happened to Zane. She'd also been thinking about the lifelong impact of trauma as severe as what Zane had experienced. Her issues could only be described as atypical. Jaina smiled as she considered her own atypical set of skills—quite possibly the perfect fit for Zane.

Jaina had been intimate with more women than she could count, but none had ever been allowed to touch her, not in that manner. She touched, but never opened herself up to being touched in return. That would have required that she let someone in. It would have required that she leave herself open and vulnerable. Eventually, and most likely with considerable effort, Zane would be her first.

Jaina had established a set of rules for her own protection. They were there to keep her safe and prevent her from ever being hurt again. As she slipped on her transparent nightgown, she knew with certainty that she didn't need rules anymore. She knew that she was safe with Zane.

Zane had endured enough pain for a lifetime. The horrible things that had been done to her had left her terrified and so vulnerable. Jaina wanted the first time they made love to be only about the pleasure and not about the pain. For that to occur, she knew that her plan had to be perfectly executed. Zane would need to be in total control and anything that occurred would need to occur at her own pace. It was tricky, but doable. Jaina felt confident. She knew she'd had a lot of practice. All she needed to do was do what she'd always done well.

***

Jaina slipped into the darkened master bedroom, her hair still damp from a shower. Her skin was still damp, too. The shear nightgown clung as if it knew her. It left nothing for the imagination. She caught the scent of her own cologne as she approached the bed.

Zane was on the far side, facing the wall. Jaina could tell by her breathing that she was still awake. She knew that she had to have heard her come in. She was lying quiet and barely breathing—obviously trying her best to hide in plain sight. But Jaina was good at this. She knew exactly what she was doing. She also knew that she had Zane's undivided attention.

Jaina lay down on the bed, careful to stay on her own side. She palmed down her abdomen and began to caress herself toward climax. It had been so long. She had needs. Soft moans escaped her lips as her breathing quickened.

Zane's did too.

Jaina pressed and stroked a little faster. Her body writhed under her own touch and she gasped.

Zane sucked in a breath.

Jaina smiled. She could feel Zane's desire from across the bed. She dipped inside her opening and felt her wetness. She stroked hard and fast until her body stiffened and she collapsed.

Zane's eyes were wide open, staring at the wall. "Did you forget to tell me about your ornery streak when we were first getting acquainted, Ms. Wakefield?" she asked softly. She took another breath.

"Oh, I'm sorry," Jaina said. "Did I wake you?"

Zane rolled over to look her in the eye.

"A girl's got to do what a girl's got to do," Jaina said with a smile. "It was my own little version of sex therapy." She chuckled. "What did you think, sweetheart?"

Zane's eyes twinkled, but she didn't respond. What could she say? *It worked well. Thanks, I'm aroused?* Then what?

***

Jaina made stretching sounds at the buzz of the alarm. She rolled over. "Good morning, handsome. I feel rested and refreshed. How about you?"

Zane knew Jaina was being ornery again. Before she could form her answer, Jaina kissed her and popped out of bed—in her very skimpy nightgown. Zane watched her prance toward the bathroom and an increasingly familiar surge bolted through her body. "You're killing me here."

A low sexy voice called out from the shower. "Just be happy I took pity on you this morning," Jaina said. "I only did because I know you have to have your wits about you to preach."

Then, the most beautiful laugh that Zane had ever heard erupted from her bathroom.

Zane shook her head and smiled.

***

Jaina heard Miss Bonnie's bedroom door open. She poked her head out of the bathroom to let her know that she was almost ready to go. "Wow!" Miss Bonnie's outfit was really something. High heels with a black ruffled cream-colored dress. "You packed that fancy thing for your trip to Illinois?" Jaina smiled. "You look beautiful."

"Thank you, and I certainly did," Miss Bonnie said with a wink. "A single woman, especially one my age, needs to always be prepared. A person never knows when they might get asked out on a date."

Jaina chuckled as she glanced down at her own attire. "I'm just thankful I managed to piece mine together."

"With a body like yours," Miss Bonnie said, "I don't think you have to worry regardless of what you wear."

***

It was a beautiful old church with more stained glass windows than a single glance could take in. They stood in the center aisle toward the back, people-watching. It's what social workers did. The congregation seemed to be happily chatting in their pews. After all, it'd been a week since they'd been together. You could tell that they were friends and had missed each other. The pipe organ hummed softly in the background.

Jaina held her breath as long forgotten memories flooded from her past. "I've been here before."

Miss Bonnie looked over her glasses. "Well I figured you had, child."

"No," Jaina clarified. "That's not what I mean. I mean that I was here before, in this sanctuary when I was a small child." She pointed to a pew, just two back from the pulpit. "I think we sat right over there." Her eyes brimmed with tears. "We went to church here." A shiver traveled down her spine toward the floor. "I just know that was our pew." Jaina walked over and ran her hand lovingly across its smooth top edge.

Miss Bonnie followed. She laid her hand gently on Jaina's shoulder. "God works in mysterious ways," she said softly. "Don't you think?"

Jaina nodded and smiled. "Yeah, I do."

***

They scooched into the familiar pew and chatted softly until just before the service was to begin. They talked about everything and Jaina reminisced. Then the organ resounded and Zane walked reverently down the aisle. Her black robe flowed. Her stole trailed. She carried the Bible. Her eyes found Jaina's.

Jaina beamed with love and pride.

When the service was over, Jaina and Miss Bonnie stood off to one side. They watched until the last one in a very long line shook Zane's hand.

"Oh my, Pastor," the older woman with the cane said. "What a moving sermon on forgiveness you preached this morning. I felt the spirit in our midst when you talked about how humbling it is to be unworthy, and yet forgiven."

Zane smiled and squeezed the woman's hand. "I'm glad you found meaning in my words. May God bless you and keep you this week." As Zane shook that

123

last hand it dawned on her that it was almost time for Sunday dinner. Her nervous stomach began to churn and her eyes locked on to Jaina's.

Chapter Fourteen

Zane's level of anxiety rose with each mile that the old Thunderbird rolled south. In her head, she was counting the number of times she'd seen her mother since she'd left home at 17. That must have been about four. They hadn't shared a meal together since breakfast that last morning. The wheels turned as she prayed.

***

Jaina did her best to keep the conversation light as they drove toward the farm. She was afraid it would be no use, but she had made the decision to try anyway. Inside, she was literally seething. Zane probably sensed it. Jaina was angry with Zane's mom, angry with Jim, angry that Zane had been victimized, angry with most everyone these days, except Zane. All of their transgressions just looped round and round in her head. She wanted to, but hadn't been able to let any of it go. Today, she knew that was exactly what she needed to do. She was about to be put in a situation where she had to make nice with Nancy Winslow over a plate of fried chicken, of all things. Patience, forgiveness, and self-control had never been her strongest suits, but she resolved to do all three for the remainder of the day. The last thing she wanted to do was make this visit more difficult for Zane.

The Thunderbird parked and Jaina took hold of Zane's arm. "It's a beautiful farm." She smiled and held Zane's gaze. "I love that you grew up a country girl."

Zane breathed in the country air. "It is beautiful out here." She pointed to the acres of ground all around them. "That's all ours…I mean, my mom's. We farmed it when I was a kid. She farms it now." They stepped onto the third step of the old front porch. It creaked. Zane clenched her jaw. "That really needs to be fixed one of these days."

***

The door opened before they had a chance to ring the bell.

"Hello, Zane. I didn't know you'd be bringing someone with you. If we're lucky, we'll have enough." Nancy held the door open, but didn't smile. "Come in."

Zane turned to Jaina. "This is my mom, Nancy Winslow."

Nancy turned her head and body toward the kitchen.

Zane shut her eyes and took a breath. She hadn't even been allowed to finish her introductions.

Jaina first noticed shock and then pain flash through Zane's eyes. Again, she was furious. She couldn't help herself. She just reacted. She thrust her right hand forward and locked eyes with Nancy Winslow. "Zane's girlfriend, Jaina Wakefield. Pleased to meet you, Ma'am." She smiled a satisfied smile and cocked her head. It was nice to see that Nancy had been sharp enough to catch the sizzle in her words.

Jaina promptly went back to playing nice as Nancy laid out a fine meal on the table. She really did want the day to go well for Zane, for all of them. "Now I know where Zane gets her talent for cooking." Jaina looked to Zane, then Nancy, with a grin. "It's from you, Mrs. Winslow. That was the best fried chicken I think I've ever had…and that apple pie." She made a face with widened eyes. "Oh my, now that was to die for."

Nancy looked up with a squeezed expression that had to be painful. "I doubt that Zane got anything from me, but thank you for the compliments."

Zane looked like she'd just been stabbed in the heart. Her eyes moistened. "I'm going to the garage for a minute. I want to see if the extra mirror that dad had for the Thunderbird is still out there on the tool bench." She slid her chair back, stood, and walked away.

Jaina heard Zane choke a sob as the screen door slammed shut behind her. She leaned back in her chair, clenched her jaw, and sucked in a breath. She felt her face flush and knew she had to be beet red. "Okay, now you and I need to get a couple things straight. We might as well do it while we have this time alone."

Nancy met her gaze. She leaned back, sat up straight.

Jaina's shoulders tipped back. Her chin tipped up. "Your daughter is very special to me. In fact, I love her."

They locked eyes.

Jaina glared. "I won't have you treat her like a piece of garbage. I simply won't have it. I know you're used to doing it, but it will not happen again. Do you understand me?"

Nancy swallowed, but didn't say a word. Her expression was that of a small child being reprimanded for breaking her mother's cherished vase.

Jaina took a slow deep breath and released it. "We'll be leaving as soon as Zane gets back inside. That'll give you extra time this afternoon for some reflection." She slid her chair back, stood, and headed for the garage.

***

The dirty dishes remained on the table. Nancy didn't move. She just sat there with her eyes fixed on the handle of the back screen door, reflecting.

***

Zane turned the key and the Thunderbird rumbled. "My mom's manners seemed to improve dramatically during my brief visit to the garage," she said as she glanced to Jaina. "You didn't happen to have anything to do with that, did you?" She raised an eyebrow.

Jaina tried, but couldn't suppress her grin. "Now, what could I possibly have done to change your mom's demeanor in that short period of time?"

"Uh-huh," Zane said. "I thought so."

***

It was a gorgeous afternoon for a ride—crimson and gold leaves falling from the trees, bright blue sky, feathery clouds. The Thunderbird, with her soft leather seats and cream-colored top, was one sexy car. The car was sexy, but Jaina couldn't keep her eyes off the driver.

For some reason, this afternoon Jaina felt delicious in her scoop-necked sweater. She wanted Zane to want her—so bad. She adjusted her clothing to reveal a little more skin and waited for Zane to notice. Finally, she glanced her way. At first she looked surprised, then Jaina was certain she looked aroused.

Zane stretched her arm out and laid it on the back of the seat behind Jaina. Jaina moved closer so that Zane's hand dropped over her shoulder. Both took a breath as she reached up to lay her hand over Zane's. They held steady that way for the next few miles.

Zane sucked in a breath when Jaina guided her hand downward to cup her right breast. She squeezed. Her fingers flicked across the hardening nipple.

Jaina moaned. "Mmm, that's nice...I love your touch."

Zane sucked in another breath as she slipped inside the scoop-necked sweater. Her fingers touched Jaina's breast, skin on skin.

Jaina moaned again.

Zane whipped the Thunderbird over and parked underneath a nearby tree. Zane turned the key and the engine fell quiet. She pulled Jaina into her arms. They kissed, passionate and probing.

Zane pulled back. "I'm sorry." Her eyes brightened with dampness. "I can't do this." The engine rumbled and her mind sped a million miles away.

Jaina knew exactly where it had gone. "You don't need to be afraid," she said softly. "I won't hurt you, Zane."

Zane's eyes were glued to the pavement. "I don't know if I can." Her eyes darted to Jaina. "I'm not sure I'd know what to do. I'm afraid that with me, you'd be in for a lot of disappointment."

Jaina smiled a tender smile. "There's no rush. You took a step today. You'll know when it's time for us to take the next."

Zane relaxed her tense shoulders.

"When the time is right," Jaina said, "you'll know exactly what to do." She laid her hand on Zane's thigh.

Initially Zane flinched, but then the muscle relaxed.

"That's good," Jaina said softly. "One step at a time."

***

Jaina simply could not bring herself to call Jim. It felt strange because she'd thought about him her whole life, dreamed that one day she'd find him. Now that she had, now that she knew exactly where he was, she couldn't bring herself to call. And an in-person visit was absolutely out of the question. She just couldn't do it.

"You didn't call again today," Zane asked. She looked Jaina squarely in the eye. "You need to at least call your brother."

Jaina didn't answer. She just watched the ice cubes floating in her glass. Zane knew where she stood. There was really nothing new to say.

Zane stepped behind her. She bent down to kiss the hollow of her neck. "Tomorrow, we'll go up and see him…together. Okay?" She nuzzled. "Don't worry, I can handle it."

Jaina sighed. "I know you can. It's me, I can't handle it." She tipped her head back and looked into Zane's eyes.

Zane brushed Jaina's cheek with her thumb. She pulled her close.

Jaina pushed away. "I'm enraged. I couldn't stand to look at him or hear his voice." She sucked in a deep, angry breath. "And I can't understand how you can."

Zane put on her pastor-like expression. "Anger destroys a person. It'll eat you alive if you let it. The only way to avoid being eaten is to forgive." She touched Jaina's cheek. "That's the only way to heal." She smiled that sweet smile. "It's the only way to move on."

Jaina sighed. "I'm not sure I can do that." She pursed her lips and shook her head. "I'm not sure I can do that at all."

***

Zane flipped the kitchen light off and went to find Jaina in the parlor. "You coming to bed pretty soon?"

Jaina looked up from the lesbian mystery she'd been reading. "I am." She smiled. "I certainly am." She laid the paperback down on the coffee table, turned the switch on the table lamp off, and followed Zane upstairs.

Zane paused just outside the guest bedroom doorway.

Jaina did too. She furrowed her brow—confused.

"I'm here to help you gather your things," Zane said. "We can't have you running down the hallway in those skimpy night clothes that you wear." She raised a playful eyebrow. "Why, there was barely enough material in the one you wore last night to cover anything." She smiled. "I wouldn't want you to freeze." Zane threw a bag over each shoulder.

Jaina picked up the remaining items and followed her into the master bedroom.

Zane set Jaina's bags on the bed and began to rummage through her top dresser drawer for sleeping attire. Once the desired items had been located, she walked into the bathroom and shut the door.

Jaina heard the lock click and the shower spray turn on. She was annoyed that Zane thought she'd walk in on her without an invitation. Zane should know that she wouldn't do that…not yet, anyway.

***

Ten minutes passed before the bathroom door opened and Zane padded back out in her t-shirt and boxers, red and green this time. She flopped down next to Jaina on the bed. "Can we talk?" Her expression was serious.

"We can," Jaina said. She turned, propped up on her elbow, and waited for Zane to begin.

Zane held her breath for a moment and then exhaled. She did it again. "What happened in the car…well, nothing like that has ever happened before, not to me. It got me thinking, thinking that we need to talk. We need to talk before we take this thing, whatever it is, any further. I want you to listen to what I have to say before you say anything." Zane met Jaina's gaze. "I mean, really listen."

"Okay," Jaina said. "I'm listening. Talk to me."

Zane swallowed and ran her fingers through her hair. "I've never been with a woman," she said softly. "I know I told you that before, but I felt like I needed to say it again, to be sure that this time, you really heard me." Zane's eyes locked with Jaina's. Her gaze was so intense. "I'm 36 years old and I have never been with a woman. Never. I've wanted to on occasion...and I've tried. Never, not once, have I ever been able to follow through to a successful outcome. I tried to have normal dates when I was in college. I tried, but they never worked out. Dates always ended up the same way; a beautiful woman would become enraged and leave after I left her hanging. My last date, before you, was just before I graduated with my bachelor's degree."

Zane took a breath and released it slowly. She smiled a sad smile. "Ashley. She left in a firestorm, screaming that I was a sexually-stunted freak." Zane shook her head, then met Jaina's gaze. "I can still hear her words. She still screams in my head." Zane swallowed and looked up. "I'm afraid to try again."

***

Jaina took a moment to consider what Zane had said. "Sweetie," she said softly, "we all have baggage. You know I do." She smiled and shook her head. "My goodness, aren't we the pair? You've been with no one and I've been with more women than I can remember." She pursed her lips. "I didn't know many of their names, but I slept with them anyway. I think we're a perfect match for each other." She paused and took a breath. "I thought I was protecting myself from being abandoned again. I thought if I just didn't let anyone in, they couldn't hurt me. I was wrong." She touched Zane's cheek. "You changed my life, Zane. You changed my life and we haven't even had sex—not once. Sex isn't everything, you know. Without love and commitment, it's actually no more than a collection of techniques designed to induce orgasm. I know those techniques well." She winked. "I can teach you if you want. When you're ready." She stroked Zane's cheek again. "We all have baggage, sweetie."

***

Zane lay quietly for a moment before responding. "Well now, I certainly didn't see any of that coming." She raised an eyebrow and turned up the slightest smile. "I trust you'll be patient with me as I struggle to come up to speed." There was a twinkle in her eyes. "Who knows, I could be a slow learner."

Jaina shifted her position and they locked gazes. "Oh, I doubt that. You've actually made remarkable progress already." She smiled, sat up in the bed, and pulled her nightgown over her head. It dropped to the floor on her side.

Zane was taken by surprise. She released an audible "squeak."

Naked, Jaina settled back on an extra pillow. "You thought last night's attire was skimpy? Ha! Now you really know what skimpy is, don't you?" She'd planned her moves very carefully, knowing that Zane would need to be the one to touch first. It was easier to touch than to be touched. Jaina expected that at least initially she'd have a very bashful pastor in her bed. If Zane's color was any indicator, she knew she'd been right. Her plan tonight was simply to break the ice. Zane

134

could take as long as she needed. Jaina was prepared to give her time.

***

Zane wanted to run, but she had to stay. Jaina was naked and gorgeous beside her. She tried to control her eyes, but she couldn't. It was like they had minds of their own, traveling much lower than they should. Her breathing became heavy and she didn't know what to do. Her eyes had backed her into a corner. They'd left her no choice. All she could do was square her shoulders, take a breath, and push through.

Zane pulled Jaina into her arms, kissing her everywhere—above her shoulders, that is. She paused to gently suckle one ear, and then the other...over and over and over.

"Mmm, feels good...so good," Jaina murmured. "See, you know what to do."

Zane's tongue flicked wildly.

"Take me," Jaina moaned. She arched to Zane while gently pushing her downward.

Zane held firm and kept kissing above the shoulders to her neck, mouth, eyes, forehead, ears....

"Mmm, that's nice," Jaina said. "Now let's move a little lower. Come on, sweetie." She gave Zane another nudge. "Go down." Jaina arched again. This time she moved her breasts upward.

Zane's breathing became more rapid and Jaina could feel the intensity of her desire. She cupped the back of Zane's head, guiding her down to her sensitive nipples.

Zane took hold of one and then the other with such suction that it was almost painful.

Jaina nudged again, determined to break through Zane's resistance. She took a breath of frustration when Zane didn't budge. Jaina cupped her hand and urged it down her abdomen, pressing Zane's fingers into her wetness.

Zane groaned. "God, it's so warm…so wet."

"That's it, baby," Jaina murmured. "You've got it."

Zane stroked and suckled.

"Oh God," Jaina gasped. "So quick. I'm almost there."

Zane thrust inside, first with one, then two fingers. Her strokes were steady and deep.

Jaina closed her eyes, concentrating on her impending climax. It started high, then rippled deep. It was so different, having someone you love pleasure you.

"God…that's unbelievable," Jaina murmured. She thrust her pelvis upward to take in more of Zane. The spasms grew stronger. Her body stiffened. Her toes curled. She screamed and collapsed into Zane. In a few minutes, Jaina recovered and shifted her position. She expertly worked her thigh between Zane's legs.

Zane's loving demeanor disappeared in an instant. Without a word, she got up and left their bed.

Chapter Fifteen

Jim lay in his hospital bed, troubled. Jaina hadn't called for days. She hadn't called him and she hadn't called for an update on his condition. He knew because he'd checked. Jaina wasn't calling and she wasn't answering her cellphone. Jim was worried.

A nurse popped in, as they often did. "Good morning, Mr. Johnson."

Jim looked up. "Good morning. My sister hasn't called, has she?"

The kind nurse smiled. "No, I'm sorry sir, she hasn't." She moved to check Jim's blood pressure and other vitals. "How are you feeling now that you're on your new medications?"

Jim faked a smile. "Better I think. At least I'm not so depressed." He shook his head. "If I could just shake this feeling that the accident was somehow my fault, that God was punishing me or something." He swallowed the pills and handed the small plastic container back to his nurse. "Did you put me on the visit list like I asked you to?"

"I certainly did," the nurse said as she turned to leave. "I even called." She stopped just outside the door and looked back over her shoulder. "Getting better takes time. You just need to be patient with yourself."

Jim nodded. "I know." He took a breath and exhaled. "I'm trying, but patience isn't my strongest suit."

***

Zane parked the Thunderbird and went inside. "Good morning."

"Well, good morning to you, Pastor," Irene said as Zane bounced through her work area.

"There's a couple things I need to do," Zane said. "Then, I'd like to discuss a personal matter." She paused and smiled. "That is, if you have time."

The smile was contagious.

"Of course I have time," Irene said. "But before you go, I have a message for you, another patient to put on your hospital visit list. He doesn't attend here, but I guess he used to when he was a child." Irene handed Zane the slip of paper. "I didn't catch his first name, but I do have his room number.

"That'll work," Zane said as she whistled her way into her office. "I should be over there later today." She shut the door.

Irene shook her head and chuckled. Not only was God allowing her to watch her prayers being answered, but he'd given her a seat in the front row.

***

At about the same time that morning but a fair piece south, Nancy Winslow loaded the last of her breakfast dishes into the dishwasher. She stood up and the room went swimming. Nausea overcame her and she choked. She stumbled forward, trying to reach the kitchen chair. She didn't make it. Instead, she collapsed face-down with a thud onto the ceramic floor.

***

Zane got back home a little before noon. She felt good, better than ever, better than she dreamed possible. Having Jaina had made all the difference in the world. She'd literally blinked and everything in her life had changed. The dull had brightened.

That morning, Zane's thoughts had wandered, as they often did. She'd been thinking about the couples that she'd counseled through the years, couples who had drifted apart, couples who'd eventually taken their love for granted, and couples where one had shared intimacy with another. That morning, as Zane sat alone in her office, she'd taken a personal vow—a vow to Jaina, a vow to always be true, a vow to never take their precious love for granted.

***

Jaina heard the Thunderbird pull in the driveway and met Zane at the door. Her welcome home kiss was quite passionate. "You slipped out early." She nuzzled Zane's neck, enjoyed her scent. "I missed you."

"I left you a note," Zane said. "I didn't want to wake you. We got to sleep pretty late last night." Their eyes met and Jaina took a breath.

"Yeah, I know." Jaina said with a lick of her lips. "And the reason we did is all I've thought about all morning."

Zane blushed. "Me too."

***

The ambulance flew down the county road, swung around the corner, and skidded to a halt in the driveway of the old farmhouse. Two paramedics jumped out. They unloaded the stretcher and one jogged inside. He dropped to his knees beside the woman in her upper-60s. His medical bag was open. Another woman, slightly older, hovered. The other paramedic took the older lady aside. "You're Mrs. Gallagher, right? A neighbor?"

"Yes," the woman answered nervously. "I live right across the road in that big white house." She pointed to the two-story with the weatherworn paint. She shook her head. Her eyes were wide and her mouth hung open. "I came over just like I always do." She smiled a nervous smile. "It was our coffee break time. I knocked on both doors—front and back. I rang the bell too. When Nancy didn't answer, I knew something had to be wrong. She always answers the door." The lady pursed her lips. "So I got the key she leaves under the mat and let myself inside." She took a breath as she looked to the floor and pointed. "I found her, right there, just like she is right now."

"I see," the paramedic said as he jotted down a couple notes. "Do you know Mrs. Winslow well? I mean, do you know her well enough to give us her medical history or information about her family? I'm afraid she's not alert enough to give us much on her own."

"A little, sir," the neighbor said. "I know that she's a widow lady, like me. I know she has a daughter. I think the daughter's a pastor somewhere in town." She shook her head. "The daughter doesn't come around much. It's a shame. Her number's Nancy's ICE contact on her cellphone. Nancy spends most of her time alone, just taking care of this big old house. That's all I know, I'm afraid."

The first responder smiled. "Thanks, what you've told us helps a lot. We'll do our best to take care of her, Ma'am."

When they were satisfied that Nancy was stable enough for transport, they loaded her onto the stretcher and rolled out to the ambulance. The driver radioed before they pulled out of the driveway. Mrs. Gallagher stood watching as the emergency vehicle sped off with lights and siren.

***

Jaina snuggled against Zane's shoulder as they drove across town toward the hospital. It felt so good to feel her body against her own. Their love for each other was deepening. She could never have imagined opening up to anyone like this until Zane. Overnight, everything had changed. Now this love, this intimacy, was her whole world. She nuzzled closer. She loved everything about this woman and respected all that she stood for. Jaina took a breath, breathing in the distinctive scent of her lover, her soul mate. She gave her one last squeeze and sat up as the Thunderbird pulled into the parking garage.

"You sure you're okay with this?" Jaina asked. "Because I'm still not sure I am."

"I'm okay. I need to do this," Zane said. "I need to do this for me…for us." Their eyes met. "He's your brother. Now come on," she urged, "you need to forgive him." The deep blue eyes locked with the lighter ones. "You need to move on."

Jaina watched Zane square her shoulders. She took a breath and squared her own. If Zane could get through this, surely she could too. She could, but she didn't want to and felt pressured by Zane. "Okay…" Jaina opened the passenger door. "It appears I don't have a choice, so I'll try."

***

Zane walked a step behind Jaina as they made their way across the medical campus. She watched her in a way she couldn't remember ever watching a woman before. She filled her lungs with a breath of fresh fall air. It felt as if a new day had dawned. She opened the door for Jaina and they headed for the elevator. The ding announced that they'd reached their floor. It hissed to a stop and the doors opened.

Jaina reached back for Zane's hand. She was quiet, and Zane knew that she was struggling with what they'd come to do. They made their way down the long corridor, turned, and Zane opened the final door.

Jaina paused outside the first door. "How about I stay in the visitor's lounge while you do your visit? When you're done, you come back here and we'll go to Jim's room together."

"Sounds good," Zane said. "I shouldn't be more than 15 minutes or so."

Jaina ran her finger from Zane's clerical collar downward. Their eyes met.

"Yeah," Zane said with a smile. "I know. You think I'm hot in the collar. You told me." She chuckled and turned to walk down the hall.

"It's not just the collar I like," Jaina called out as Zane walked off. "I like the swagger, too."

***

Zane reported to the nurse's station as the message had directed. The nurse on duty stopped what she was doing and looked up. "Good to see you again, Pastor." Her gaze lingered much longer than it should.

Zane got directions to the room and headed down the corridor, preoccupied. That just didn't happen, not to her. She wondered if she'd done something to bring it on—the flirting. She strolled on into Mr. Johnson's room, but panicked and almost bolted when she realized where she was. She'd thought she was ready. Maybe she wasn't.

Jim looked up and met her gaze.

Zane swallowed, sucked in a breath, and prayed.

"Hello, Pastor," Jim said. "Thanks for stopping by. I just felt like I needed to have a prayer with someone."

Zane exhaled. He didn't know who she was. Her mind stirred the horrid memories and she struggled to remain composed. How could it be that he didn't remember her? Had she changed so much? He and four others had destroyed her life. They'd crushed her soul and reduced her to less than human. How could it be that the bully didn't remember his victim? He didn't remember his victim after all he'd done. She extended her hand. "Good afternoon, Mr. Johnson. I'd be happy to pray with you."

Jim smiled a depressed smile. "You see Pastor, I hit a rough patch and I'm still trying to get through it. After I lost my wife and little girl, I attempted suicide. I just can't stop thinking that my family died because God needed to punish me for something I did." He met Zane's gaze. "That's crazy, right?"

***

The shift happened in less than a millisecond. Maybe it wasn't actually a shift, but rather a conversion. Regardless, Zane watched it occur. She watched, but didn't have time to say a single word. It happened too quickly, like a knife slices a finger on the cutting board. It slices, and you look down to see you're bleeding. Jim's eyes had widened. The color had drained from his face. The bully had recognized his victim.

"Oh, my God," Jim said. "Oh, my God, please forgive me." He dropped his face into the palms of his hands and began to sob uncontrollably.

Zane sat down on the hospital bed and placed her hand on his shoulder. His breathing was labored. She felt his wide shoulders heave with every sob. She took a breath, released it, and spoke softly. "You are forgiven, my son. God is here. He loves you and forgives you. I forgive you." Zane rubbed Jim's back. "Your wife and little girl fell victim to an awful accident, an accident that you had nothing to do with. You are forgiven, my son. Go and sin no more."

An entire lifetime of remorse flooded from eyes the color of Jaina's as they locked on the deep blue eyes of his victim. "I'm so sorry…"

Without any hesitation at all, Zane opened her arms and pulled him close.

***

Jaina had waited the 15 minutes they'd agreed upon and then had come looking for Zane. She'd found her just in time to watch the scene unfold. Jaina couldn't hear the words that her brother and Zane had spoken to each other, but knew nevertheless what had transpired.

Zane must have sensed her presence because she looked up. She extended her arm and invited Jaina to join their embrace. Just then, a nurse stuck her head in the door.

"I'm so sorry to interrupt," the nurse said, "but Pastor, you have an urgent call on hold at the desk."

Zane apologized for having to leave so abruptly and headed for the door. She met Jaina's gaze on her way out.

"You're an extraordinary woman," Jaina said, "and just when I think I love you all I can, I love you more."

Zane smiled. "Ditto."

***

Jim had regained most of his composure by the point that Zane left his room. His eyes followed her to the door and then returned to Jaina. He tilted his head as he absorbed the new information. "So…you and the pastor… are..." He appeared puzzled. "I'm not sure what term to use."

"Together," Jaina spit. "We'll just go with together." She gave him a sizzling glare.

Jim's eyes widened. His brows furrowed.

"You know I love you," Jaina said as she paced around the room. Her glare resumed when she took a position beside the bed. "You're my big brother and I can't help but love you."

Jim started to speak, but Jaina trampled his words.

"I am so furious with you, more furious than I've ever been with another person in my life." Jaina spun toward the door, but once again returned. "Zane said I needed to work on it, so I am." Her nostrils flared as she tried to rein in her emotion. "I'm working on it, but I'm not there yet."

Jim's eyes glistened. This time, he didn't try to say a word.

Jaina turned for the door again, then paused to look back over her shoulder. "One day, but not yet." She held her brother's gaze. "So, you work hard and continue to get better. I love you, but I don't like you much at all. That's going to take me quite some time."

Chapter Sixteen

Zane stumbled away from the nurse's station and collapsed into a nearby chair. She slumped over and stared at the message in her hand. It surprised her that this event had hit her so hard. She never thought it would.

Jaina spotted her as she came out of Jim's room. She saw Zane's reaction and could tell from the distance that something was wrong. She picked up speed. It wasn't until she got much closer that she realized just how shaken she was. She dropped on one knee in front of her and reached up to brush the lock of hair that dangled in her eyes. "What's going on, baby?"

Zane didn't respond. She just sat there, crying.

"Zane, use your words," Jaina insisted. "Tell me what's wrong."

"It's my mom," Zane choked. "The neighbor found her. They think she had a heart attack. She's on her way here now." Zane swallowed hard. "I don't know if she's alive."

"I'm so sorry, sweetie," Jaina said as she gathered Zane into her arms. She stroked her and ran her fingers through her hair.

Zane held her hand up to her mouth and tried to pull herself together. "We have so much left unsaid between us. We've scarcely seen or talked to each other in years."

Zane had kept in contact with her dad, but not her mom. Nancy had always been too difficult to deal with. She choked back another sob. "My dad and I always got along." She looked into Jaina's eyes. "He got me, you know? He loved me for who I was. With my mom, it was always different." She looked away again. "No, not always, just since I was 11 or 12. It was like a switch flipped when I hit adolescence. All of the sudden, she hated me." Zane furrowed her brow. "I don't think she did, though—not really." The tears had slowed to a trickle. "When I came out that day, I could tell she couldn't stand to look at me anymore, so I left." Zane laid her head into her palms. "Please, God, let her still be alive."

Jaina wanted to be sure they got there in time. She kept urging that they make their way toward the ER before the ambulance arrived. Finally, after considerable nudging, Zane put her arm around her and they walked to the elevator.

***

Nancy's stretcher was wheeling through the double doors as they approached the reception desk. The doors hissed shut and she raised her head. Zane caught her gaze and exhaled the breath she'd been holding for the last several steps. An hour passed before the nurse came to tell them that they could go on back to see her.

"I'll just stay here," Jaina said. "You go see your mom. She'll be more comfortable if it's just you."

The nurse turned around. "I'm sorry, but I just happened to overhear." She looked to Zane. "Your mom specifically asked for you and your partner to be brought back to see her. She was very clear about that. She wanted to see you both."

Zane stood and shook her head. "Must have hit her head on something." She looked to Jaina. "Okay…if that's what she wants."

***

Jaina trailed behind Zane as she navigated her way down the long corridor. Zane paused at the door closest to the nurse's station. She peeked first and then stepped inside. By choice, Jaina waited in the hall. She wanted Zane to have a few minutes alone with her mom before she joined them.

Nancy must have sensed that Jaina had hung back. "Are you planning on joining us, Ms. Wakefield?" She spoke loud enough to assure that Jaina heard.

Jaina stepped into the room and Nancy continued her description of what had happened. "So, it was definitely a heart attack, but not the big one. It was just big enough that they're making me stay in the hospital, hopefully for just one night." She rolled her eyes. "And of course, there'll be multiple tests." Nancy looked up to Zane. "Your old mom's going to live, which is good because we've got things to talk about." Nancy spoke to Zane with a kindness that Jaina already knew to be atypical.

Jaina met Nancy's gaze.

Nancy responded. "I've been reflecting, just as you suggested." She smiled a warm smile. "Thank you for the nudge."

Jaina leaned down and put her arms around Nancy's neck. Her voice cracked. "Get better, okay?"

***

After several hours in the ER, Nancy was finally taken upstairs and settled into her room. Zane never left her side and Jaina never left Zane's. Some may have been irritated that the wait had been long, that the chairs had been uncomfortable, that the time had been wasted. It's funny how perspectives on the same event can be so different. Zane felt these hours had been more precious than any she could remember. The time, all of it, had simply passed too fast.

It was late when Zane and Jaina finally bid farewell and made their way toward the parking garage. They walked in dark and silence. It was a beautiful autumn night—clear, cool and crisp. Both were lost in their thoughts.

Zane unlocked Jaina's door. "Can you believe the change in my mom since Sunday? Come on. What did you say to her?"

Jaina slid into her seat and met her gaze. "Oh, nothing much. I guess she just had some time for reflection."

***

Nancy Winslow sat in the chair beside her hospital bed. She'd been there for hours just looking out the window and reflecting upon her life. She knew she'd be okay this time. There was just something about having a near death experience that had made her think about all the things she wished she'd done, and about all she wished she hadn't. She vowed she'd do better with

Soul Mates

whatever time she had left. It would all start with honesty—honesty with herself and with those she loved. Nancy closed her eyes as she felt a slight twinge pinch inside her chest. She leaned back and hoped that it would pass as her mind drifted to a happier time, a time when she was young. The twinge passed and she smiled. Those days as a young girl were the last days that she remembered feeling happy. Ahh, first love. She'd been happy and her mom had ruined everything. "I failed my daughter," Nancy sobbed out loud, "just as my mother failed me." She prayed that God would allot her enough time to undo the damage.

***

Jaina was waiting for Zane as she came in the door. It had become their unofficial tradition. It wasn't that Zane expected it or anything. It was just that when she was gone, Jaina missed her.

"Mmm…that's a nice welcome home," Zane said. "Kiss me like that again and you just might make me forget that I was going to take you out to dinner."

"Well now," Jaina said as she popped another quick kiss on her lover's lips, "we can't have that, can we?"

Zane laughed. "I should say not." She grinned. "I have big plans for you."

Jaina raised an eyebrow. "Ahh…now that sounds interesting."

***

Zane had put tremendous thought and planning into this evening, and of course, into how she'd do what she was about to do. Everything had to be perfect—extrordinary. It had to be an experience of a lifetime. How often does a person get to propose to their soul mate?

The Thunderbird cruised into the church parking lot and Zane parked in her usual spot near the back door. "I thought we'd stop by here on our way to dinner. I want to show you something that I've been working on." She got out and walked around the car, opened the door for Jaina, and she got out too.

Zane pulled out her keys, selecting the one that opened the door, and slipped it in the lock. The building was dark except for a sliver of light peeking out of the church library. "Come on."

Jaina followed Zane down the hallway, perplexed when they passed her office. When they paused just inside the library, she was perplexed again. The overhead lights were off. A table lamp provided the only lighting. Romantic jazz played softly in the background. A dining room table had been positioned in the center of the room.

Zane pulled out a chair for Jaina and she sat down. Zane met her gaze with a tender smile.

Jaina held her breath as Zane lit the solitary candle on the table. Its tiny light was amazing. It flickered on the china, the silverware, the crystal glasses, and throughout the room. Red and yellow rose petals blanketed the floor. In her heart, Jaina knew what was coming.

Zane stepped over to the serving table. She lifted one lid at a time and allowed the tantalizing aromas to escape their containers. "On the menu this evening:

Tuscan porterhouse steak with red wine peppercorn jus, mashed cheese potatoes, crisp lettuce salad with warm dressing, and creamed asparagus." She grinned. "Dessert is your favorite—key lime pie."

After dinner, Zane walked around the table. She dropped to one knee at Jaina's side and peered deeply into her eyes. The room spun and the world stopped turning on its axis. Tears streamed and Jaina brushed them away. The blue eyes locked on, each pair seeing enough love for a lifetime in the other.

Zane reached into her jacket pocket to retrieve a small velvet box. She opened the lid and held it out to Jaina. "Your love has made me whole. I can no longer imagine my life without you." She touched Jaina's cheek. "Drew once told me that she believed a person only got one chance at a soul mate. You're mine. And in this place where we first spent time together, I ask you to walk beside me, to be my lover, and to be my wife." She took Jaina's hand into her own. "Jaina Wakefield, will you marry me?"

Jaina pressed into Zane's arms. She kissed her neck and ran her fingers through her hair. "Yes," she whispered through happy tears. "Of course I'll marry you."

***

To say that Nancy was anxious to be discharged from the hospital would have been an understatement. She was just one of those people who couldn't tolerate being under the control of someone else, even when that control was for her own good. She'd been absolutely miserable and had done her best to make sure that everyone else had been too.

Zane had no doubt that the nurses were probably more anxious to move her mom on down the road than she was to go, and that was saying something. She felt their pain. She'd been there before. "I'm sure they'll be in soon, Mom. We just need to be patient with them. They have other patients and I'm sure they're doing the best they can." She pulled over an empty chair, hoping Nancy would sit down. She didn't, but at least for a moment, she stopped her frantic pacing.

Nancy's blue eyes met Zane's. She raised her hand to touch Zane's cheek, suspending her trail of IV tubing in mid-air. Her fingers slid across Zane's collar, the symbol of her calling. Nancy smiled the smile of a mother who was proud of her only child.

Zane smiled back and scooted the empty chair an inch closer to her mom. Their eyes met again. This time, Nancy sat down.

Zane raised an eyebrow. "Thank you, Mom."

Nancy raised hers in return. "You're quite welcome, Zane."

***

Jaina hadn't visited or called her brother for days. She knew she should, but she hadn't. Today would be the day. They were already at the hospital. It just made good sense to go ahead and get it done. She willed her feet to walk into his room. It wasn't easy because they didn't want to go. Neither did Jaina. She looked up as she stepped inside the door. Their eyes met. His were brimming with relief, while hers were bursting with rage.

"I was hoping you'd stop by," Jim said. "I know you don't want to hear me say it, but I have to say I'm sorry one more time."

"I know you are," Jaina said, "but sorry will probably never be enough." She glared through tears that she willed not to come. "You robbed Zane and me of things that you can't even imagine."

"I know," Jim said, "I know I did, and I'm…."

Jaina glared and the conversation shifted to the only safe topic that they had—Jim's health. He looked better and obviously felt better too. She was pleased that he was improving. Jaina didn't wish him harm. In fact, she wished him well. He was her brother, after all. She loved him. Maybe one day, if Zane had her way, she'd even like him again.

"What's that I see on your finger?" Jim asked. His gaze had zeroed in on Jaina's left hand.

Jaina looked into his eyes, but didn't respond.

"It's new, right?" Jim asked. Their gazes locked. He kept on. "Is it from the pastor?"

Jaina leaned back in her chair. She inhaled and exhaled twice in a row. "Yes, it's from Zane."

Jim grinned a grin that took Jaina by surprise. "Congratulations, I'm happy for you."

He looked as if he'd hug, but Jaina backed away. She set her jaw. "Are you," she asked, "happy for me? How about us? Are you happy for us, too?"

"Yeah," Jim said. "I am."

Their eyes locked one more time.

Jaina wasn't certain, but she thought she caught a glimpse of sincerity.

Chapter Seventeen

Irene kept busy at her desk as she listened for the rumble. She'd been the first to know of Zane's plan to propose to Jaina. She had to know. Zane had needed her help. At least, she'd needed her kitchen. Irene had come through. Now, she waited. She wanted to know the outcome of their efforts. Was it a "yes" or was it a "no?" Her fingers froze on the keys when the door opened. "So? 'Yes,' right?"

Zane grinned. "It was a 'yes,' and we've got a date too. December 31st at noon."

Irene threw her arms around her pastor's neck and squeezed. "Congratulations," she exclaimed. She stepped back and peered over her plastic frames. "Now, you know Pastor, the congregation will want to be involved in your wedding."

Zane nodded. "Of course they will." She smiled a loving smile. "And I'm sure you'll see to it that they are."

"I will," Irene said cheerfully. "You can count on me to see to everything."

***

Nancy settled into the parsonage and what she was sure would become her favorite chair over the next several days. It was a comfy chair, well suited for taking naps, and centrally located in front of the large flat screen TV. Naps had become her new way of life since the heart attack. She hoped that her strength would return and the need for them would lessen with time. She was thankful that she once again had family who cared enough to help during her recuperation.

"Here you go," Jaina said as she handed Nancy a steaming cup of coffee.

Nancy took a sip. "Thank you. It's perfect." She caught a glimpse of Jaina's ring and raised an eyebrow. "That's beautiful. Are we destined to become family?"

"We are," Jaina said. "How do you feel about that?"

"Proud," Nancy said with no hesitation and a grin. "I feel very proud."

Jim's reaction and now Nancy's had taken Jaina by surprise. She wasn't sure exactly what she'd expected, but it wasn't happiness or pride. People change.

Nancy leaned forward in her chair. "I've decided to share some things with Zane. I'm going to do it this evening if you approve." She pursed her lips. "What I have to say may upset her."

Jaina met Nancy's gaze. "You already know where I stand with regard to Zane. I am fiercely protective of her. I won't have her hurt unnecessarily."

"Hear me out," Nancy said. "If you don't want me to share what I'm about to tell you with Zane, I won't.

"Fair enough," Jaina said. She listened with an open mind. When Nancy finished what she had to say, Jaina looked into the eyes of her future mother-in-law. "You, like your daughter, are an extraordinary woman." She kissed Nancy on her cheek. "You both make me very proud."

***

The rumble in the driveway was followed by tennis shoes thumping down the stairway toward the kitchen door. Nancy startled awake. She heard voices and tilted her head to listen. The voices were Zane's and Jaina's. Their tone was soft and intimate. Their words were private. Their love was like only one she'd ever known. She tried to shield herself from those bittersweet memories. She tried, but the words she'd overheard had called them home.

Nancy had always been a tough woman with a tender heart, and a rock-hard shell. It was a shell she'd nurtured layer by layer for most of her life. She'd nurtured it more than she'd ever nurtured her own daughter. She had to. It was the only way she'd found to survive. That shortcoming, along with one other, had haunted her for much of her life. The other, the seed from which the shell had grown, was buried deep. It was deep, but those intimate words unearthed it. Nancy was reminded of Zane's courage, her courage to be who she was meant to be, and to love who she was meant to love. She'd always resented that courage and had tried her best to beat it down. She'd tried, but she hadn't been successful. Nancy shut her eyes, leaned back in her chair, and thanked God. Her eyes opened again when Zane tiptoed into the room.

"Sorry," Zane said. "I didn't mean to wake you. I just wanted to let you know that dinner was about ready." She cocked her head. "Are you okay?"

Nancy met her daughter's gaze. "I was just thinking about some things that I wished I'd done differently." She flipped the lever and her feet dropped to the floor. She smiled. "I think there's still time."

Just then, Jaina popped around the corner. She too cocked her head to study Nancy and then sat down beside her. The more time she spent with Nancy, the more she liked her. It wasn't too surprising since she reminded her so much of Zane.

***

It's odd how something unexpected can come out of nowhere and shift your world, your views, and your experience. You think you've got it all figured out, why things are the way they are. Then, boom—something happens and everything's changed. For better or worse, it doesn't matter, because by that point, your thoughts are spinning out of control. You're spinning at the speed of light. All you can do is hold on, because you're going for one hell of a ride.

Zane had sensed something in the air that night. It was something big. It was something that both Jaina and her mom knew about, but she didn't. She waited, knowing that soon, one of them would tell her what it was. Jaina stood to collect the plates. Nancy met her gaze and she sat back down. She reached over to hold Zane's hand. Fur Ball jumped into Nancy's lap. He pawed, softening, and then laid down. She stroked him gently. As he purred, she began.

Nancy explained that there were things she needed to say, things that should have been said long ago. She hadn't said them because she'd lacked courage. She was a coward. The heart attack had been a clarifying moment in her life, its impact more good than bad. It had forced her to reflect on her life, her family, and her priorities. In her reflection, Nancy had found courage, a courage that had always been there, just buried deep inside.

"I know I've not been a good mother to you," Nancy said. She shook her head and pursed her lips. "I know that, and I'm sorry. If I could, I'd turn back time and start all over again. You deserved a mother who accepted and encouraged you, but you didn't get one. Instead, you got me, and I'm sorry."

Nancy had always acted as if Zane was her father's child, as if her conception hadn't taken two. Zane couldn't remember her mom ever acknowledging any quality that she'd gotten from her—not her looks, not her smarts, not even her interest in cooking. Nancy had denied their connection, their similarities, from the very beginning. Zane had always known the denial was a lie. She knew her mom did too.

"We'd known each other forever," Nancy said. "We went to school together, did chores together, laughed together, and cried together. She was my best friend and I loved her. Everything changed that day, the day a piece of my heart died." A tear or two rolled down her cheeks. "We were only 12. Times were so different back then. Girls were just expected to marry. I'm not even sure I knew the word 'gay' existed. I knew that we were different, though. I knew that we had feelings for each other. I knew that our feelings grew stronger in adolescence." She looked away. "We touched each other in ways I'd never imagined with another girl." She paused to smile at a memory. "That day we were nestled in the straw in dairy barn. I can still smell the straw, feel it prickle my skin." She caught back a quiet sob. "My mother walked in on us. She was disgusted and enraged." Nancy shook her head as her tears began to tumble. "She was my love, my only love, and my mother made sure I never saw her again."

Zane squeezed her mom's hand.

"Your grandma drug me inside, beat me black and blue, and quoted scripture. She broke my heart." Nancy paused and took a breath. "Eventually, I met your father." She smiled at another memory. "He understood the situation, and I married him. We had sex one time." She looked into Zane's eyes. "Our wedding day was the day you were conceived." Nancy swallowed hard. "I never forgot her though, never forgot our love, not in all these years. The day you were born I held you and looked into your tiny blue eyes. I loved you and named you for my other love. I named you Zane." She touched her daughter's cheek. "I didn't know your eyes would be a constant reminder of my loss. I didn't know they'd inflict that stabbing pain. I wasn't strong like you are." Nancy met her daughter's gaze. "Please forgive me. I'm so sorry, Zane."

Zane struggled to maintain her composure. "I do, Mom. I forgive you."

***

Zane stumbled up the stairs, down the hallway, and collapsed onto the bed. Finally…her mom and Miss Bonnie were in their rooms, she was alone with Jaina, and the house was quiet.

"You doing okay?" Jaina asked as she slipped off her jeans and lay down on the bed.

"Yeah," Zane said, "I'm okay. It's just a lot to take in." She shook her head. "Never in a million years did I expect to hear what I heard tonight." She put her arm over her eyes. "I'm okay with it, but man…"

Jaina scooted closer. Her fingers brushed lightly across Zane's nipple as she moved to hold her.

Zane's entire body stiffened and she sucked in a gulp of air.

Jaina sighed and rose up to meet her gaze. "What was that about?"

"I've got a lot on my mind, that's all," Zane said. Her eyes looked away.

"Okay," Jaina said. "Let's talk about it."

Zane sighed again and rolled to face the wall. "It's been a long evening. Can we just deal with this in the morning?"

"Sure." Jaina tugged her t-shirt down over her panties and rolled to her back. She lay there a few minutes before her feet hit the floor. "You just let me know when you're ready." She stomped into the bathroom, slammed the door, and slid down the wall. She sat with her knees pulled tightly against her chest and cried. A few minutes passed before she peeled off her clothes, stepped into the shower, and cried some more.

***

Zane studied the ceiling fan as she tried her best to mute the sound of the heart-wrenching sobs. Then, she squeezed her eyes shut as if shutting them would deafen her ears. It didn't. The sobs were breaking her heart, but she didn't move. She wasn't courageous. She was a coward, too. Finally, the water stopped, the sobs ceased, and the bathroom door opened. She exhaled and waited, expecting Jaina would join her soon.

Zane's mind raced as she tried to figure out what she'd say. She tilted her head, listening. The knob turned. The door opened. It clicked shut. She was left with unsettling quiet, alone and afraid. It wasn't rational, but she was afraid that Jaina was going to leave.

***

Soft sobs escaped through the guest room door. Zane paused to gather her thoughts, knocked softly, and then stepped inside. A sliver of street light peeked under the shade. She sat down on the edge of the bed and gently laid her hand on Jaina's thigh.

Jaina rolled over and looked at her with the saddest eyes she'd ever seen.

"I told you I had a problem," Zane said softly. She swallowed down her emotion. "Please don't leave me when you know how bad it is."

Jaina sat up. "Okay…so you have what you think is a serious problem. That doesn't mean I'm going to leave you. It means we need to work on the problem." Her eyes were like lasers. "Did you think that I couldn't see how scared you were? My goodness, all I have to do is look like I might touch you and you flinch."

"I know," Zane said as tears began to tumble from her eyes. "I need help."

"Then let's figure this out," Jaina said. "I wasn't pushing you, sweetie. I just wanted you to talk to me about what was going on."

Zane hiccupped a sob.

Jaina pulled Zane close to rock her against her body. "I'll help you." She kissed her forehead. "Whenever you're ready."

Zane lifted up to look into her eyes. "What if I'm ready now?"

Jaina smiled as she fingered a lock of Zane's hair. "Then we'll take it slow." She kissed Zane and gently reached underneath her shirt.

Zane began to tremble.

Jaina caressed and soothed, pausing to give her time to settle, and then did it again.

Zane whimpered as fingertips brushed across her nipple.

"That's right, baby," Jaina whispered. "Feels nice, doesn't it?" She kissed Zane with tongue. "I won't hurt you, sweetie. Just relax."

Zane did. She arched toward the pleasure. Her hips rocked and she moaned.

"Okay...I'm gonna reach inside your shorts to touch you." Jaina paused to be sure that it was okay, then followed through. "Mmm, nice." She pressed into her.

Zane's breathing quickened. She stiffened slightly and released a gasp.

Jaina stilled. "Still okay, baby?"

Zane nodded as she took a breath.

Jaina slipped out and upward, her fingers still slick with Zane's arousal. She began to stroke, steady and fast.

Zane groaned and stiffened again, this time in climax.

Jaina moved to hold her, but Zane pushed away. In those moments that followed, Jaina came to realize that her lover's issues were far more complex than she'd ever imagined.

"I need to finish," Zane said. Her expression was dead serious.

"Okay," Jaina said in an uncertain tone.

Zane left the bed, pausing as her palm reached the doorknob. "Give me a few minutes, then join me in the shower."

Chapter Eighteen

Jaina listened to the water running for several minutes before she knocked on the bathroom door. She waited for an answer before turning the knob. The room was foggy, but she could see Zane's silhouette in the shower, facing the wall.

"I'm so proud of you," Jaina said softly as she stepped under the hot spray and slipped her arms around her. She felt Zane catch her breath. Jaina kissed her back and squeezed. "You're safe with me. I won't hurt you." She nudged Zane, urging her to turn around. "My eyes are shut." She nudged again.

Zane trembled as she turned.

"That's good," Jaina said. She lathered her hands. "See, you're okay." She kissed Zane lightly and began to explore her nakedness with her fingers.

Zane sucked in a breath. "I'm ready."

Jaina opened her eyes to meet the most fearful gaze. "It's okay, honey. You don't have to be afraid." Her eyes just naturally trailed downward. What she saw sucked the wind from her chest and she struggled to breathe. "Oh, God, Zane."

***

Afterward, they snuggled under the blanket. There was much to say.

"I'm so angry," Jaina said. "I could kill him. Them. I know you think that's a sin, but it's the way I feel." She touched Zane's cheek. "I can't stand that someone hurt you that way." She squeezed her eyes shut. "I don't know what to do."

Zane brushed a curl from Jaina's eyes. Her voice was low and tender. "After it happened, I left home, and thank God, found Pastor Kate. She helped me to survive during the most difficult days. For me, survival was a process, a process that occurred over the last 20 years. I can only speak for myself, a pastor and a victim." She took a breath. "Over time and through my call to the ministry, my rage has lessened. Eventually, I was able to forgive the people who'd hurt me. But as you know, I still have a ton of baggage to work through." Her eyes met Jaina's. "You helped me, are helping me…finish. It takes time, honey. It takes time and sometimes help to work the rage out of your system." She kissed Jaina's forehead.

Jaina peered into Zane's eyes. "I don't know if I can stand to know all that happened to you, but I think I need to." She needed to know so that she could deal with it and move on.

Zane paused. Her voice softened. "They don't hurt…the scars. They did at first, but they don't anymore. The ones that look like punctures are bite marks. They're mostly on my breasts, but other places too. The boys passed me around, one to the other. It was like a game." She shook her head. "They were sick, you know? That one…" She pointed. "Just below the hairline is a brand. You never think about hair not growing back where there's been a burn, but it doesn't. It was from a small homemade branding iron made in the shape of a 'Q.' I heard them laughing about how they'd made it special, just for the occasion. It was quick, just one time. It was a long time ago." Zane pulled Jaina close. "They're just scars now. They don't hurt anymore."

Jaina struggled free. Her feet hit the floor at a run, making it to the toilet in time to vomit.

***

Zane's eyes opened before dawn. She felt different, lighter, as if the weight of the world had been lifted from her shoulders. She held her breath as Jaina stirred beside her. Zane didn't want to wake her, not this early, not after such a rough night. Zane watched as Jaina burrowed into her pillow. She twitched her delicate nose like she was being tickled by a feather. It twitched and then it stilled.

The sleepy eyes fluttered open and Jaina rolled over with a kiss. She stretched and yawned. "Good morning. What time is it?"

"Hey there," Zane said with a kiss on the tip of her nose. "Just a little before 10:00." She smiled. "I was letting you sleep."

Another stretch. "Our guests are probably sitting at the kitchen table," Jaina said. "With a fork in their hand."

"I'm sure they are," Zane said, "but this morning, your sleep was more important." She raised her eyebrow. "Plus, I seriously doubt that either starved in our absence."

Jaina chuckled. "You're probably right about that, but we should get up to check on them anyway."

Zane grinned. "As you wish, my dear."

***

They found the kitchen quiet, and the rest of the house too. Zane flipped the light switch and pushed "start" on the coffeemaker. "Huh...they're gone." She plucked the note in her mom's handwriting off the table. "It seems they went out for breakfast."

Jaina opened the curtains. "In my Echo, I might add." She couldn't help but shake her head and smile.

"Well, I'll be darned," Zane said, "they did. I told you they wouldn't starve."

"Nope," Jaina said, "guess not. They probably had a lot to talk about with all the commotion last night."

"Yeah, they probably did," Zane said as she caught Jaina's eye. "Probably wanted to go somewhere where they could talk in private."

***

The dishwasher hummed and swished the breakfast dishes as Jaina poured her third cup of coffee. She'd just sat back down to resume her crossword puzzle when the door opened. "I thought you two would come back sooner or later."

"We had to," Miss Bonnie said. "Nancy needed a nap." They chuckled, but as is often the case with humor, it wasn't far from the truth. She poured herself a cup of coffee and sat down.

Jaina looked over her glasses. "You up for a chat? Zane thinks I need to talk to you about something."

"Of course I am," Miss Bonnie said. Her eyes took on concern.

Jaina pursed her lips and began. "I know you heard us last night. You had to. We were loud enough...and right next to your bedroom, too." She smiled a thin smile and met her gaze. "Don't worry, we're okay. It's something else."

Miss Bonnie leaned back in her chair. She took a sip of coffee.

Jaina held nothing back. She told it all, of the struggle to be intimate with Zane, of the victimization, of her own all-consuming rage.

Miss Bonnie didn't interrupt. She just listened.

"They tortured my sweet, gentle Zane," Jaina said through tears. "The sadistic bastards tortured her because she was different. How could someone...how could my own brother have done that to her?"

Miss Bonnie swallowed hard. "I don't know, but I do know that Zane's right about you needing to find a way to let it go." She reached across the table and squeezed Jaina's hand. "Sometimes, it helps if you can find a way to turn a negative into a positive."

Jaina nodded. She understood. In fact, she'd been thinking the very same thing. "Zane was victimized, just as many kids in the LGBT community are victimized." She took a sip of coffee. "I feel a pull toward them and back to social work." She shook her head. "You think I'm crazy?"

Miss Bonnie smiled with pride. "No, sweet girl, I don't think you're crazy. I think you hear your call, just as Zane once heard hers." Jaina had grown since the last time she'd tried. This time, the profession would be a perfect fit for her.

Jaina leaned back in her chair. "I've decided to pursue my MSW." She slid her application packet across the table with a smile. "In a couple years, this won't just be your alma mater. It'll be mine, too."

Miss Bonnie grinned ear to ear. "I think there's enough of the University of Illinois for both of us."

***

Jaina lumbered through the back door and dropped the mail onto the counter. She popped the top on a can of Fancy Feast, dumped it in the bowl, and flopped down into a kitchen chair. It was only noon. She'd already been to Indy, fought the airport traffic, and made her way back home. It'd been an exhausting morning, but her mission had been accomplished. Miss Bonnie was in the air.

It struck Jaina as funny that Miss Bonnie had put off telling her that she wanted to go back home for a while because she thought Jaina would be upset. Ha! Relieved was more like it. This way, Miss Bonnie would be able to oversee the moving company as they packed Jaina's things for transport to Illinois and still be back in time for the wedding. It couldn't get much better than that.

***

Nancy had been snoozing in front of the flat screen all afternoon, that is, until Fur Ball jumped into her lap. "Are you still in there?" she called out. "How long can it take to update a resume?"

"I am," Jaina said. "I'm almost done, but I think I'm ready for a break. Can I interest you in a cup of coffee?"

"I'd love one," Nancy said, "that is, if you'll join me."

"Sure I will," Jaina said. She brought the steaming cup to Nancy and then sat down beside her. "You look like you're feeling better this afternoon." She pursed her lips. "In fact, you're looking stronger by the day. As much as I hate to admit it, I think you're about ready to go back home." She smiled and met Nancy's gaze. "I'll miss having you around, but at least you'll be here for Thanksgiving."

"I'll miss you too," Nancy said. "It feels so good to have family around me again. I was stupid for too long."

"We all do things that we regret," Jaina said. "What's most important is that we correct what we can and try not to make the same mistake again." She touched Nancy's hand. "You've done that." Jaina gave her a hug. "You're going to be the best mother-in-law ever."

Nancy's face broke into a smile. "And you're going to be the best daughter-in-law a mother-in-law could ever have."

Chapter Nineteen

Zane bounded through the back door and into the kitchen with her arms full of groceries. "This should be the last of it." She set the bags onto the counter.

Jaina was amused at Zane's level of excitement. It was literally off the chart. Drew and Stacey would be arriving in a few hours. Before they did, Zane had plans to complete much of the early preparation for their Thanksgiving dinner. Some might have dreaded that task, but not her. She was absolutely giddy.

"This is going to be so much fun," Zane exclaimed as she searched out the necessary utensils and lined them up neatly on the counter. "I really think you guys will hit it off. They're just regular folks, easy to have fun with. You'll like them."

"I'm sure I will," Jaina said as she leaned around to give Nancy a wink. It was fun seeing Zane so happy and relaxed. She slid her arms around Zane, laid her head against her back, and pulled her close.

Zane laid her paring knife on the cutting board beside the pile of chopped celery and arched back into the embrace. Then she set the next chopping victim, a Vidalia onion, onto the cutting board.

Jaina returned to the kitchen table and popped open her laptop. It was time to resume her search for a tiny needle in a very old haystack. Here, she could be with Zane and still get something accomplished.

***

Zane loved to cook. She loved to cook so much that had she not been called to the ministry, she could have been one happy chef. "Alright," she chirped, "the chopping's done. The cranberry salad's prepared and chilling in the refrigerator. All that's left to do is clean the turkey." She plunged her arm deep into the bird and pulled out the bag.

The doorbell rang.

"Can you get that, sweetie," Zane called out as she plopped turkey parts into the sink. "It should be Drew and Stacey."

"On my way," Jaina called out as she sailed around the corner in sock feet. She turned the deadbolt and opened the door. "Uh…oh, my God…uh…you're Stacey?" Her eyes must have been as big as saucers.

"I am," Stacy said with her million-dollar smile. She extended her hand. "And you must be Jaina."

Jaina swallowed and felt her face flush. "Uh…I am." She shook her head. "And I'm so embarrassed. I'm really not the spluttering idiot that I probably look like at this moment." She pursed her lips and frowned. "Zane didn't tell me…on purpose." She scanned the area near the front door for something. The newspaper would do nicely.

"Quite possibly, darling," Stacey said with a chuckle. "Zane probably wanted to save me as a surprise." She chuckled again.

"Please come in," Jaina said as she folded the *News Gazette*. "If you'll excuse me, I need to have a quick word with Zane." Jaina marched into the kitchen and raised the newspaper. SWAT!

"OUCH," Zane said as a grin spread across her face. "I take it you've met Stacey." She laughed.

"You didn't have the decency to warn me that when I opened the door I might find Anastasia Shanning standing on our porch?" Jaina asked. The newspaper went up again and came down. SWAT!

"OUCH!"

"Anastasia…friggin'…Shanning!" SWAT!

"OUCH!"

"Just regular folks huh? I opened the front door spluttering like an idiot," Jaina said. "You are in so much trouble, Zane Winslow!" SWAT!

"OUCH!"

By the time Drew stepped around the corner, Zane was laughing so hard she could barely catch her breath.

"She's a feisty little thing, isn't she?" Drew said as she stepped into the kitchen. "You sure you can handle her?"

Zane grinned, shook Drew's hand, and then pulled her in for a hug. "Oh yeah, I can handle her." She shook her head. "You two are going to love each other."

Drew caught Jaina's eye, struggling to suppress a laugh. "So…I understand that you've already met my adorable wife."

Jaina locked her gaze. She folded the newspaper, aimed, and swatted.

Drew dodged, but not quickly enough. Jaina landed her target.

"OUCH!"

***

Zane brushed the last of the graham cracker crumbs from the counter and into the trash. One by one, the guests had all made their way upstairs, and the house was quiet. It was quiet, except for the occasional moan that resonated through the walls. Drew and Stacey were obviously making up for lost time. Zane poured herself a final cup of coffee to the tune of another round of orgasmic screams. She locked eyes with Jaina and they laughed. It'd been a fun evening—special people gathered together, pumpkin cheesecake, a crackling fire, and a competitive game of Charades. It was the perfect start to a festive holiday weekend.

"I had a great time tonight," Jaina said. "Your friends are a hoot."

Zane chuckled. "They are, aren't they? I knew you guys would hit it off."

"Well we did," Jaina said with a smile and a raised eyebrow. "But don't think you're out of trouble just because I had fun."

Zane faked serious concern. "Oh no," she said, "I know I'm still in terrible, terrible trouble." She cocked her head and raised her eyebrows a couple times. "But I'm pretty good at asking for forgiveness. Heaven knows, I've had a lot of practice over the years."

"You are, huh?" Jaina said with a smile that was quite seductive.

"Yeah, I am." Zane stood to put her cup in the dishwasher and held out her hand. "Come on, let's go upstairs. I'll show you."

Zane couldn't have been more relaxed as she climbed the stairway toward their bedroom. She squeezed her brain trying to determine the exact moment when the change within her had occurred. She couldn't. She only knew that somewhere between pumpkin cheesecake and watching Jaina try to guess Bambi in charades, she knew. She could feel it deep inside. She was ready to take the next step. Tonight would be the night. She closed her eyes and took a centering breath as she opened the bedroom door.

Jaina met her gaze. It lingered until Zane moved to hold her, to kiss her, to share what was on her mind. She filled her hands, her mouth, and her mind with Jaina.

Jaina tipped back to expose her neck. "Mmm, that feels nice. Someone's in the mood."

"I am," Zane whispered as she nibbled on Jaina's ears and neck. "Take a shower with me."

"Now you're talking." Jaina peeled off her t-shirt and unfastened her bra. They dropped to the floor. Her remaining items of clothing fell on their way to the bathroom. She slid the door open, stepped in, and turned on the water.

A lump caught in Zane's throat as she prepared to follow. After a moment, she stripped and stepped in too. It felt so good—the water and Jaina.

"I want you to make love to me tonight," Zane said softly. "I mean…all the way." She held Jaina's gaze. "I'm ready."

"Oh, God," Jaina whispered. "I've wanted to hear you say those words for so long." She pressed her body into Zane, nuzzled and kissed her under the warm spray.

***

Jaina settled her iPhone into the dock and selected a playlist of soft jazz. The volume was low. She lit candles and their tiny lights flickered on the walls of the master bedroom. Jaina wanted everything to be perfect, romantic.

Zane had slipped on her robe, and by that point was watching Jaina from the chair beside the bed. Before long, Jaina came to her and lowered her body between her knees. Zane hissed in a breath filled with fear as well as anticipation.

Jaina reached up to untie her robe. She heard Zane swallow. "Just let go, baby," she whispered. "I'll take care of you." She began to lick her way up Zane's inner thigh. "Lean back and enjoy."

Zane gasped in another breath and groaned. "Oh, God…"

Jaina kissed along the way. "Just relax," she soothed. "It'll feel good."

Zane thrust upward to meet Jaina's mouth as Jaina took her in. She bit her lower lip and groaned.

Jaina spread Zane's folds and dipped her tongue inside. "Mmm, you taste good."

Zane began to pant. "Oh, God…"

Jaina focused on Zane's hardness. She licked, and kissed, and suckled.

Zane choked as spasms took hold. "I love you," she gasped.

Jaina pushed in, deep, and pulled out slow. "I love you too," she murmured. She pushed in again.

Zane's body stiffened and she began to tremble. She moaned a high-pitched moan and then relaxed.

Jaina lightened her touch and shifted her position.

Zane reached down to lay her palm on the back of Jaina's head. "Don't pull out…stay…I want you to stay inside."

***

Zane was in the kitchen by 4:00 that next morning. It was Thanksgiving and she was stuffing and prepping the Butterball. Soon it would be ready to pop in the oven. It'd be several more hours before the slow roasting turned out a tender bird. Everyone else in the grand old house slept as she poured a freshly brewed cup of hazelnut coffee and padded to the parlor. Her fledgling fire had just begun to crackle and warm the room, to warm memories of Thanksgivings from long ago.

They were special times, cherished reflections from childhood that she'd treasured for a lifetime— watching the parades, smelling crisping turkey in the oven, bowing heads as a family at the dinner table. Toasty warm memories of good times before everything changed. Zane stoked the fire as an image of her dad securing a Christmas tree to the top of the old Thunderbird drifted through her mind. She missed him as if he'd passed only yesterday. She wondered if the void would ever fill, if the pain would ever deaden, if the holidays would ever feel the same. She took a slow sip of coffee as her thoughts catapulted forward in time—to her mom—to Drew and Stacey—to Jaina. She'd bowed her head, silently thanking God for his many blessings, as familiar arms slipped around her shoulders.

Jaina nuzzled, planted tender kisses on Zane's neck, and moaned. "Happy Thanksgiving." She kissed again. "You're deep in thought this morning."

"Mmm," Zane said as she tipped her head back for another. "Just thinking about Thanksgivings, the love of family and friends, blessings." She smiled reflectively. "A little bit of everything."

Jaina made her way around and settled onto Zane's lap. She laid her head against her shoulder and snuggled close. "I don't remember much of my family at Thanksgiving. I guess I was too little." She smiled tenderly and met Zane's gaze. "Never thought much about what I'd missed, until you. Now, I think about it all the time."

Zane tipped her lips down to meet Jaina's in a gentle kiss.

"Someday, I want us to have a family," Jaina said. "I want to have our baby."

Zane kissed her lover's forehead. "Yeah," she said with a faraway smile, "and I want you to."

The rustling upstairs and on the stairway disturbed the private moment and the couple sighed in unison.

"Time to get to work on breakfast," Zane said as she shifted her position to steady Jaina as she stood up. "Maybe later on we can pick up where we left off."

Jaina's eyes glistened. "Yeah, I'd like that...a lot."

Chapter Twenty

They ate a simple breakfast, the kind you eat before a holiday feast. When all had been consumed, the guests moseyed in to watch Santa arrive on his New York sled. The hosts cleaned up the kitchen.

"Okay," Jaina said, "the breakfast dishes are all put away. I'm at your service." She looked up expectantly awaiting her Thanksgiving dinner job assignment.

The stirring spoon stilled and Zane looked up. Her eyebrow raised in playfulness. "Hmm, now I'm not sure how that would work—you being at my service." She grinned. "It sounds fun, though." She put a finger to her chin in contemplation. "Give me a minute, I'll come up with something." Her eyes did an obvious pass over Jaina's body.

Jaina smacked Zane with the dish towel. "Stop it," she reprimanded. "We have people all around us." Her eyes widened. "Your mom's in the next room, for goodness sake!"

"Alright, alright," Zane said. "If you insist." She nodded toward the clear plastic bag filled fresh green beans. "Break away."

"Uh-huh," Jaina said with a smile, "I get it. You get in trouble for misbehaving and I get assigned the crap job." She shook her head in exaggerated disgust. "Frozen would've been a whole lot easier."

"Possibly," Zane conceded, "but not nearly as fresh, nor as much fun."

***

The group sat down to a feast fit for royalty. Zane made sure of that. After all, it was an important occasion—a first Thanksgiving of sorts. It was special in so many ways.

Drew finished off a second plate of turkey, dressing, and trimmings. She was diligently scooping out a third. "Wow, I still can't believe you cook like this." Her gaze met Zane's and they smiled together.

"I can't either," Nancy piped in with a chortle. "Zane didn't touch a cooking utensil when she was growing up, not one, just tools and footballs. In that respect, she was just like her father." Nancy looked across the table to meet her daughter's gaze. Her smile turned tender. "In other respects, she was just like her old mom."

Zane's eyes moistened and Jaina reached under the table to squeeze her hand. They met each other's gaze and smiled.

"I'm stuffed," Jaina said as she pushed her plate toward the center of the table.

"Me too," Stacey echoed with a nudge of her own. "God, I'm glad all the bikini scenes are done. I may never get into that skimpy suit again." She smiled at Zane. "It was a wonderful meal and worth every last pound."

Soul Mates

***

The guests scattered and the hosts cleared off the remnants of another fine meal. Drew made her way to the parlor, a task not as easy as one might think, considering the quantity of food she'd just consumed. She unzipped her pants, dropped onto the sofa, and groaned.

The crackling fire popped as Stacey lowered herself to the floor between her knees. Legs tucked underneath her body, she rested her chin on Drew's thigh. "Poor baby ate too much." Her look suggested no sympathy whatsoever.

Drew grimaced. "I did," she moaned. "Why'd I have to take the third helping?"

Stacey shook her head. "I'm sure I have no idea."

Drew moaned again and shifted to what she hoped would be a more comfortable position. "Me neither."

Stacey snuggled inbetween her legs. "Zane and Jaina seem happy." She rubbed her cheek against her wife's pre-washed denim.

"Yeah, they do," Drew said softly. She'd never thought she'd see Zane like that, like she was with Jaina. "She seems content; satisfied."

"She is," Stacey said as she popped a kiss on Drew's knee. "And Jaina is too."

"Good," Drew said. "And they're so into each other." She chuckled. "Did you hear them last night?"

"Oh yeah," Stacey said with a face, "What do you think got me all revved up for round two?"

"Ahh," Drew said as she raised an eyebrow, "and all along I thought it was me."

"It was, darling," Stacey said as she stretched up for a kiss "The sound effects just sped up the process."

***

Zane cleared her throat as she stepped through the parlor door.

Jaina followed with four champagne glasses. "We have an announcement to make," she said as she set the long-stems on the table nearest the sofa.

Zane popped the cork on a bottle of pink bubbly and began to pour.

Stacey zeroed in on Jaina's ring finger. She'd clearly sensed that happy news was in the air. She smiled at the fine diamond perched upon white gold. "It's beautiful." She nodded toward the jewel and squeezed Drew's hand. "Look at that."

Drew's eyes fell to the diamond as well. Then they met Zane's gaze. "You guys are getting married."

Zane slipped her arm around Jaina's shoulder. "We are."

A contagious grin spread across Zane's face and throughout the room. The engaged shared plans for their wedding. They'd have a traditional nuptial, celebrated at Faith United, and officiated by Pastor Kate. Their chosen colors would be pastel shades of the colors of Zane and Drew's alma mater, orange and blue. The wedding party would consist of their closest friends.

"Miss Bonnie will be standing up with Jaina," Zane said as her eyes caught Drew's. "I was hoping you'd stand up with me."

"I'd be honored," Drew said with a handshake that quickly turned into a hug. She lifted her glass. "To soul mates."

The glasses raised and clinked. They sipped champagne.

Zane lifted hers again. "To life-long friends."

***

Jaina felt like a completely different person. She attributed the change within herself to love—of Zane, of family, of newly found friends. In a relatively short period of time, she'd grown to love, to trust, and to enjoy being with others. She'd grown to treasure being part of a family. Jaina had evolved in ways she'd never dreamed possible. One of the most noticeable was her newly found delight in holidays.

"I want to do something special for your mom's birthday next week," Jaina declared.

Zane looked up. "Sure. Whatever you want to do is fine with me," she said with half attention. "Good idea."

"I kind of have something special in mind," Jaina said as she kissed the back of Zane's neck. She was trying her best to draw Zane's attention away from the church budget and to their conversation.

"I'm serious," Zane said. "Whatever you want to do is fine." She chuckled. "You two are crazy about each other. I trust you'll plan something she'll enjoy." She shook her head. "Go figure, the mom I thought couldn't stand me because I was gay, turns out to be gay, and I think she loves the woman I'm going to marry. Of course, I understand," Zane said as she tipped her head back for a kiss, "because who wouldn't love her?" Another chuckle and her attention returned fully to the work at hand.

"Okay," Jaina said with a smile. "I'm leaving, but you'll beg me to tell you more before it's all over." She whistled on her way back to the kitchen table.

***

It takes time and practice to learn to put another's needs before your own and to function as a couple. Sometimes, even if you're a kind and considerate person by nature, you fall flat on your face. Zane was still early on the learning curve.

"I'm ready whenever you are," Zane said as she prepared to head for the hospital.

"Are you absolutely sure about this?" Jaina asked. She couldn't help but scowl. "You don't need to do this…certainly not for me."

"I know I don't," Zane said, "but he's our family. He did a terrible thing, but he's our family and it's the right thing to do. Besides, they won't discharge him unless he has someone he can stay with for a few days." She put her hands on Jaina's shoulders and looked into her eyes. "This is who I am. Your brother asked for forgiveness. I forgave him. My home is his home. That's all there is to it."

Jaina pursed her lips. "Well, I haven't forgiven him. In my opinion, you're taking 'turning the other cheek' to the extreme." She sighed. "Well, it appears your decision is already made. I guess I'll just have to deal with it, huh?" Jaina slammed her makeup case down on the vanity hard enough that it cracked. "It'll be a few minutes, *dear*. You might as well go work on your sermon."

Jim sat in the chair adjacent to his hospital bed. He was nervous and could barely keep down his breakfast. He was a bully, at least he used to be, and he was waiting for his kind-hearted victim to take him home with her. That reality had sent his thoughts spinning out of control. He tried not to tick through the things he'd done to Zane, but in the end, he couldn't help himself. He shut his eyes and squeezed his forehead with his hand. Nothing provided any relief. The regrets just looped round and round and round.

Zane popped her head in the door. "You ready to get out of this place?"

Jim startled from his obsessions and looked up. "I sure am," he said with a forced half-hearted smile. "Good to see you, Pastor." He leaned over to peer into the corridor. It was empty. "Jaina didn't come with you?"

"Actually, she did," Zane said. "She just decided to wait in the car, that's all."

"Oh," Jim said. His voice and eyes dropped toward the floor. "My paperwork's not done yet. You don't have to wait."

Zane touched Jim's shoulder. "But I will." She smiled the kindest smile. "Of course I'll wait for you."

***

Jaina was a quiet passenger on their way home from the hospital. Her mind and emotions were a jumble. She knew what Zane expected. She knew what she wanted. She knew how to please her. She just wasn't ready. Maybe she never would be. Jaina knew she was

KA Moll

supposed to forgive, to move on, and to let go of her anger. She just couldn't. That's all there was to it. Thanks to Zane, the man who'd sexually tortured her would be staying in their home. He'd be sleeping steps away from their bed. He'd be close enough to hear the sounds of their lovemaking. She was angry that Zane had been so inconsiderate of her feelings. Jaina wondered if that's what she had to look forward to in their marriage.

Jim was Zane's guest. Jaina stayed in the kitchen while Zane settled him in. She listened as the two chatted about the game that would be on later that evening. They chatted like they were old friends. It made her sick to her stomach…made her feel like a caged animal…made her furious. She marched up to the master bedroom. The door slammed.

Jaina dropped onto the bed, hoping to sleep away the evening. No such luck. She got back up to dig through her side of the closet. There they were—the jeans. Now to check the back pocket. It was still there. She stared at the scribbled number for several moments.

***

Jaina began scanning for her potential companion the moment she walked into the pancake house. She'd dialed her cell, but her call had rolled to voicemail. She'd figured correctly that Emma would be working.

"Hey there," Emma said from behind. "Coffee?"

Jaina's gaze lingered. "Yeah…join me?"

Within moments, Emma was on break and at her table. They talked for a while about nothing in particular. When Jaina got up to visit the restroom, Emma followed.

She caught up with Jaina in the hallway and leaned into her from the rear.

Jaina felt Emma's breasts against her back. This was wrong. Why was she here? She knew why…because she was angry. Because for a moment, she'd wanted to get even, to hurt Zane because she'd hurt her. She turned with the intention of telling Emma that she had to go. Before she got the chance, Emma pressed into her and kissed her with tongue.

Jaina pushed away. "I can't. I'm sorry."

Emma grabbed onto Jaina's wrist. "Did I do something?" Her eyes filled with emotion. "I thought this was what you wanted."

"It was, but not anymore." Jaina brushed the back of her hand against Emma's cheek. "It's not you. It's me. For a minute, I thought this was still who I was." She gently removed Emma's hand from her wrist. "I can't, Emma. I have someone at home."

***

Nancy heard Jaina come in the back door. "Come here," she called out.

Jaina's nausea increased as she walked in to join her.

Nancy patted Jaina's hand and met her gaze. "Are you and Zane having problems?"

Jaina smiled unconvincingly. "No, not really. We just had a disagreement over whether or not to bring my brother home with us." She tilted her head and raised a shoulder. "I lost and went for a drive to think about it. That's all." She smiled again, hoping that she'd been convincing enough for Nancy to drop the subject. Thank God she did.

***

The house was quiet except for the velvety voice of the sports announcer as he called the final plays of the fourth quarter. Zane's mind wasn't really on the game. It was on Jaina. She assumed that she'd already gone to bed. Jaina had been distant—gone much of the evening. Zane had decided to give her space. It was a bad decision.

Jim passed the almost empty bowl of popcorn across the sofa to Zane. "I still can't believe Anastasia Shanning is upstairs." He shook his head. "Wow…she's really something, isn't she?" He drank his last slug of beer. "I think I've seen every one of her movies."

"Yeah, she's a great actress. She's also a really good person," Zane said as her eyes flitted to Jim and then back to the screen. The pass had almost been intercepted. "Drew and my mom are good people too. I think you'll enjoy getting to know them."

Zane pulled her eyes from the game, over and over, as Jim yammered on.

"I never knew Anastasia Shanning was gay," Jim said with yet another shake of his head.

Zane sighed. Her frustration escaped. "Well she is, Jim." She looked over and her eyes pinned her chatty guest to the sofa. "A lot of people are."

"I know. I know," Jim sputtered. "I didn't mean anything by it. I just didn't know, that's all."

"It's okay." Zane shifted her position and was just about ready to give up. The Bears were losing anyway.

She couldn't concentrate. It was probably time to head for bed, time to face Jaina.

"Do you think my sister's ever going to talk to me again?" Jim asked somewhat hesitantly.

Zane switched off the TV. She took a breath and released it slowly. "I do," she said softly. "But you've got to give her time." Her eyes were like penetrating lasers. They met Jim's head on. "She's got a lot to work through. You and I, we've had 19 years to deal with what happened. Jaina hasn't. Give her time."

"I'm so sorry," Jim said for what Zane believed was the fifth time that night.

Zane's intake of breath was audible. "Stop apologizing to me," she shouted. "I don't want to hear one more apology from you. What happened... happened. You did what you did. God forgives you. I forgive you. Now stop apologizing and move on. We need to move past this. We need to move past this for us, but mostly for Jaina."

Jim sat, staring, not uttering a word. It was the first time he'd been quiet since they'd gotten home from the hospital.

"With Jaina," Zane added, "you may need to continue apologizing for sometime, possibly years."

Chapter Twenty-One

Zane slowly made her way up the winding staircase and down the hall. Jaina was already in bed. The light was off. She was acting as if she was asleep, but her breathing and soft chokes gave her away. Zane stripped down to her boxers and slid in bed beside her. Her stomach was churning, sick that she'd hurt Jaina through her own stupidity. Now, she was afraid it was too late to make things right.

"I know you're awake," Zane said. "Do you want to talk?" Silence. "I know you're angry too, mostly at Jim, but some at me." Silence. "I can hear you crying, sweetie. I know you're awake. Wouldn't you rather just come over here, lay on my shoulder, and talk about it?" Silence. "You know we'll end up talking sooner or later. If it's sooner, we'll both sleep better tonight. Come on…what do you think?"

The bed groaned as Jaina flipped to her opposite side. She glared red and tears streamed down her face. They puddled onto her pillow. "You're right. I am angry. In fact, I'm almost crazy with rage. The man who viciously assaulted you is two doors down from our bedroom. How can that be? How could you let that happen?" Jaina sucked in an angry breath. "I may work through this, I may not. Either way, you and God don't get to snap your fingers and tell me to deal with it. That man is in my home and I'm furious. I don't give a damn that he's my brother. And you, Zane Winslow, don't get to dictate that I just get over it because you and God think it's the right thing to do." A series of choked sobs echoed through the room. "You're damn right I'm angry."

Zane was initially speechless. Then, her eyes met the angry, hurt ones in her bed. "I'm sorry, baby. I don't know what I was thinking, but whatever it was, it was inconsiderate. Your needs and feelings are what's most important." She shook her head, threw the covers back, and prepared to get up. Zane would get up to do what went against her beliefs, against the heart of her ministry. "He goes tonight. Surely Jim has friends he can stay with. Don't worry, I'll take care of it"

"I love you," Jaina whispered.

Zane stilled and met her gaze. She'd do anything for this woman, anything. In a way, that realization scared her. She pulled Jaina close and kissed her forehead. "I love you, too."

***

The oppressive weight of the anger, and of course, the guilt, lingered for some time afterward. Damn Zane, why did she have to be so perfect? How could she always know just the right thing to say? Jaina thought she'd never fall asleep, but finally did.

She wasn't really sure what time Zane had made her way back to their bed. She only knew that she'd slipped under the covers sometime in the wee hours of the morning. Jaina had awakened, but hadn't said a word. She'd lain there, breathing as if she was asleep, silently beating down an overwhelming urge to confess. But she didn't confess. Confession might have eased her own guilt, but it would've ruined everything. No, she couldn't confess. If Zane knew what she'd set out to do that evening, it would shatter their relationship and destroy her trust in Jaina forever. Confession was out of the question. Jaina would just have to live with what she'd done…alone.

***

The darkness had lifted by morning with the new day holding a promise of light-hearted fun. Jaina didn't usually enjoy errands, but these would be different. Stacey was excited too and they giggled together as they prepared to leave. Kisses. Goodbyes. Promises to be home in time for lunch.

"I think they're up to something," Drew said as the Echo chugged out of the driveway.

"They are," Zane said with a wink. "I believe they're off shopping for a wedding dress." Her eyes widened. "God…and I still need to get fitted for my tux. If I don't do it pretty soon, I won't have one. I can't believe it'll be just over a month."

"Yeah, it won't be long now." Drew smiled. "You two are so cute together. I'm so glad you found her."

"It's like a dream, a dream that I never dared to have," Zane said, "until Jaina. It just came out of nowhere—hit me, hard and fast." She swallowed. "I can't imagine life without her. I look into her eyes and see our babies and their babies. Is that weird?"

Drew smiled a tender smile. "Soul mates."

"Yeah," Zane said. "I think that's what we are."

The bridal shop was very small and quaint. It was located in the center of the old downtown, not far from the parsonage. Their selection of attire was in a range from traditional to contemporary. The place was like no other within 50 miles. Jaina hardly knew where to begin, but Stacey did. She knew the world of fittings very well.

"Oh, darling," Stacey exclaimed. "That's the one. God…that strapless sheath." She grinned. "Mmm, it shows off your curves…very nice." She ran her fingers down the almost invisible seam. "It's breathtaking. Absolutely breathtaking."

Jaina beamed. "This one is really pretty, but its way out of our price range."

"Oh, no it's not," Stacey said with a shake of her head. "It's not out of your price range at all, because it's in mine."

"It's too much," Jaina objected. "I can't let you do that."

"Sure you can," Stacey said as their eyes met. "You see, we have plenty of money and we enjoy spending it. This morning, Drew and I were discussing what we wanted to give you two as a wedding gift. We decided that what we wanted to give you most was your wedding. In fact, I expect that just about now, Drew is having this very same conversation with Zane."

Jaina barely knew what to say or how to react. She had no point of reference for this. A survivor, she'd always made it on her own. She had to. It'd been her only option. Everything was so different now.

"Thank you," Jaina said softly. The two words didn't seem like enough, but they were.

Stacey smiled. "You're welcome."

***

Stacey paid as if the enormous bill was nothing. The pair cheerfully made their way out the door and down the brick sidewalk toward the car. They chatted as good friends do about everything that mattered and things that didn't matter at all.

"I still can hardly believe this is real," Jaina said as she inserted her key. The old car door creaked open and she got in. "One minute I'm on my own. I'm not in a relationship and don't expect that I ever will be. It's just me. The next minute, I'm moving across the country to be the wife of a pastor."

"It's all real," Stacey said. "Soon, you'll marry that handsome pastor, the love of your life." She smiled and her eyes twinkled as one who knew. "This love you share, the one that sparkles in your eyes right now, it's priceless. It's a treasure that most will never be lucky enough to experience in their lifetime." She tugged the door a second time to get the latch to catch.

Jaina started the engine and headed east toward Urbana, a city as different from Champaign as one could possibly be and still be so close. It was the heart and soul of campus-town. "One fun errand down, one to go."

Jaina slowed and turned into the old residential neighborhood. It was a neighborhood filled with two-story homes, virtually all of which were dwellings of past and present professors. The homes were impressive and perfectly maintained. The Echo swung a sharp left, pulled into a driveway, and parked under a tall red oak tree. The homeowner was expecting them.

"Thanks for agreeing to meet with me, Professor Lantry," Jaina said. "I hope it's alright that I brought a friend."

The intelligent woman's eyes widened in surprise. "Of course. It's perfectly fine that you brought your friend." She chuckled. "But you might have warned me that you'd be bringing a celebrity." Another chuckle as she looked to Stacey. "I believe I'll need an autograph before you leave, Ms. Shanning. Without it, my bridge club will never believe that you joined me for coffee." The grand front door opened wide. "Come in, make yourselves at home. I'll put on a pot."

***

To say the morning was fun would have been an understatement. Jaina was certain that she'd ride high on this outing for days. Most likely, Stacey would too. Shopping for her wedding dress had been a once in a lifetime experience, the kind that a person never forgets. Jaina knew she never would. The fact that the dress was literally plucked from her dreams just made it all the better. Yes, shopping had been fun, but what followed had been incredible. The pair still giggled as they stepped through the back door.

Jaina called out to Zane.

"They're not home yet," Nancy shouted from the far end of the house. She flipped the lever to lower her feet and padded toward the kitchen. "Did you two have a nice time?"

"We did," Jaina said excitedly. "We found it, my wedding dress." She met Stacey's gaze and they giggled.

KA Moll

Nancy smiled and raised an eyebrow. "I'll bet it's beautiful." She studied the younger women as if she suspected they'd been up to something else. "Now, you know Zane's not supposed to see it until your wedding day. It's an old superstition, but we don't want to take any chances."

"Don't worry," Jaina giggled again. "She won't see it."

***

Zane got up early, prepared to take her mom home on her way to work. It had felt good to have her stay with them so that they'd have a chance to become reacquainted. As a side benefit, they'd grown close. Yes, it was good to have her here, but better to have her well enough to go back to her own home.

"Ready to go?" Zane asked as she peeked around the corner to what had become her mom's chair. Either Zane looked sad or her mom thought that she should be.

"Don't worry," Nancy said as she met her gaze. "I'll be back. In fact, I'll be back before you know it—just a couple days, to be exact." She looked sternly to Zane and then to Jaina. "Now, don't you two go and buy too much for my birthday because I don't need a thing. You'll just have to pack it all up someday after I croak, so let's not add to the pile."

Zane pinched her lips. Her eyes narrowed.

Nancy shook her head and smiled. "Just a joke. Your old mom's fine. Sometimes she's got a twisted sense of humor. You just never had many opportunities to see it until now."

"We hope you'll stay overnight on your birthday," Jaina said as the two stepped out the door.

"I will," Nancy said as she made her way to the car. As it rumbled south she looked to Zane. "I meant to tell you that I enjoyed your sermon yesterday." She said it in a matter of fact tone. "You have a nice church." She waited for Zane to look her way. "And I've decided to transfer my membership."

Zane's mouth fell open and her eyebrow raised.

Nancy raised one in return. "What's the big deal? Don't you think this old gay lady needs to belong to an ONA church?"

Zane shook her head. "Absolutely, Mom." She laughed. "But lately…you are full of almost more surprises than I can handle."

Nancy chuckled. "Well if it makes you feel any better, lately I've been surprising the both of us."

Chapter Twenty-Two

Jaina thought about her duplex in Sarasota as she pulled on a black pair of dress slacks. The packing of her possessions should be well underway by now. She was certain that Miss Bonnie would have the situation well under control, but made a mental note to check in with her later that afternoon. She thought about Key West as she buttoned her white silky blouse. Jaina smiled. She could almost feel the sand between her toes and the sun on her back. It was a place she'd never visited before, but had always wanted to. Now, she'd have the chance. Key West was a gay-friendly hot spot and her dream destination for their honeymoon. She was still smiling as she slipped on her new pair of stylish boots. The wearing of boots was an added benefit to living in Illinois. She scooped the School of Social Work packet off the counter, inserted the Bluetooth into her ear, and headed for the driveway.

The Echo groaned as the engine started in the frosty temperature. As Jaina backed out, she initiated her first call, a call to Professor Lantry. These were days that required constant multi-tasking. It was the only way she knew to get it all done. "I'm just calling to check in. I wanted to be sure we were all set for our little birthday surprise." Jaina's smile grew wide. "Good deal…I'll pick you up Wednesday at 4:00." She terminated the call as a giggle escaped her lips. "This is going to be so much fun."

***

As Jaina plugged the parking meter, three blocks over from the School of Social Work, Zane stood reverently near the altar of Faith United. It was the place she always liked to start her day. It was a place she felt centered and close to God. Somehow, Irene had an uncanny sense of her presence there. It didn't matter how quietly she came in or where she parked her car, Irene always knew she was in the building and appeared. This morning was no exception.

"Good morning, Pastor," Irene said as she made her way cheerfully between the pews and down the aisle. "You really have been full of the spirit lately. Yesterday's sermon, oh, my..." Her eyes lit up and she smiled. "Everybody's noticing." Irene sat down in the front row.

Zane watched the older woman with fondness. She smiled, knowing what would come next. It had happened so many times before.

As expected, Irene patted the seat beside her.

Zane sat down.

"How's that wedding planning coming along?" Irene asked. "Anything your church ladies can do to help?"

Zane shook her head. "No, I think we've got everything under control. The fittings are all done. The honeymoon reservation's made." She took a breath. "And I've prayed without ceasing."

Irene reached down to brush a piece of lint from her navy skirt. "You know, the Women's Fellowship would like to take care of decorating the church for your wedding and reception. You're our family and we want to somehow be involved."

Zane smiled. "We wouldn't have it any other way...thank you."

***

Zane was certain that she and Jaina had been sucked into a whirlwind. Between wedding planning, her mom's heart attack, and company galore, the time they spent together other than when they were in bed seemed to always be on the fly. Just the thought of having an entire evening alone with Jaina had kept her jazzed all day.

"I can't believe we're here all by ourselves," Zane said. "It seems like it's been forever." She cocked her head in an obvious listening pose. "The house is so quiet." Her eyebrow rose. "Makes me want to make some noise." She lunged.

The lunge took Jaina by surprise. She squealed and sprinted.

"Run if you must," Zane called out, "but you're just making it hard on yourself." Their eyes met and Zane sprang again. "It's going to result in lots of torment."

Jaina paused to laugh at Zane's most recent failed attempt. It was the pause that did her in.

"Gotcha," Zane said with satisfaction and a grin. She slipped her hand inside Jaina's bra.

"Mmm," Jaina moaned. "Don't forget you promised torment."

Zane laughed. "Oh don't worry, you'll be tormented alright."

***

Jaina scurried around that next morning preparing for the birthday party, and of course, the big surprise. By lunchtime, all the decorations were hung, the balloons were inflated, and the cake was cooling on the counter. The house literally screamed, "HAPPY BIRTHDAY!"

It was all coming together as planned, just like clockwork. Jaina had just stepped back to admire her handiwork when a familiar rumble summoned her attention to the door. Zane was home early, as promised. She exhaled and smiled.

Before she knew it, Zane was in the kitchen, and dinner prep was down to the final count. The champagne was on ice. The glasses were chilling. The dining room table was being prepared for company. Zane laid her spoon down and peeked around the corner just as Jaina was tweaking the last place setting.

Zane crinkled her brow. "We're expecting a fourth?"

Jaina folded the remaining cloth napkin. She placed it underneath the silver and looked up. Her smile was a satisfied smile. She didn't say a word.

"Uh-huh, still not talking, huh?" Zane said as she stepped back into the kitchen. "It'll be common knowledge soon enough. I can wait."

Jaina sent Zane to pick up her mom a little before 3:00. She delayed her own departure by 40 minutes to assure that Zane had enough of a head start to make it back first. The event had all been carefully planned right down to the very last detail, just like clockwork. Nancy was to think she'd be joining them for a simple dinner and homemade birthday cake—nothing more, nothing less, and certainly nothing special. Zane was to serve her a drink and seat her by the fire. Then, she was to return to dinner preparation. Jaina hoped that all her planning would pay off. She wanted a very special evening for Nancy.

***

The special guest stood at her front door awaiting Jaina's arrival. As Jaina rounded the corner and turned into the cobblestone driveway, the woman stepped onto the porch and secured her front door. Her heels clicked as they made their way down the winding sidewalk toward the car. Jaina studied her as she approached. Her hair was cut with style. Her attire was a tailored suit that smacked of sophistication. Her character was decent and scholarly. Professor Lantry was an eye-catching woman.

The passenger slid into the seat with a noticeable exhale. "I'm afraid I'm a bit nervous," Professor Lantry said as she tugged the seatbelt gracefully over her shoulder. "I've been trying to mentally prepare myself for this all day. I thought I was ready." She took another quick intake of breath. "But I guess I'm not."

Jaina smiled a reassuring smile. "It'll be okay. We'll just take our time getting across town. You'll be ready by the time we pull into the driveway." She smiled again and reached out to touch the special lady's hand. "I'm glad you decided to come."

Kind eyes met each other. "I am too," Professor Lantry said. "I've been looking forward to seeing Nancy again after all these years. It should be fun to meet her family, and of course, to wish her a happy birthday." She looked away. "But it's been a very long time. Just because she's remained special to me, doesn't mean that I…" She paused and took another breath. "Oh well, as I said, it's been a very long time."

Jaina shifted to a lighter subject, hoping to help her guest relax. "So tell me more about your cruise. It's next month, right?" Jaina shook her head as her eyes watched the road. "I'm not sure I'd have enough courage to head off to the Bahamas all by myself."

The gentle woman shifted her position to look at Jaina. "If you're alone dear, you either find the courage or you sit home. It's as simple as that." She smiled. "I tend to be a person who likes to go for the gusto."

***

It all came together for Jaina as she drove toward home that afternoon. It wasn't that she didn't understand that what she was about to do was special, because she did. It was more that she suddenly realized that her actions might alter the course of two lives. It was that tomorrow might be better than today, because of something she'd done. That realization sent chills running up her spine. She settled her nerves with a breath as the Echo pulled into the parsonage driveway

"Well, here we are," Jaina said. "Sit tight and I'll be right back." She exited the car and tiptoed into the house. She wasn't surprised to find Zane already totally re-immersed in dinner preparation.

Zane looked up when the back door squeaked open and Jaina stepped in.

"I hope you're at a good stopping point with dinner," Jaina said with a smile, "because you're going to want to see this."

"Ready anytime you are," Zane said with a raised eyebrow. She shook her head as Jaina zipped back out the door.

In moments, Jaina returned with her guest.

The trio met each other's gaze.

"Professor Lantry," Jaina said. "This is my fiancée and Nancy's only child, the Reverend Zane Winslow."

Zane appeared perplexed when the older woman's eyes teemed with tears.

Jaina smiled and continued. "Zane, this is your mom's childhood friend...*Zane* Lantry."

Zane paused. It took an extra moment to process what had just occurred. "Well, well...it's nice to meet you," she said with a tender smile. "I believe I'm your namesake."

Chapter Twenty-Three

Jaina took hold of Professor Lantry's hand and led her toward the parlor. The older woman was moving slowly and Jaina paused to allow her time to catch her breath. This was clearly an emotional experience.

Nancy was seated beside the crackling fire, sipping her drink and listening to Jaina's specially selected arrangement of romantic jazz. She looked up, surprised, yet her gaze immediately locked on to Professor Lantry. There was instant recognition.

Jaina fought back tears. She released the professor's hand and watched as time screeched to a halt, then reversed. The blue eyes were 11 again.

"Oh, my God," Nancy cried as the love of her life pulled her close. "Zaney."

Zaney shut her eyes, nuzzled, and kissed Nancy's neck. "I never thought…" she choked. "I never thought I'd see you again…hold you in my arms…hear anyone call me Zaney."

The women were once again lovers. The soul mates had been reunited. They'd been separated for a lifetime and now clung together as if there'd been no separation at all. They also clung as if there'd be no tomorrow.

As Jaina watched, her mind filled with Zane. She couldn't help but feel the weight of what she'd almost done. It was as if her secret had driven an invisible wedge between them. What was she going to do? She reached over to squeeze Zane's hand.

Zane smiled and pulled her in for a kiss. "I love you, baby."

Jaina swallowed. "You too."

***

Zane padded back into the kitchen to lower the cooking temperature. Dinner could wait. What was occurring in the next room was far more important. Jaina had done something special, something that Zane would never have thought to do in a million years. It wasn't that Zane wouldn't have wanted to, just that it wouldn't have crossed her mind. Jaina and Zane complimented each other. Each brought something different to their relationship—a different set of skills and a different perspective on life. Together, they were well rounded. Together, they were whole.

Zane looked lovingly into Jaina's eyes. "You're an amazing woman." She kissed her lips. "And I'm so lucky to have you in my life."

Jaina leaned into Zane, resting her cheek against her chest. "It's me who's lucky." Her voice cracked. "And I don't know what I'd do if I lost you."

Zane kissed the top of Jaina's head. "You're not gonna lose me, sweetie."

Jaina caught back a soft sob.

Zane stroked her hair and pulled her close. "What's wrong?"

"Oh Zane," Jaina said. "There's something I have to tell you."

Just then, Nancy appeared in the kitchen doorway. Her eyes left no doubt what she had on her mind. She'd come to talk with Jaina. Jaina wiped her eyes and managed to pull herself together. God, what had she almost done?

"Zaney told me you searched until you found her," Nancy blurted out. "She told me you did that for me. You found my first love and tonight I feel like a school girl again." Nancy tried desperately to swallow her emotion. "I feel desire that I haven't felt for decades, desire that I thought I'd never feel again." She opened her arms and pulled Jaina tightly against her breast. "My words are inadequate," she whispered. "No words would be enough to thank you for all you've done."

***

After dinner was served and consumed, Zane raised her glass to propose a toast. It was a toast she'd been composing in her mind for virtually the entire evening.

"To that moment in time," Zane said softly, "when one pair of eyes looks to another and recognizes the reflection of their own soul." She met each pair of eyes in the room. "To the one true love of our life, our soul mate."

The glasses clinked. The clinking was followed with activities typically associated with a birthday celebration—the blowing out of the candles, the eating of the birthday cake, and of course, the singing of the happy birthday song.

Zane stepped away to light the candles on the cake. She crept back slowly so that they wouldn't go out, pausing for a moment at the parlor door. There they were, sharing a single cushion at the end of the sofa, her mom's head resting against her first lover's breast. She hated to interrupt but unfortunately had no choice, unless she wanted wax to become a second layer of cake icing.

Nancy smiled as her daughter padded into the room. Zane dropped to her left knee, and held out the flickering offering. Nancy closed her eyes and did what was expected of her. She made a wish, sucked in the deepest of breaths, and blew. The candle flames were promptly extinguished.

"Good job," Zaney said with a big smile. "What did you wish for?"

"I'm not telling," Nancy said. "If I did, it wouldn't come true."

Jaina nodded toward the console piano as Zane prepared to carve the cake.

Zaney acknowledged the communication and nodded back.

"I think we should ask our guest to accompany us on the piano," Jaina said. "It's not every day we have an emeritus professor of music in our midst." She winked at Zaney. "I assume you're able to pick out 'Happy Birthday.'"

Zaney smiled and raised an eyebrow. "Well, I certainly hope so." She stood, briefly met Nancy's gaze, and then walked over to the piano. She stroked the instrument once, as if it were an old dear friend, and then sat down.

Nancy watched Zaney as she stretched her long slender fingers and rolled up her sleeves, remembering Zaney's first piano lessons. Nancy beamed with pride and pleasure when those fingers danced across the keys and voices raised in song. Zaney played, and played, and then she played some more. She played until the old clock on the mantle chimed 12:00.

"If you'd like, you're welcome to stay with us," Jaina said. "I think you're about my size so I'm sure we can find you some sleepwear."

Nancy answered before Zaney had a chance. "That's really nice...and I hate to disappoint you, but I believe what might suit us best," they giggled like girls, "is if you take us on over to Zaney's."

Zane met Jaina's gaze with a wink. "I'll get my keys."

***

The coffee was brewed and a plate of soft oatmeal cookies had been placed in the center of the conference room table. As usual, Irene had everything ready before the first elder arrived for the meeting. Zane was thankful for many things and that was one of them.

"Let's hope for a brief one this morning," Zane said as she positioned a copy of the agenda in front of each place. "I still have scads to get done before tonight's Christmas Eve service." She nodded to Irene. "It all looks good."

Before Irene had a chance to blink, Zane was gone. She was headed in full stride toward the sanctuary. Lately, she'd become a person who didn't waste a minute. She had only a few to spare and she used them all wisely. This morning, she was using them to check out the most recent additions to the altar, the poinsettias.

Irene sprinted down the hallway after her. "I didn't get a chance to tell you that you have a message to call Pastor Kate before your meeting this morning. I think it's about her motel reservation." Irene pursed her lips and shook her head. "I hope she can find one at this late date."

Zane was already shaking her head. "She doesn't need a motel reservation. I already told her that she could stay with us." She made a quick lap around the sanctuary, nodded her approval to the poinsettias, and headed back to her office. If she hurried, there'd still be time to make the call.

***

The fire spit and the seasoned log shifted position. Blazing hot flames tickled the damper. The parlor smelled of freshly cut pine and twinkled with tiny multi-colored lights. Jaina snuggled against Zane's chest. "It was a really nice service tonight. Your mom was so proud." She tipped her lips upward. "And she looked so happy. I've never seen anyone look as happy as she does with Zaney."

"Yeah," Zane said as her fingers brushed a lock of blonde hair from Jaina's eyes. She leaned in to kiss her. "You did that. You gave her that happiness as a gift."

"Speaking of gifts," Jaina said softly, "I have an unusual one for you."

Zane shifted her position to meet her gaze. "You do, huh?" She kissed her forehead.

"It's something unusual, but special," Jaina continued. "Something you can't actually have until our wedding night." She kissed Zane's neck. "It's something I need to tell you about though, later when we're in bed."

"Okay," Zane said. Her curiosity was peeking off the chart. "Sounds interesting." She wanted to know more, but chose not to push. At some level, she sensed the significance of the moment and the significance of the gift.

***

Jaina's emotions were a constant swirl of extremes. She'd always been prone to mood swings, but this was so much worse. It seemed like she was either over the top with excitement, swallowed by guilt, or wild with fury. Jaina could tell that Zane didn't know what to expect from her. In fact, she looked as if she was tiptoeing around in a field of eggshells most of the time. Jaina prayed that Zane would be able to sustain that level of patience until she got through it.

Jaina wanted things between them to be fun and easy again. Once again, she pushed the thought of telling her about that night out of mind. Mostly, the problem was Jim. She knew it. Zane knew it. Heck, probably even Jim knew it. Sooner or later, she'd have to call him. Ultimately, their silence would have to be broken. Jaina decided that today was as good a day as any. She picked up the phone and dialed.

***

"You look good," Jaina said as she slid into the corner booth. "Looks like you feel better, too."

"I do," Jim responded, "a lot better. And I'm back to work, too."

"Good," Jaina said as she sucked in a breath. She could already feel herself reaching her limit for nice chitchat with the man who had assaulted her lover. "I'm glad."

Jim sat quietly across the table, waiting. It was as if he knew that today, there'd be more. "I'm sorry."

Jaina bit the inside of her lip and tasted blood. Her eyes bore into Jim with the fire she'd been carrying inside. Her intention that day had not been to be cruel. She'd come to say what she had to say and that was all. All she wanted was to say it and move on. She sucked in a breath. On exhale, she couldn't seem to stop her tirade. "You're my brother, but I no longer like or respect you. I don't know if I ever will." She sucked in another. "Zane and I are getting married on the 31st at noon. Come or don't come, it really doesn't matter." She stood. Without another word, she exited the restaurant.

Jaina marched across the almost empty parking lot as her eyes began to fill with angry tears. She dropped into the seat, started the engine, and sped off. She was pissed and almost late for her next appointment. Talk about piling on stress, this appointment and a meeting with Jim were all in the same day and just a couple days out from her wedding. She had to be crazy.

***

These were busy days with one appointment dovetailing into the next. Some were definitely more fun than others. This was one of the fun ones.

Jaina's eyes lit up as the passenger she awaited walked through the gate. It hadn't really been that long since she'd seen her, but with all the recent uproar, Miss Bonnie was a sight for sore eyes. She threw herself into her friend's open arms and they hugged.

Miss Bonnie eventually pushed back and cocked her head. "Is everything okay?" She pinched her brow. "Are you and Zane having problems?"

Jaina hesitated. "No, we're fine." She looked down to the ceramic tile. "It's just been nerve-racking lately. That's all." Her eyes rose to meet Miss Bonnie's concerned gaze. "You know how I get."

"That I do, child," Miss Bonnie said. "That, I know quite well." She put her arm through Jaina's as they walked toward the luggage carrousel. "Are you being honest with me?"

Jaina swallowed. "Not totally."

Miss Bonnie paused. "Okay, that's good enough for now." She knew Jaina would talk when she was ready. "I'm here if you need me."

Jaina forced a smile. "I know…and I'm glad."

***

Zane had taken the important phone call while Jaina was at the airport. It was a call they'd been expecting all day. Jaina had missed it by less than 15 minutes, but it really didn't matter. She'd handled it, jotting down the most important details—the when, the where, and the time.

Jaina spotted the note on the counter the moment she came through the door and smiled. Miss Bonnie lumbered in right behind her, said a quick hello to Zane, and then as Jaina read her note, made her way upstairs. Miss Bonnie's behavior had seemed a bit odd. Jaina had assumed that she was just tired.

That wasn't it at all. It was that Miss Bonnie wanted to put an end to her dread. She wanted to slip her dress for the wedding over her head and confirm what she already knew—that it wouldn't fit. She wanted to get her confession to Jaina out of the way. That the dress didn't fit because the measurements were two inches shy. That the unfortunate situation wasn't exactly the result of an error, but rather a few extra pieces of key lime pie. Miss Bonnie shouted down the stairway for Jaina.

Jaina cocked her head. It was odd. "Coming," she called out as she laid down her crossword puzzle. She climbed the stairs two steps at a time worried that something was wrong.

"I'm in my room," Miss Bonnie called out from behind her door. "Don't come in though. Just stand where you are."

"Okay," Jaina said. "Are you alright?"

"Yeah," Miss Bonnie answered, "but you might not be in a moment." She'd been turning every which way since squeezing into the dress, turning and talking to herself in the full-length mirror. She'd tugged the dress down on her left hip. It rose up on her right. She'd pulled the strap up on her right shoulder as the left one fell. The silky-smooth monster was in cahoots with her roly-poly body. They clung and rolled together as if they had a mind of their own. "I just don't know why they can't design these dressy clothes for full-bodied women. Not everyone's meant to be a skinny twig." Another tug was accompanied by a grunt and then a groan. She sounded like a large wounded animal. "Some of us actually have womanly curves." She tugged again, wiggled, and released a roll. "Please don't be upset," she whimpered through the door, "but I think we may have a slight problem."

By that point in the conversation, Jaina was already pacing the hall. She knew the problem and she knew the cause. Her wedding was the day after tomorrow. It was the holidays. Who in the world could she get to let the seams out of that dress in time?

Miss Bonnie heard the familiar sigh. She braced for more, but it didn't come.

"Don't worry," Jaina said softly, "we'll figure something out. It's okay."

Not that there was any doubt, but it was at that moment that Miss Bonnie knew with all certainty that Jaina was a different woman. She'd grown.

Chapter Twenty-Four

The striking couple stood at the terminal window. They'd been there for some time, watching as the airplanes took off and landed. They were waiting for the one that carried their friends. Both were queasy with anticipation. Their guests were arriving. Their wedding day was almost here. It was good, a relief in a way, to spend this last day before the big day with their two best friends. Heaven knows they needed the distraction, and no one, absolutely no one, was a better distracter than Stacey.

Stacey called out a greeting the moment she saw them. It was the very moment she stepped through the terminal gate. Intentional or not, she was immediately the center of attention. Her voice projected like a pro. It was distinctive and easily recognizable. The fans within earshot swarmed. There was no time to escape.

Zane watched the spectacle in amazement. She'd never witnessed anything quite like it before. In a way, it was a moment of insight into a life so different than her own. Stacey was an authentic celebrity, the real McCoy. She was as suited to be in the middle of a crowd of adoring fans as Zane was to be standing in a pulpit. It was who she was.

"Sorry," Stacey laughed as Drew swept her up and out the door. "Guess I should've worn my sunglasses. For some reason that always seems to throw them off."

***

The snow was pounding down hard. It had been since they'd got home from the airport. It wasn't supposed to have amounted to much. Ha!

"Don't worry," the weatherman had said, "there'll be little to no accumulation."

Zane stepped on the back porch and stomped. Frozen chunks of slush fell from her boots. She shook and more fell from her hair. "Little to no accumulation. Ha!" She leaned her shovel against the porch wall and dripped her way into the kitchen. Normally, a blanket of snow wouldn't have bothered Zane in the least. But this one, at a time when guests were traveling to their wedding, was a totally unwelcome event.

Jaina met her at the door. "Looks pretty nasty out there to me. It's 79 in Sarasota." She flashed a grin and kissed Zane's wet, cold nose. "I just thought you might want to know."

Zane raised an eyebrow. "It's not a good time to be a smarty-pants," she said as her eyes met Jaina's in challenge. She lunged and caught her by surprise. "You make this too easy on me." Zane held on tight with one hand as she bent down to retrieve a handful of slush with the other.

Jaina squealed as she tried to escape.

Zane slipped her cold hand down the front of Jaina's shirt and dropped the slush inside her bra.

Jaina screamed until she finally wormed free.

Zane roared with laughter and sprinted after her up the stairs, down the hall, and into the master bedroom.

"You are so bad," Jaina said as she slowed purposely to allow herself to be caught.

Zane was amused. "I've noticed a pattern. Bad turns you on."

***

Pastor Kate was one of the most important people in Zane's life. It's funny how that happens. You never know when or where you'll meet one of those significant people. You just do and it takes you by surprise. She'd met Pastor Kate the day she'd left home, the day that everything had changed. Zane hadn't realized back then what she did now, that she'd been in the midst of a divine intervention. At the time, she'd felt nothing extraordinary. She'd simply been walking for hours, was tired, and needed to sit down.

Zane had come to believe that it was God who'd placed her before Pastor Kate just as her legs were giving out. She'd collapsed just as the pastor had stepped outside. Had Kate not caught her, Zane would have hit the sidewalk hard. Who'd have guessed that that catch and the talk that followed would destine them to become lifelong friends? Who'd have guessed that being caught would turn out to be Zane's first step toward the ministry? Who'd have guessed that that catch would be the one thing to which she attributed her survival?

Zane jogged back down the stairway. "She should be here by now. The roads are probably a lot worse around Chicago. Maybe something happened."

Soul Mates

Jaina patted the seat beside her. "I'm sure she's fine. The snow's slowed way down. Snowplows are out and I'm sure the roads are getting better by the minute. She probably just got a late start." Jaina leaned over to kiss Zane's lips. "Don't worry, honey. I'm sure Pastor Kate is fine."

Zane stood, took a breath, and walked back to the front door to watch for her friend.

***

Zane spotted the beams of Pastor Kate's headlights as her compact car slid around the corner. She opened the door to wait. Finally, Pastor Kate crunched her way up the sidewalk and stepped inside. It had been a long haul from Chicago to Champaign and the slightly older woman looked tired.

Jaina smiled as she watched Zane welcome her mentor to their home.

"We really appreciate you getting out in all this," Zane said. "I know the roads had to be awful."

Pastor Kate's eyes twinkled. "Are you kidding?" She shook her head. "I'd have come by snowmobile if I had to." She smiled as she pulled Zane and Jaina into her arms. "I wouldn't have missed officiating your wedding for the world."

Jaina felt as if she knew Zane a little better each time she met another of her friends. She wondered if Zane felt the same when she got to know Miss Bonnie. Jaina made a mental note to ask her later on. Getting to know Pastor Kate and watching the two interact was the most enlightening of all. They were clearly the best of friends and yet they kept a certain distance, almost professional. They were friends, but first and foremost, they were pastors.

Pastor Kate looked over the top of her wire rim glasses to Zane. "I'd like to talk privately with the both of you before tomorrow." Her smile was warm. "You know the drill. We need to discuss your love, your decision to marry, and your ceremony. I want your special day to be just as you envision it."

"Certainly," Zane said. "I anticipated as much." She smiled back. "I don't officiate a marriage ceremony without meeting with the couple first." She frowned a bit and nodded. "I feel it's our responsibility."

Pastor Kate nodded back. "As do I."

***

The latch on the master bedroom door had barely snapped shut when Jaina began. She'd obviously waited as long as she could. "So, what do you think?"

Zane smiled, sat down on the end of the bed, and kicked off her loafers. She leaned back on her elbows and met Jaina's gaze. "I think it went well. Pastor Kate undoubtedly thinks we're a good match. How about you? What do you think?"

Jaina grinned. "I think our ceremony will be wonderful," she said as she sucked a deep breath into her lungs. "And, I think I'm so nervous I can hardly stand it."

Zane chuckled. "Yeah, me too. Whatever possessed us to abstain the last week before the wedding?" She shook her head. "Sex is our best form of relaxation."

Jaina grinned. "Yeah, I know," she said. "We were idiots."

Zane rolled to her side and pulled Jaina close. "I don't think showers count." Her fingers brushed lightly across Jaina's nipple, unintentionally, of course.

Jaina leaned in for a kiss. Her gaze lingered a moment before she rolled to her back and then popped out of bed. "Me neither."

Zane watched Jaina head for the bathroom. She heard the water turn on and then...

"You coming, sweetheart?"

Zane smiled and swung her legs over the side of the bed. She peeled off her shirt and dropped her shorts. "On my way."

Chapter Twenty-Five

The alarm sounded. Two pairs of eyes opened and adjusted to the dark. Two pairs of lips kissed. Zane and Jaina rolled out of bed, dressed, and crept downstairs. All was still. The guests were still asleep. Zane gently lifted her jacket from the coat rack and put it on. Jaina did the same. Like kids slipping into the night, they opened the front door without a sound and stepped onto the porch. The crunch underneath their feet made them smile. They'd come to see a sight that they'd never see again. They'd come to watch their wedding day sunrise.

"It won't be long now," Zane whispered as she threaded Jaina's fingers through her own.

Jaina held a breath. "No, not long at all." Her voice cracked. "Before it sets, you'll be my wife."

Zane nodded. "And you'll be mine."

Jaina laid her head on Zane's shoulder.

Zane gathered her close.

They kissed and nuzzled as they marveled at the beauty of the winter sunrise.

***

By the time they stepped back inside, their guests were wide-awake and their home was a bustle of activity. All would play a part in the wedding that was now just

224

hours away. All had at least some level of anxiety—all except Pastor Kate, that is. She was cool, calm, and collected. Zane spotted her as she hung her jacket back on the coat rack.

Kate stood at the counter with a most serious expression on her face. She was obviously in the process of making a very important decision, the selection of the perfect pecan roll. Zane had baked them last night. She chuckled and supposed that the one with the most goo and nuts would win. She supposed right. Zane poured two cups of coffee and sat down.

"I think I'll follow Jaina over this morning," Kate said as she took her first bite. "I always like to get settled in and dressed before it gets too busy."

Zane sipped the steaming beverage and set her cup back in its saucer. "I know what you mean. I'm the same way when I officiate." She shook her head. "I don't know what I am today."

Kate looked up from her roll. "Are you doing okay?"

"Yeah, It's just that it feels weird, you know, to be the one getting married." She sucked in a breath. "Weddings never make me nervous, but today…man," she exhaled. "Plus, I feel like I should be doing something. I can't stop the wedding to-do list from ticking through my head." Another breath and exhale. "Then, I remember Faith United's yours for the next couple weeks and that all I really have to do today is show up."

Kate laid her hand atop Zane's. "That's right, all you have to do is show up." She smiled a tender smile. "It's your special day and you don't have to worry. I'll take care of everything."

Zane knew her friend spoke the truth. And she knew that taking care of everything for the next couple weeks wasn't exactly an imposition. It was more like a vacation that her friend had been looking forward to for weeks. It was her chance to not only officiate a wedding, but to preach two sermons in a row, both things that she'd missed desperately since leaving her pulpit to teach at the Chicago Theological Seminary.

"Well, since showing up in anything other than my tux isn't exactly an option," Zane said, "I suppose I should go up and get ready." She grinned. "You, on the other hand, have plenty of time to sit and read the newspaper."

Kate grinned. "That I do. Yet another benefit of the collar and the robe."

***

The hours between breakfast and departure were occupied by clothing—taking it from the closet, slipping it on, and checking it out in the mirror. There were, however, some exceptions. One such exception occurred just down the hall, the other, on the opposite end of town.

Drew stood, admiring her reflection before the full-length mirror. The light blue tux fit perfectly and she looked good.

Stacey considered Drew from her perch at the foot of the bed.

"Hey," Drew scolded as Stacey reached in for a squeeze. "You're gonna wrinkle my tux."

Stacey reluctantly pulled back her hand. "I can't help it. You're so handsome." She squeezed her wife's butt cheek again.

Soul Mates

This time, Drew cocked her head, and gave her the look.

Stacey sighed. "You're no fun."

Stacey's pouty expression was effective and Drew leaned over for a kiss. "How about I ravish you later?" She smiled. "Say, the minute we get home?"

Stacey grinned. "That'll work." Her mission had been accomplished.

***

At nearly the same moment, Zaney stood at the doorway of her large master bedroom. She was watching Nancy slip on her wedding outfit for the fourth time. The process had started well before the crack of dawn. It was an important day and Nancy obviously wanted to look her best.

"You're a beautiful woman," Zaney said as she moved so that their breasts touched. "And that navy suit...mmm. It brings out the indigo in your eyes." She leaned in for a kiss. "I remember what else used to bring out that color."

Nancy looked interested. "You know we need to finish getting ready."

Zaney pulled her close. "Uh-huh, but we started really early." She unbuttoned the top button of Nancy's blouse. "I'm sure we'll have plenty of time."

***

The first hours of the morning flew by at record speed; at least, they did from Jaina's perspective. One minute, she was holding hands with Zane on the front porch watching the sunrise. The next, she was in the limo with Stacey and Miss Bonnie headed for the church. It was almost as if she'd time traveled to the current moment.

Jaina sucked in a breath as she tallied what was left to do and how little time was left to do it. No wonder she was stressed. She knew that what she needed most was to clear her mind and let her wedding day play out as planned. In rational moments, she knew that she had nothing to worry about, that everything would end up being fine. Jaina tried her best to relax as they drove toward the church. She tried to steer her thoughts away from everything that could possibly go wrong. She tried to push the nagging guilt out of her mind. She tried to get her mind to listen to the waves as they crashed against the shores in Key West. She tried to feel the sand squish between her toes. She tried, but she couldn't. Her mind simply wouldn't let go of all the "what-ifs." What if her wedding gown ripped as she slipped it on? What if she couldn't get her make-up to look right? What if she got to the altar, looked into Zane's eyes, and forgot her vows? Jaina sucked in another breath. This time she closed her eyes. What if she blurted out what she'd almost done?

"How you doing over there?" Miss Bonnie asked with a squint and a cock of her head. "You look a little sick to me."

Jaina exhaled the breath she'd been holding. "I am." She moaned. "But don't worry, I've been this way all week." She exhaled. "It'll pass…I hope."

"I was like that before our wedding, too," Stacey said. "But when I looked into Drew's eyes as we said our vows…" A smile crept across her face as she remembered. "In less than two hours, you'll stand like that with Zane." She slipped her hand behind Jaina and gently rubbed her back. "You'll pledge your love and it'll all be okay."

***

Zane sat pencil-like on the edge of the parlor sofa. Drew sat with a bit more relaxed posture beside her. Their tuxedos were on and they were ready to go. They were ready, but they couldn't leave. It wasn't time. The day and its activities had been carefully planned right down to the very last detail and moment.

"Dashing," Drew said. "That's what we are, we're dashing." She grinned and hoped Zane would too.

"Yep," Zane said as she sucked in a breath. "Dashing." She exhaled with a moan. "Oh, God, please don't let me throw up."

"You'll be fine," Drew said, "and you're not going to throw up." She looked at her watch again. "Especially now that we can hit the road."

***

The Lamborghini rumbled in to park near the door.

"What in the world," Zane blurted as she swung the door open and exited the car. She pointed to the roof. "Where did those come from?"

Drew came around to join her. "I don't know, but they're cool."

"Yeah, cool, but where'd they come from?" Zane shook her head in puzzlement. "To install flag poles on the roof would be a church council decision and I'm at every meeting. There's been no discussion of flag poles."

Drew patted her friend on the back and grinned. "I think they're in honor of your wedding. Rainbow flags flying for your big day. How sweet."

The flying of rainbow flags wasn't unusual for ONA churches. In fact, many flew them. They were like ONA welcome signs that waved in the breeze for all to see. *No matter who you are or who you love, you are welcome in this place.* Faith United lived that welcome, but didn't fly the flags. Zane wished they did, but hadn't pursued it because their purchase and installation would've been an extra, and Faith United simply couldn't afford extras.

"I think you're right," Zane said as tears filled her eyes. "They know me well." She wiped one away. "And they couldn't have chosen a more perfect gift for our wedding."

***

Irene watched from the window as the Lamborghini roared into the parking lot. She'd been charged with keeping Zane clear of Jaina's dressing area and had been waiting for her to arrive. She smiled as she watched Zane's first reaction to the flags.

When Zane made the move to head inside, Irene met her at the door. She threw her arms around her pastor's neck. "It's your wedding day."

Zane chuckled at the greeting. "Yeah, I know." She winked. "But thanks for the reminder." Her grin evolved into a locked gaze. "I don't suppose you know anything about the flags?"

Irene's eyes twinkled. "I might…it's possible that the church counsel had one more item of business to conduct after you left the last meeting." She winked. "It's also possible that the item was *inadvertently* left off of the meeting agenda."

Zane choked up. "You guys…"

Chapter Twenty-Six

The quartet played softly as the guests filed in and took their seats. Late morning sun filtered through the tall stained glass windows and candles flickered in every nook and cranny. Romantic jazz and wedding bells were in the air.

Zane stood beside her mom in the rear of the sanctuary. At three minutes before noon, the musicians quieted their instruments. At two before, the guests began to look around and whisper. At one before, the performer made her appearance and they hissed in a collective breath. Anastasia Shanning was creating quite a stir as she made her way down the aisle to the microphone. Like a pro, she lifted it the moment her eyes lifted toward her audience. She nodded and the instruments awakened. She raised the microphone to her lips and the music played. She sang a mix of romantic classics from the 80s. It was a one-time performance in honor of two dear friends. Pastor Kate nodded when Stacey finished. The ceremony was about to begin.

Nancy took hold of her daughter's arm.

Zane walked her down the aisle to her front row seat beside Zaney. Her love stood to receive her.

Zane continued up two steps to the altar.

Drew stood by her side.

Soul Mates

The first notes of "The Wedding March" rang throughout the sanctuary and the rear doors opened. Zane's eyes fell on Jaina as she began to make her way down the aisle on Miss Bonnie's arm. She watched her graceful movements in the cream wedding gown. It was a perfect choice for her body; Zane knew that she was about to marry the most beautiful woman in the world. Their gazes met and Jaina took her side.

"We're gathered together in this beautiful house of God," Pastor Kate announced, "to join these two women in the bonds of holy matrimony. The joining in marriage is the apex of a relationship, an intimate act of love, and commitment. Jaina and Zane have written vows to one another." Pastor Kate nodded to Zane.

Zane turned to take Jaina's hand into her own. She looked into her eyes. "Today, we begin our lives together, walking side by side, and hand in hand." She squeezed the hand within her own. "I promise to love you always. I promise that you'll always be my only one. I'll comfort you and look to you for comfort." Her eyes moistened and she blinked. "I promise to walk beside you, not in front of you, nor behind. Today Jaina, you become my wife and my partner. Today, we become one." Zane smiled. "Today is our beginning. It's the day I choose to be your wife. Anyone who knows me knows that beginnings have always been hard, but not this one. This one is easy."

Drew reached into her pocket for the ring. She handed it to her friend.

Zane met Jaina's gaze as she slid the white-gold symbol of their love and commitment onto her finger. "With this ring, I thee wed."

Pastor Kate smiled and looked to Jaina with a nod.

"Today," Jaina said, "we begin our lives together and I choose to be your wife. I make this choice with full knowledge that to be your wife means that I will be a pastor's wife. As I look into your eyes at this moment, I promise I'll always love you. I promise to be faithful until our last breath. I promise to support you and to put my heart and soul into your ministry." She wiped a tear as it trickled down her cheek. "I love you, darling." Jaina placed the band that matched her own on Zane's finger. "With this ring, I thee wed."

The couple turned toward the rear of the church. They joined hands.

Jaina caught Jim's eye. He was there, alone, seated in the last row.

Pastor Kate lifted the newlywed's clasped hands high. "By the power vested in me by this church and the State of Illinois, I now pronounce you wife and wife." Her eyes looked upward and then fell upon the guests. "What God has joined together, let no one put asunder." She grinned and looked to Zane and Jaina. "You may each kiss your bride."

Zane leaned down as Jaina tipped up. They kissed.

Once again, the pastor smiled. "It's my pleasure and honor to introduce my dear friend and her bride. I present the Reverend and Mrs. Zane Winslow.

The music played.

The guests stood.

The relaxed couple smiled to one another and then made their way back down the aisle.

Soul Mates

***

The fellowship hall was decorated in the couple's chosen colors. The seats were filled as virtually the entire congregation had attended the wedding. All had been invited to stay. Jim didn't. The reception included a light lunch that was followed by wedding cake. The wedding cake was beautiful. The mutual feeding was messy.

Jaina wore a tad of icing as she positioned herself for the next activity, the traditional tossing of the bouquet. Those inclined to be catchers of the item supposed to foretell the future gathered close. Jaina met their gaze. She closed her eyes and tossed. The flowers flew over her shoulder and sailed well above the heads of the hopeful. She watched the daises soar as if on autopilot. Like torpedoes, they bulleted toward their unsuspecting target. The woman looked up with a startle as they descended. She raised her hands to catch them. In a swish, Nancy held her prize. The delight on her face was priceless. It made Jaina smile.

***

The white limo had parked just outside the rear entrance. The driver had left the engine running. Zane and Jaina opened the last of their wedding gifts and bid farewell. They had a flight to catch and it was time to slip away. Drew signaled to the driver, who in turn, stepped out and opened the door. The couple climbed inside. It would be a relatively short ride to the airport.

Jaina scooted across the smooth leather seat. "I've never been in one of these before." She pointed. "Look, it even has a wet bar."

Zane couldn't help but grin at all her cuteness. "Well now, isn't that something."

Jaina's head settled onto Zane's shoulder. "I think people were surprised when I took your name," she said softly. Her brow furrowed. "But I don't know why. Who in the world would think I'd want to keep my adoptive parents' name?"

"I don't know," Zane said. "I definitely wouldn't." She leaned in for a kiss. "Especially when Winslow suits you so well."

Jaina smiled and snuggled closer. "It does, doesn't it?" She caught her wife's eye and winked. "All ready for our big night?"

Zane raised an eyebrow. "As long as you brought the supplies."

Jaina raised one in response. "Oh I did." She grinned. "Every last one of them."

***

Drew and Stacey had gone far above what most would have done to assure their friends had a wonderful wedding. It felt like getting married inside a fairytale that was chock-full of beautiful things and romance. It was an amazing day and these newlyweds were having the time of their life.

"I can't believe we have a private jet flying us to Key West," Jaina said as she made her way up the ramp. She stepped inside the cabin door and looked around. "Now, this could almost make me like flying." Then, she made a face. "Almost, but not quite."

Zane's eyes were wide. "It's like traveling in a luxury apartment."

Jaina chuckled nervously. "Yeah, a luxury apartment that's 12,000 feet above the ground."

Zane's smile became seductive. "Ahh…but it has a king-sized bed."

"Uh-huh," Jaina said. "Well, you can forget about using it. I'm not falling out of the sky with no clothes on."

Zane laughed, and then kissed Jaina's forehead. "I know, and I wouldn't ask you to."

Jaina tipped up to kiss her lips. "Good."

They took their seats as the engines began to roar.

"Did you see him?" Jaina asked. "In the back row?"

Zane raised her wife's hand to her lips. She planted a soft kiss on the new ring that now graced her finger. "I did."

They sat in silence for a few moments.

"I think I'm moving on," Jaina said softly.

Zane nodded. "I'm glad."

***

It was late afternoon by the time the Key West International Airport became visible in the distance. Jaina noticed the airplane begin its descent and sucked in another breath. Her fingers threaded through Zane's, squeezing at the sound of wheels hitting the pavement and locking when brakes were applied. She didn't exhale nor release her grip until they'd rolled to a complete stop. When she did, Zane gingerly retrieved, and stretched her fingers.

"Sorry," Jaina said. "Are they okay?"

"Yeah," Zane said. "Don't worry, I'll have circulation back in no time."

Zane looked up and noticed the crew had begun to flutter about the aircraft. One was gathering their luggage and loading the cart. Another was preparing to escort them to the awaiting limo. Zane stood and waited for Jaina to step into the aisle.

"Looks like we're on our way," Zane said with a smile.

"We are." Jaina smiled back. "And we're still on schedule."

Fifteen more minutes and they were in the back of the limo speeding toward the first of their two destinations. The driver parked in a restricted zone near the door and Jaina jumped out. She ran into the building, rode the elevator up to the third floor, and continued toward the reception desk. The 30-something brunette had been awaiting her arrival. She checked Jaina's two forms of ID and handed her the parcel. Back on the elevator and out the door, Jaina got in and the car zipped back into traffic. So far, everything was on schedule. With any luck, they'd be checked into their hotel and on the balcony in 30 minutes.

Zane grinned as Jaina handed her the small rectangular package. "You got it."

Jaina winked and grinned back. "I sure did."

Chapter Twenty-Seven

Zane and Jaina had never stayed in a five-star luxury hotel. Since this one was one of Stacey's favorites, Zane assumed that it would be over-the-top. It was. Jaina likened the accommodations to a bee colony, where a multitude of drones buzzed at the door awaiting your arrival. Once inside, you were crowned queen and the drones buzzed around, fanning you with their wings. Their sole purpose was to be at your beck and call, to serve you the moment you had a need, and to assure that you never had to lift a finger. This luxury hotel was like nothing these two had ever imagined. It was way beyond their wildest dreams. Once again, their friends had totally outdone themselves.

When the check-in process had been completed, a pair of drones escorted Zane and Jaina to their room. One inserted the key to open the door to the newlywed suite. The other placed their luggage on the bed and asked if assistance with unpacking would be required. Zane declined the offer of assistance. The drones turned to leave.

"Wait a minute," Zane said as she reached into her back pocket.

The first drone paused and smiled. "Thank you Ma'am, but gratuities have already been taken care of." He nodded and joined his comrade in the hall.

Zane shut the door and extended her hand to Jaina. She smiled. "It's almost time. Ready to go check out the balcony?"

Jaina grinned and took her hand. "I am."

The glass door slid easily and the couple stepped outside. The view was absolutely breathtaking. Zane met Jaina's gaze and squeezed her hand. "This day and this sunset are the most incredible of my life." She pulled Jaina into her arms. "I love you, darling." Their lips met and they kissed. They kissed deeply until the afterglow of the red-orange orb was replaced by the shine of street lights.

***

Key West was known for its gay New Year's Eve celebrations. Some were the largest in the world. The hotel was known to be the best in town and the newlywed suite overlooked the festivities. It couldn't get much better than that.

By the time Jaina stepped inside, party-goers had already begun to gather five floors down. "Looks like fun. It's way bigger than I imagined."

Zane met Jaina's gaze. "It does. We can go if you want."

Jaina looked at her wife, shook her head, and smiled. "Are you kidding?" An eyebrow raised and she pointed to the floor. "My party's right here."

Zane chuckled. "Mine is too. Maybe next year." A thoughtful expression crossed her face. "In fact, maybe we just need to start an anniversary tradition."

"Mmm. Maybe we do," Jaina said, "but right now, what we need to do is order room service." She kissed Zane's neck. "Hang the 'Do Not Disturb' sign on the door." Her hand slid inside her wife's waistband. "And get down to business." She met Zane's gaze. "I told you patience wasn't my strongest suit."

Zane gave her wife a kiss. "I know, but I love you anyway."

Jaina grinned and kissed Zane's nose. "Good, I'm glad that you do."

***

Zane and Jaina had been looking forward to this night all day, and not just because they were anticipating hot sex. They'd had that before, and hopefully would again. No, looking forward to this night wasn't about the sex any more than watching the sunrise and the sunset had been about the sun. It was more about being present in the moments of their wedding day. It was about making memories that would last a lifetime.

Jaina had given considerable thought to what she was going to wear on their wedding night—thoughts that didn't materialize into lingerie. In the end, Stacey had taken the matter into her own hands. Secretly, Jaina had been relieved, but when the items came home, she'd been almost afraid to open the box. Eventually, she had. She wasn't disappointed.

Jaina turned to examine her reflection in the bathroom mirror. She couldn't remember ever feeling so delicious. That lasted for all of one minute. Then, she sat down on the edge of the whirlpool and leaned forward with her head in her hands. *Please not now. It's our wedding night, for God's sake.* Her tears didn't obey. She had to tell Zane. The secret was eating her alive. Funny, in the old days, Jaina wouldn't have thought she'd done anything wrong. Everything had changed.

After several minutes, Jaina returned to the bathroom mirror. She adjusted her make-up and then opened the bathroom door. Wanting this night to be sexy, Jaina struck her most provocative pose. She waited for Zane to notice. It didn't take long.

Zane looked up and swallowed hard.

Jaina watched her as she adjusted her position to relieve pressure.

Their gazes locked.

"Come here," Zane said in a low, seductive tone.

Jaina did, but not too fast. She wanted to coax her wife's arousal to an all-time high.

Zane watched Jaina from across the room. She watched her trace her nipples with her fingertips. She watched them darken and become prominent under the sheer fabric. She watched Jaina's fingers brush across her center. Zane wet her lips and waited.

"Need something?" Jaina asked.

"Of course I need something. You're killing me here," Zane panted. She leaned back, unzipped her trousers, and motioned with her finger. "Come here."

Jaina took another step in Zane's direction. "What do you want, darling? You can have anything, you know." She touched herself again. "All you have to do is ask for it."

Zane slid to the floor, reached, and lightly tugged at the waistband of her wife's panties. "Take 'em off and come over here."

Jaina peeled the delicate lace, slipped it over her spike heels, and moved to stand above her wife. She spread her legs and assumed a wide stance.

Zane licked her lips again. She kissed and nibbled Jaina's sex. "Mmm, you taste good."

Jaina moaned and tipped her head back.

Zane surged with passion. She spread Jaina's folds with her fingertips as her lips encircled and suckled her hardening bud.

"Oh, my God," Jaina moaned. Her body stiffened and her pelvis thrust forward as the first waves of what would be a mighty orgasm crashed through. She slipped her hand down to hold Zane in place. "Right there, baby. Stay right there."

Zane lightened her suckle for a moment and then resumed with greater intensity.

Jaina screamed as the pleasure overtook her. Her knees weakened and she collapsed to the floor in a puddle beside Zane. "Oh baby, that was good." She gasped. "So good."

Zane gathered Jaina into her arms. She loved this woman so much.

***

Zane lay back against the pillow—no clothes, no covers, just nude. It was something she still didn't do very often. Zane knew Jaina would like it. She did.

Jaina settled in beside her.

"You're gorgeous," she said as her eyes absorbed her wife's nakedness. Jaina began to trace Zane's lines and curves with her fingertips.

"Mmm," Zane murmured. "Feels good. I love it when you touch me." Her mouth found Jaina's mouth and Jaina's tongue slipped beyond Zane's lips.

Jaina rolled to top her and they kissed. They kissed until Jaina's tongue and lips moved on.

"Come on, baby," Zane urged as she pushed her wife lower. "Make me come."

Zane began to whimper as Jaina gently separated her. Jaina's warm lips swallowed the sensitive spot that her fingertips had exposed. The sensation tingled throughout her body.

Zane moaned.

Jaina's suckle was gentle at first, then she bared down with tongue.

Zane's breathing became labored. In no time, she was close.

Jaina slipped inside. Her thrusts were deep and steady as she took Zane toward climax.

Zane's cries became whimpers again as her strong vaginal muscles clamped onto Jaina's fingers.

Jaina stilled, allowing them to hold on.

Afterward they held each other—intimate moments and quiet conversation—afterglow.

"This kind of connection," Jaina whispered, "like we have, I never thought I'd have it with anyone." She kissed Zane's forehead. "And then, whoosh. I have you. I have us. And it feels like the most natural thing in the world."

Zane propped onto her elbow. "Yeah, I know what you mean. I always thought I'd be alone too. I never dared to dream that I'd find what we have." She choked up. "I never dared to hope that I'd have a family of my own." She kissed Jaina's ring. "It all changed in the blink of an eye."

Jaina smiled. "It did."

***

It was almost midnight when the noisemakers began to call to one another on the street. Fireworks cracked and popped in the distance. It was time for round two.

Zane re-checked the items that Jaina had carefully arranged on the nightstand. "You ready?"

"I am," Jaina said as she slipped off her robe and crawled back into bed.

Zane lowered on top of her. Her kisses were loving; her carass, gentle.

Jaina moaned.

Zane's kisses deepened and her fingers slipped down to find Jaina's wetness.

"Let's make a baby," Jaina whispered.

Zane kissed down Jaina's neck and suckled each of her nipples. "Let's do."

Jaina whimpered as Zane's tongue dipped into her navel. Her pelvis began to rock as Zane moved toward her center. "Man, you've gotten good with that tongue."

Zane paused briefly to raise an eyebrow and smile. She resumed, and then paused again, to position two pillows at the foot of the bed and gather the necessary items. "Ready?" Zane asked softly.

Jaina caught a wave of emotion. "Yeah, more than ready." She slid down in the bed, placing her bottom on the pillows.

Tender eyes met one another as Zane dropped between her knees. Jaina held her breath as Zane inserted the cervical cap. She released it when she positioned the tube. Without a moment's delay, Zane took Jaina into her mouth to finish what she'd started.

Jaina gasped and her breathing quickened. Zane knew she was close. She nibbled on the swollen organ until it twitched with spasms. Then, she emptied the syringe.

Jaina reached out and Zane pulled her close. She held her still and quiet until they fell asleep. The would-be parents had done everything possible to assure that conditions were ideal for conception. Now, the only thing left to do was wait and see.

***

Zane hadn't slept long before she awoke to the sound of quiet sobs. She rolled to her back. "What's the matter, baby?" She nudged Jaina onto her shoulder. "You having second thoughts?"

"No," Jaina choked. Her sobs intensified and she coughed.

"Aw, sweetie," Zane said as she rubbed Jaina's back. She ran her fingers through Jaina's hair and kissed her face. "Tell me what's wrong."

Jaina wiped her tears on the sheet. "What if we can't get pregnant?" she whimpered. "I'm 36." Her teary, red eyes met Zane's. "What if we don't have enough time left to make a baby?"

Zane smiled and kissed her forehead. "I think we'll have plenty of time because I think we made our first baby tonight. If we didn't, we'll try again or we'll adopt." She closed her eyes to pray. Seconds passed and they opened.

"I'm just scared," Jaina said. "I'm scared you might be wrong."

Zane sat up to meet her wife's gaze. "Didn't the doctor say she saw no problem with you getting pregnant? Didn't we inseminate you at the right time and just like she said? Didn't donor number 95 have a remarkably high sperm count?" She grinned. "That, plus dark brown hair, blue eyes, and musical ability?"

Jaina cracked a tiny smile. "Yeah, she did."

"Okay then," Zane said, "we've got nothing to worry about." She gave Jaina a nudge. "Now roll over. I'll spoon you and we can go back to sleep."

Chapter Twenty-Eight

The 10-day honeymoon was amazing. The sex was hot and frequent. The sight-seeing was crazy-fun. The water was warm and the beach was relaxing. But now, the lovely honeymoon was over. It was time for the newlyweds to go back home.

"Alright, I think that's everything," Zane said as she walked through the suite one last time.

A familiar drone showed up at the door and loaded their luggage onto a cart. "It's been a pleasure to have you with us." He smiled. "We hope your stay was truly one-of-a-kind."

Jaina met Zane's gaze.

Both were barely able to suppress snickers.

"Oh, I assure you," Jaina said, "it was."

"Good," the drone said as he rolled their luggage cart onto the elevator. The newlyweds followed along. He pushed the button and a nasally, feminine voice responded.

"First floor," she said.

The rectangular carriage moved, then thumped, to a stop. The bell pinged. The doors hissed open. The drone unloaded the cart and placed the luggage into the trunk. The limo driver loaded the newlyweds into the backseat.

Jaina leaned into Zane as the car picked up speed. "It's been the best 10 days of my life." She slipped her arms around her wife's neck. "I love you."

"I didn't know anything could feel this good," Zane said. "I love you too."

Jaina looked to her wife. "I hope you're right about our baby." Her head lay gently on Zane's shoulder and she fell silent.

"Me too, sweetheart," Zane said. "Me too."

***

People always tell you not to worry when you go on vacation. "Don't worry," they say, "the place will get along just fine without you." In a way, you want that to be the case because you want to go on vacation. But, in a way, you don't. You want them to miss you, to need what you have to offer. The congregation of Faith United missed Zane while she was gone. They missed her, but they and Pastor Kate had gotten along fine. By the 10th day, however, all were ready for Zane's return.

Irene smiled as she scurried to answer the phone that last morning. Tomorrow, everything would return to normal. "Faith United. How may I help you? No, I'm sorry, our pastor's not in. She's due back today, but won't actually be in until tomorrow...yes, we had an adoption agency years ago. Okay, I've got it...I'll have her call." Irene hung up. She stood and slipped on her sweater. The call and the caller had given her the chills.

***

The aircraft wheels set down on the runway. The limo rolled to a stop at the front door. The luggage and the newlyweds made their way through the terminal. It'd been a wonderful stay. They'd enjoyed it thoroughly, but it was time to go home. Zane spied their friends as they neared the gate.

Drew extended her hand.

Zane took hold.

"Welcome aboard," Drew said. "You look good." She stepped back for a better look. "Maybe a bit more fit," she added with a laugh and a slap to Zane's back. "Nothing like a little honeymoon exercise, right?" Still grinning, she leaned over to kiss Jaina on her cheek. "Beautiful, as always, my dear."

Jaina giggled and smiled.

Stacey floated to Drew's side, draped her body around her neck, and flashed that smile. She caught Jaina's eye and winked. "Did you have a good time? I'll bet Zane liked your outfit."

Jaina blushed and her friend raised an eyebrow.

"Well, I guess so," Stacey said as she allowed her gaze to linger. There was something different about Jaina. Initially, she couldn't figure out what it was, but then it came to her. It was a glow. She stepped aside. "Come in, make yourselves comfortable." Her eyes twinkled as she met Jaina's gaze. "And tell us all about your sexy honeymoon."

***

Careful what you ask for, Zane thought as she settled in beside Jaina. She knew both were dying to share. Once that cork was popped, it'd be difficult to get it back in. Drew and Stacey would be lucky if they got a word in edgewise. As it turned out, they didn't, but they didn't care. They were just pleased to know that their gift had been enjoyed and thrilled to see their friends were having so much fun together.

***

Zane opened the front door of the parsonage as the limo backed out of the driveway. She took a breath. God, it was good to be home. She'd had fun, but the comfort and familiarity of home was the best. Zane turned without notice, lifted Jaina into her arms, and swung her over the threshold.

Jaina giggled all the way across. "You're so funny."

Zane raised an eyebrow. "I am, huh?" She grinned. "Do you still love me?"

Jaina's eyes moistened. They'd been doing that a lot lately. "Of course I do."

"Good," Zane said as she slung one bag over each shoulder and picked up the other two. "Now that we've got that settled, I'll be right back."

***

Fur Ball wrapped his body around Jaina's leg as she headed for the kitchen.

"Did you miss us?" Jaina asked. She reached down to scratch behind her cat's ears. "Because we missed you." Fur Ball purred and Jaina burst into tears. The can of Fancy Feast sat on the counter.

Zane heard Jaina's familiar sobs. She left the pile on the bed and came running. "Aw, sweetie, what's the matter now?" She rubbed Jaina's back. "You're having quite a tough time these days."

"I know," Jaina blubbered, "but I don't know why." She made an attempt at being funny. "Maybe you married a crazy woman."

Zane put her arms around Jaina and held her tight. "I don't think so, sweetie." A smile crossed her face and she kissed her wife's forehead. "What I think is that my wife is pregnant."

***

Zane settled in at her desk to open the mail that had come while they were gone. The messages could wait until tomorrow. Jaina was still out of sorts, but Zane felt she had to come in, at least for a few minutes. She picked up the wrinkled letter, the one from the state correctional facility first. She didn't have a reason, she just did.

"Oh, my God," Zane said as she jumped out of her chair, grabbed her coat, and ran. It was 3:15. She ran out of her office, out of the building, and toward the car.

Irene hopped up to follow.

"I've got to go," Zane said. "Got to get home before 4:00."

Irene stayed right with her. "Is something wrong?" Her voice rose in alarm. "Is there something I can do to help?"

Zane shook her head. "Not now. I'll call you."

"Be careful," Irene called out.

Zane looked back. "Don't worry, I will."

Her tires squealed backward and she raced down the road.

***

The Thunderbird flew much faster than usual—fast enough to get stopped.

"Crap," Zane growled as her tires slid around the corner. A rust bucket, most likely *the* rust bucket, was sitting in the middle of her driveway. "Damn thing." She squealed to a stop in front of the parsonage and jumped out of the car.

Zane heard loud voices and she sprinted. One of the voices definitely belonged to Jaina. Her adrenaline rushed into overdrive and she took her front steps in one leap. Then, she bound through the door.

"You need to leave," Jaina screamed at what Zane was sure was the top of her lungs. "I never should've sent in that paperwork."

"But you did and I found you. I'm not going anywhere," the rough blonde yelled back. "I've waited all of these years to see you again." She leaned into Jaina's space. "And you, little girl, are gonna talk to me." She looked enraged. "I'm your mother, for God's sake. I gave birth to your sorry ass." The woman pushed her finger into Jaina's chest. "You owe me that much."

Jaina spotted Zane and ran to her.

"Do as my wife asked," Zane shouted. "You need to leave."

Janice Grayson smirked. "Well, well…aren't you just something, a dyke and a preacher. Well how about that. Jaina's got herself a preacher girl." She reached up to touch Zane's collar.

253

As quick as a snake can bite, Zane grabbed the woman's offending wrist. "I wouldn't do that if I were you."

"Don't get me all wrong now, baby," the old blonde said. "I'm down with it—girl-on-girl, I mean. Even had me a couple, just like you, when I was in the joint." She wrinkled up her nose. "Cock's better, but in a pinch, pussy'll do." She smiled a disgusting, almost toothless smile.

Zane felt the vein in her neck twitch. "Look, here's the way it is. We've asked nicely that you get out of our home." She felt heat flush through her body. "But nice isn't going to continue. In a moment, I'm going to call the police." Her glare became increasingly lethal. "Or maybe…" She took a step in the woman's direction. "Maybe I should just remove you on my own."

Janice Grayson backed up as Zane stepped forward into her space.

"Move along," Zane shouted. "Don't make me."

"Okay, baby," Janice said, "you don't have to get all bent out of shape. Saw my boy. Now there's one hunk of man." The woman's expression sickened Zane. "Just wanted to see my girl."

Zane glared. "You've seen her. Now get out of our home, and get your rust bucket out of my driveway."

The sleazy woman backed off from the much taller one. She got in her car and roared away.

***

By the time Zane turned around, Jaina's face was buried in the sofa. She sat down beside her.

"My mom's been in prison almost all this time," Jaina choked, "for sexually abusing Jim as well as some other crimes." A couple more sobs. "When he was just a little boy." She sat up and met Zane's gaze. "What kind of monster does that? What kind of God allows her to?"

Zane took a breath but didn't answer. She'd save that answer for another day. Right now, what Jaina needed most was for her wife to hold her, to stroke her, and to reassure her that everything was going to be okay.

***

Zane was relieved when Jaina was able to shake off the roughest edges of the ugliness by the time they'd finished dinner. She wasn't sure that she'd have done as well given the same set of circumstances. That woman had spewed out a whole lot of nastiness to wrap her head around.

Just when Zane thought they'd moved onto lighter topics, Jaina had one more thing to say. She shook her head, curled up her lip in disgust, and said it. "She got 25 years for what she did to Jim," Jaina spewed. "It wasn't nearly as long as she deserved. She should rot in prison for what she did to my brother." Jaina fell silent as her tears began to tumble again. "Awful things have been done to the people I love…awful things."

Chapter Twenty-Nine

Zane discharged an audible sigh of doorbell disgust. She checked her watch—7:00 p.m. "Who in the world?" She pulled the lever and dropped her feet to the floor, hoping that Jaina, who had just begun to settle down, didn't beat her to the door.

She called out to her just in case. "I've got it, sweetie," Zane said as her sock feet padded across the foyer. She turned the knob. There, arm in arm, stood her mom and Zaney. "What a pleasant surprise." Zane hugged both and held the door open. "Come in." She called out for Jaina.

Jaina met Nancy's gaze the moment she stepped into the foyer. Without a word between them, Jaina landed in Nancy's arms. There was little doubt the unexpected visit pleased her greatly.

"Just seeing you brightens my day," Jaina said.

Zane watched her mom take notice of Jaina's swollen eyes. She gave Jaina an extra tight squeeze and then met Zane's gaze. Zane mouthed that all was fine. She hoped that it was. It was time to change the subject. "So, what brings you our way?"

The guests shifted eyes and feet like kids who'd just been caught in the act. Something was definitely up. Zane watched them wait each other out.

Finally Nancy spoke. "We need to talk to you about something...as a pastor." Jaina started to leave but Nancy caught her eye. "You stay," she said firmly. "You're family."

Jaina sat back down. "Okay..."

Zane walked over to sit down beside her wife. She reached over to touch her mom's arm. "What's up? Is something wrong?"

"No, don't worry," Nancy said. "Nothing's wrong." She looked down and began rummaging through her purse. "Ah-ha." Nancy located and pulled out a marriage license and handed it to Zane. Her smile was so sweet. "I've loved this woman since I was 11 years old. I don't know how many years we have left, but we want to spend them together." Nancy looked into her daughter's eyes. "Will you marry us?"

Zane was initially speechless. It was, and yet it wasn't, a lot to take in. Finally, she found her words. "Well...now that took me by surprise." A smile slowly spread across her face. "Of course I'll marry you." She leaned over and hugged both women. "Congratulations. So, when's the big day?"

The two giggled like school girls as one met the other's gaze. "We were hoping..." they giggled again. "Tonight."

Zane raised an eyebrow. She shook her head as a smile crept onto her face. "Oh no...don't tell me one of you got pregnant." She stifled the laugh that insisted upon release.

"No," Nancy said in all seriousness. "Zaney has a cruise to the Bahamas the day after tomorrow." She pursed her lips and looked determined. "There's only one bed and I want to go."

Zane's renegade laugh finally escaped. "Well okay then, that explains everything."

Jaina gave Zane a swat. "This is serious."

Zane swallowed a couple more chuckles and met her gaze. "Of course, it's serious. These two are getting married and you're getting ready to perform your first official duty as a pastor's wife." She smiled again. "Of course, it's serious." She excused herself to go make the necessary call. With any luck, Irene would be available to serve as their second witness. As it turned out, she was.

***

Zane hung in the parlor doorway, watching, before returning to her seat. Jaina noticed, but didn't interrupt. She must have sensed that her wife needed time, and she did. She needed a moment to adjust, a moment to pray, and a moment to remember how it used to be.

Zane had always known her mom liked her dad. She'd liked him for what he was, the boy from the farm down the road and the father of her child. They all knew she didn't love him. Never, not once, had she ever let on like she had. It had been a gaping hole in their marriage, one that no one talked about. Zane remembered coming to the realization that the problem was her mom. At first, she didn't understand what was wrong between her parents. Then, as she grew older, she thought she did. Now, she realized that what she had assumed had been very, very wrong. The insight she'd gained since learning of Zaney had been almost cathartic.

"It'll be 30 minutes or so before Irene can get here," Zane said as she sat back down. Her eyes were tender. Her presence was a swirl of pastor and daughter. She looked to her mom. "Tell me a story—a story from when you two were young."

"A story," Nancy echoed as her expression became pensive.

"Hmm…a story," Zaney said. Her eyes twinkled to Nancy. "What one should we tell?"

Nancy's strayed to the fire. "Hmm…let's see. Ah, I know." She looked up and smiled. "You know the one I'm thinking?"

Zaney chuckled. "I believe so. Was it a summer night?"

Nancy squeezed her hand. "That's the one."

Zaney looked away reflectively, her thoughts returning to their chosen moment in time. Finally, she spoke and her words broke the silence. "I'd raised a grand goat that year. I just knew the ribbon would be hers." She patted Nancy on her thigh. Her gaze lingered. "I'd taken quite a fancy to you by that point." She winked at her love. "I wanted you to see her win."

Nancy squeezed her lover's hand. "Oh, you weren't the only one who'd taken a fancy." She leaned over for a kiss as a mischievous grin crossed her face. "Boy, my mom never would've let me go if she'd known what we were going to figure out that night."

They giggled and Nancy's eyes trailed back to the fire. Her voice was far away. "The Ferris wheel was really tall, but its lights were pretty, so we decided to ride."

Zaney leaned forward. "I'd never kissed a girl before, but I wanted to kiss your mom." She met Nancy's gaze." "I wanted to kiss her so bad."

Nancy blushed. "And opportunity knocked, didn't it sweetheart?"

Zaney grinned. "It did…and all because of a mechanical problem. Fate, I think." She chuckled. "We got stuck on top." They giggled and kissed again. "Well, needless to say we were considerably more experienced by the time they got us down."

The doorbell rang. That would be Irene. Zane stood but didn't move to answer. Her eyes met the one for whom she'd been named. "So, did your goat win?"

Zaney smiled with pride. "She did." Zane noticed the sparkle that ignited in her eyes. "And I did too."

***

It was a wedding with little notice, but that didn't matter. These two people had become very important to Jaina. They'd waited 56 years for this day and she was determined to do her part to make it special. Jazz played. Candles flickered. She sent Zane up to put on her best black and brand new collar. Afterward, after the pictures, she allowed Zane to take the collar off.

Zane popped the cork that night on her finest bottle of champagne. She poured five long-stemmed glasses, four bubbly and one grape juice, just in case. They toasted and sent the second pair of newlyweds on their way.

It had been a day of emotional extremes. Jaina headed upstairs while Zane finished up the remaining loose ends in the kitchen. Zane heard the water turn on in the master bathroom. She took a breath and revived. She knew they both would feel better if they made love before they said goodnight.

Zane slid the shower door open and stepped under the warm spray. "God, you're beautiful. Her eyes drifted across the planes of Jaina's body. They settled onto her stomach. Zane was almost certain that she noticed a slight swell. She smiled.

"Welcome to my shower," Jaina said. She pressed close and they kissed. "You're becoming my most frequent visitor."

Zane raised an eyebrow. "Well, I should hope so."

Jaina recoiled. "What's that supposed to mean?"

Zane stepped back, dumbfounded. "Nothing. I was just being funny."

Jaina turned off the water and jammed the shower door into the wall. "Well, you weren't." Her voice rose to a scream. "I figured sooner or later you'd bring that up." She began to hysterically sob.

Zane felt a tightening in her chest. She reached out for Jaina, but Jaina jerked away.

Zane just stood there, dripping. She ran her fingers through her wet hair. "Hey, wait a minute. We need to talk."

Jaina whipped the towel across her body. "Now I know how you really feel," Jaina choked. "True colors, they show eventually, don't they?" She slammed the bathroom door on her way out.

***

What in the world had just happened? Zane stood frozen, trying to figure it out. She dried and slipped on her robe. Jaina wasn't in the master bedroom so she padded down the hall. She turned the knob...very, very slowly. As upset as Jaina had been, Zane didn't want to set her off. She gave the guest room door a nudge and peeked inside. No Jaina. Zane poked her head around the corner to look down the stairs. Dark and quiet. Jaina was nowhere in sight. Zane was almost afraid to look out to the driveway, but she did. The Echo was gone.

Jaina was an adult woman, usually perfectly capable of taking care of herself, but not tonight. Worry had Zane by the throat and she grabbed the phone to dial. Jaina didn't pick up. She dialed her mom. Not there. Zane made calls until she'd exhausted the short list of local people that Jaina knew well enough to drop in on at this late hour. It was the middle of the night. For God's sake, where could her wife have gone? Zane sat down on the second stair. She laid her head into her palms as her imagination went wild. Surely Jaina wouldn't head back to Florida. Zane wouldn't have thought so, but Jaina had been so irrational lately—especially since Jim's discharge from the hospital. God, what was wrong? She asked the question in her mind, but in her heart, she knew. She'd felt it between them for sometime. Zane dressed and headed for the Thunderbird.

***

It took the old girl quite a while to warm up on that cold January night. Zane's teeth chattered as she took a second lap around nowhere in particular. It's hard to go after someone when you have no idea where they've gone. Then, out of the fog, Zane just knew. The Thunderbird rolled across town, parked next to the Echo, and Zane went inside.

Zane stepped quietly into the darkened sanctuary. She could see Jaina's profile toward the front—in her pew. Zane sighed relief but didn't move or say a word. It wasn't long before Jaina sensed her presence.

"You can join me if you want," Jaina said softly. "I'm glad you're here."

Zane walked down and slid in beside her wife.

"I'm not going to blame what happened on my hormones," Jaina said. "That was part of it, but there's more."

"I know," Zane said softly.

Jaina met her gaze. Her eyes were swollen. "And it wasn't anything you did or said tonight."

Zane slipped her arm around Jaina and pulled her close. "I know that, too."

Jaina swallowed. "You're perfect—more perfect than I deserve."

Zane gave Jaina a squeeze, trying to pull her closer. "No one's perfect, Jaina, except God." She planted a slow, loving kiss on her wife's temple. "I'm certainly not, and I don't expect perfection from you either."

"But I'm so ashamed…about the things that I've done," Jaina whispered through tears. "The Friday nights…"

Zane kissed Jaina's temple. "I know."

Minutes passed in silence.

"And…" Jaina covered her face with her hands. "Zane, I'm so sorry."

"I know you are," Zane said as she kissed her wife again.

Again, they sat in silence.

"Do you want to tell me what happened?" Zane asked softly. "On the night that I brought Jim into our home?"

Jaina lifted her eyes. How could Zane have known? She hadn't had the courage to say a word. She wasn't sure she'd have found the courage tonight had Zane not asked her about it. Jaina lowered her eyes and weeped as she shared the details. When she'd finished, she looked to Zane. She almost looked relieved.

Again, they sat in silence.

Eventually, Zane spoke. Her voice was calm. "We all make mistakes. And we all need to forgive others, but more importantly, ourselves.

"You're not angry," Jaina said. "That I almost slept with someone else?"

Zane's smile was tender. "But you didn't." Her lips met Jaina's. "You were tempted, and in the end, you did the right thing. I'm very proud of you, so proud that you're my wife."

***

So they settled into their routine and waited. The period was missed. The stick turned blue. They made the appointment. Finally, the day arrived.

"Have you seen my other sock?" Zane asked as she dangled a lone blue argyle between two fingers. "The one like this one."

Jaina poked her head out of the bathroom. "Probably behind the clothes basket. You've got a bad habit of that."

Zane checked the suggested location. "Oops, sorry. Guess I'll wear the solids."

By the time Zane got to shoes, Jaina had come out, dressed and ready. She met Zane's gaze.

"Seems like today should be my birthday or something," Zane said as she struggled to suppress a grin.

Jaina furled her brow in confusion.

Zane cocked her head and raised the ornery eyebrow. "It'd make sense, wouldn't it? You gave me your last pelvic exam for Christmas."

Jaina couldn't help but laugh. "Sometimes, Pastor Winslow, you are just plain bad."

***

Jaina lay back on the exam table and tried to get comfortable. Zane stood by her side.

"Ready?" the obstetrician asked.

Jaina nodded and the doctor inserted a cool lubricated wand. She gasped.

Zane stroked her hair and looked into Jaina's eyes.

"I'm okay, baby," Jaina said. "It just surprised me, that's all."

In moments, the wand was forgotten and their full attention was focused on images being projected beside the bed.

"There it is," the doctor said as she highlighted a tiny area at the center of the screen. "Do you see it?"

Zane and Jaina looked closely and nodded.

"That's your baby's heartbeat," the doctor said with a smile.

Jaina's eyes overflowed with tears. "We're parents."

Zane kissed her forehead. "Yeah, we are."

Epilogue — About Five Years Later

Zane walked out of her office just as Irene was finishing up a call. Irene looked harried. The phone had been ringing off the hook all morning.

"That's right," Irene said, "the Adoption Resource and Counseling Center is located in the rear of our building. No, Mrs. Winslow won't be back until tomorrow. Maybe one of her staff could assist you…alright, please hold." Irene transferred the call and looked up. "They've been extra busy this morning. I can't seem to get anything else done."

"That's exactly what Jaina thought would happen if she took the day off," Zane said as she handed Irene her sermon for that next Sunday. "But nothing could've stopped her from spending the day with Bonnie Kate. It's their birthday, after all."

Irene paused her multi-tasking to look up. "I'll bet they had big plans."

Zane sat down on the corner of Irene's desk. "Yeah, big plans—lunch at McDonald's and then on down to Tuscola to visit Jaina's mom in the new assisted living facility. The first one Jaina found wasn't a good fit."

Irene smiled. "Jaina really turned that situation with her mom around, didn't she?"

Zane nodded with pride. "I think she realized that what her mom needed most was a little love and a second chance. She forgave her and they moved on."

"It's kind of sad though," Irene said, "isn't it? Just when things seemed to be looking up for Ms. Grayson, her health began to decline."

Zane nodded. "It is sad. All her years of living on the edge just caught up." She looked away. "Our choices in life do have consequences, good and bad."

***

Zane walked back into her office and sat down in her chair. As was often the case, she swiveled and allowed her eyes to drift out the window onto the church grounds. The trees had already started to show their color and it made her smile. She loved this time of year, probably because it represented all that she held most dear. At the top of the list was Jaina and their beautiful daughter.

Irene appeared at the door. "I think that's wonderful. She'll only be little once and four is such a fun age." She smiled. "You should go home. Spend the rest of the day with your family."

Zane swiveled back to face her. "Oh, I plan to. I just have a couple more things to get done and then I'm out of here."

Irene eventually left and Zane put herself back on task. She didn't stay there long before the phone on the corner of her desk rang. Zane looked up, snapped her pencil, and answered in frustration.

"I'm sorry," Irene apologized. "I thought you'd want this call. It's Drew."

Zane leaned back. "I'm the one who's sorry, and I do. Go ahead and put her through."

***

It had been almost impossible, but Zane managed to get away on time. She dropped in the Thunderbird, rolled down the top, and rumbled off. With any luck, the cake would be ready, the jeweler stop would be quick, and she'd be home on schedule. Since her daughter had learned to tell time, she was quick to notice such things. Jaina probably was too. She just kept quiet.

Zane smiled as she rounded their corner. She was home early, even if by only 15 minutes. To BK, early was all that mattered. To Zane, it was making BK happy. For some reason, she glanced toward the living room picture window and caught a glimpse of their little girl standing behind the curtain. She was cute as a button, waiting with her tiny nose pressed tightly against the glass. Zane swallowed and tried to hold back a sob. It just hit her out of nowhere. Had fate twisted in a different direction, she might have missed it all. She slowed to give herself time to regain composure. Zane didn't want her daughter to see her cry and certainly not on her birthday.

***

"Mama's home," the little blue-eyed girl squealed at the top of her lungs. "Mommy, Mama's home." She ran into the laundry room and back to the window. "I see our car."

Jaina emptied her third basket into the washer and joined her daughter at the door. "I know, sweetie. She's home early, huh." They watched Zane get out of the car and come up the walk. Jaina smiled. She loved her wife so much and couldn't be happier with their life together.

Zane got to the middle step and listened for a creak.

BK giggled. She knew it was coming. Her mama did it everytime.

As Zane reached the top step, the front door flew open, and BK jumped into her arms. Jaina stood in the door, a smile on her face and a sparkle in her eye. She couldn't have held their daughter back had she'd tried.

"Mama, you're home early," the cutie said. "Did you remember? It's me and Mommy's birthday."

Zane raised an eyebrow. "Of course, I remembered. How could I forget such an important day?"

BK giggled at her mama's silly expression.

Zane set her daughter down and kissed her wife.

BK tugged at the left leg of Zane's trousers.

Zane smiled, squatted down, and looked her in the eye.

"We get to have birthday cake when everybody gets here," BK said. She put her tiny hands on her hips like Jaina. "And I get to open my birthday gifts."

Zane's smile was wide. "That you do, my little one. It'll be fun, right?"

***

The youngest birthday girl ran with each ring of the doorbell. One by one, she greeted the guests and showed them to the parlor. When all had gathered, BK announced the menu. It was all her favorites—hot dogs, potato chips, and chocolate cake.

Drew chuckled and met Zane's gaze. "Boy, has that ever changed."

Zane raised an eyebrow and gave her the eye. "I wouldn't talk. Four years from now..." Zane smiled and shook her head. "My guess is, you'll have a few changes at your house too." She scrunched her brow to tally. "Let's see...that'll make Bryson about 12." She grinned. "Oh yeah, there'll be some massive changes at your house."

Drew chuckled. "And every single one worth any adjustment that we have to make. His adoption is the best thing we've ever done in our lives."

"Yeah," Zane said. "There's nothing quite like having a child of your own." Her eyes drifted toward their kids. In spite of their age difference, the two played well together. They played like cousins.

Zane looked across the room and caught Jaina's eye. She smiled and nodded toward their little girl. BK was having so much fun. The day had shaped up to be just her kind. Her house was filled with company, junk food was on the menu, and she had someone closer to her own age to play with. The pile of packages in the middle of the room was just a bonus.

Zane motioned toward the door with her head. Jaina acknowledged and the parents quietly slipped away. When they returned, the pink bicycle that their daughter had requested rolled between them.

BK looked up with delight in her eyes.

"Happy birthday, sweetie," Zane and Jaina said as their cutie climbed up onto the banana seat. It was the training wheels that balanced her, but it didn't matter. She squealed with joy simply because she was able to remain upright.

"Can Uncle Jim take me and Bryson outside?" BK begged. "Please!"

Jaina nodded with a smile, then met her brother's eye. "Only on the sidewalk."

Jim nodded his acknowledgement and picked up the bike. "Come on, parsnip. Let's take it for a ride."

***

Birthday cake was about to be served by the time the curly-haired girl and her brand new bike made it back inside. Jaina watched her daughter sneak out of the room. She smiled when she returned dragging the old black case that was stored in the back of the master bedroom closet.

Zane looked up in surprise as the dusty item bumped her foot.

"Here, Mama," BK said. "I want you to play 'Happy Birthday' for me and Mommy."

Zane looked around and then leaned over to whisper in her daughter's ear. "Mama's shy." She kissed her little cheek. "She doesn't play her sax in front of people."

"Pleeeese," BK begged. She flashed the smile that always worked and pleaded with her eyes.

Jaina watched in amusement. She leaned to Stacey. "Watch this. She'll play. Our daughter has her mama wrapped around her little finger."

"Okay, okay," Zane said. "But if I play, you have to play, too." She looked toward Zaney and her mom. "I know that's one of the songs that Grandma Z taught you."

BK grinned and climbed onto the piano bench. "Okay…I'll play."

Zane unbuckled the old case. Her sax looked as good as it did the day she graduated. She met Jim's gaze. He'd watched her march in the band and heard her play—before that day. She propped one foot onto the piano bench and BK positioned her fingers on the keys. Together, the mama-daughter duo played "Happy Birthday."

BK slid off the bench, winked at her Grandma Z, and took a bow. She put her hands on her hips. "Anybody want to know what I asked Santa to bring me for Christmas?"

The gathering nodded and said they did.

BK grinned and continued. "A big brother…like Bryson." She giggled and ran to jump into her mama's lap.

Jaina watched her from across the room. She watched her flash that smile. She watched her bat those eyes. The piano wasn't the only instrument her daughter was mastering.

Zane kissed the top of BK's head as her eyes searched out and locked on Jaina.

***

The birthday party had become a tradition. Most years, most everyone came. This year, they had quite the full house. In fact, all the significant people were present, except for Miss Bonnie. She was floating somewhere in the Caribbean. It was her second cruise of the year. Zane wondered if her ongoing and what appeared to be quite desperate search for a boyfriend would ever end successfully. Recently, she'd added Miss Bonnie and the boyfriend acquisition to her prayers.

Soul Mates

Jaina set the punch bowl down into its box and folded the top.

Zane carried it to the garage. "Okay, that should be the last of it until next year." She shut off the lights and followed Jaina up the stairs.

They paused, as they did each night, outside what used to be their smaller guest room door. Zane gently nudged it open so they could peek inside the dark, but not too dark room.

"She's so cute," Zane whispered. "Look, she's all curled up with her little hands under her chin."

"Yeah, she's our baby," Jaina said with a smile. "And man, was she ever tired tonight. She was out like a light before we finished her favorite story." She tilted her head and met Zane's gaze. "I know what you're thinking."

Zane nudged the door another inch.

"Don't do it," Jaina said. "You wake her now and we'll be up way past midnight trying to get her back to sleep."

Zane fake pouted. "Okay." She raised an eyebrow. "But I hope you're not tired." She grinned her Friday night grin. "Because I've got lots of energy."

***

Zane propped up on a second pillow to watch her wife undress. Jaina noticed her and smiled. She loved that after five years, umpteen wrinkles, and a dozen stretch marks, Zane still found her sexy. Some days, she even felt like she was. Others, she felt every single one of her 41 years. She felt tired. Jaina dropped her nightgown over her head and padded to the bathroom.

273

"You're beautiful," Zane said as she gazed at her wife in the bathroom mirror. Jaina dipped a finger full of anti-aging cream from the jar and wiped a glob of it on each cheek and her nose. "And maybe," Zane said with a chuckle, "you will be again, once you get all your goop rubbed in." She turned back the covers on Jaina's side. "Now come on, finish up and come to bed."

Jaina screwed the top back on the jar, rubbed in the remaining smudge, and did. She slipped under the covers. "Good party. I think everyone had fun."

"Yeah, it was," Zane said as her eyes met Jaina's, "except for the command performance." She shook her head and smiled. "Can you believe she did that? I didn't even know she knew where that thing was."

"Of course I can," Jaina said. "She's proud of you. Plus, she likes to hear you play."

Zane leaned back. "I guess." She pulled Jaina close and planted a soft kiss on her forehead. "What'd you think of her Christmas list?"

Jaina rolled over to fully face her wife. "Uh-huh, I thought that might be tonight's bedtime topic of conversation." She kissed Zane's nose. "Our daughter has you so wrapped around her little finger."

Zane chuckled. "Yeah, I guess she does." The room fell silent.

Jaina swallowed. Her voice was soft. "I think trying to have another baby at my age would be pretty risky."

Zane ran her fingers over the slick silk. "Then maybe we should adopt." She smiled. "See, we've got this adoption agency in the back of the church." Her eyes twinkled. "And the director and I, well, we have a rather close working relationship."

Jaina nudged Zane's hand underneath her gown. "You do, huh?"

"Yeah," Zane said as her fingertips traced the curve of Jaina's ample breasts. "Plus, it was the only thing our little sweetie wanted for Christmas this year." Zane's fingers moved lower and found the spot.

"Oh yeah," Jaina murmured as her breathing quickened. "She really went easy on us."

About the Author

KA Moll was born and raised in snowy central Illinois. The change of seasons touches her soul. She holds a Bachelor's Degree in Psychology and a Master's Degree in Social Work from the University of Illinois. In addition, she holds a Master's Degree in Counseling from Eastern Illinois University. She is a young retiree from state child protective services, where she supervised investigations of child abuse and neglect.

KA and her wife have been together for just under thirty years and counting. Their marriage is the wind beneath her wings. She enjoys golf, bridge, and of course–reading and writing lesbian fiction.

KA can be contacted at kamollwrites@gmail.com
Website: www.kamollwrites.com
Twitter: @ka_moll
Facebook: KA Moll

Other Titles Available From
Triplicity Publishing

Coming to Terms by KA Moll. Coming to Terms is a love story—and so much more. Sawyer James is a cop. It's who she is and all she ever wanted to be. The job is all she has. To move forward into a fulfilling relationship, Sawyer must come to terms. Sage Carson is a clinical social worker. She's divorced and alone. To move forward, to not spend her life alone, Sage must come to terms—with her own sexuality and with Sawyer. In their struggle—to love—to forgive—to survive—Sage and Sawyer risk everything. But is everything enough?

Second Chance by Sydney Canyon. After an attack on her convoy, Marine Corps Staff Sergeant, Darien Hollister, must learn to live without her sight. When an experimental procedure allows her to see again, opening up the possibility for her to go back to the career that is deeply ingrained in her, Darien is torn, knowing someone had to die in order for this to happen. She embarks on a journey to personally thank the donor's family, but is too stunned to tell them the truth. When the truth finally comes out, Darien walks away, taking the second chance that she's been given to go back to the only life she's ever known, but she's not the only one with a second chance at life.

Twin Bridges by Tina Kunkle. Hadley Jameson had it all in New York City, top detective in her precinct, someone to love, and a beautiful brownstone on the East side. Life as she knew it was good, but then, in a matter of seconds, it all changed and the Big Apple she once loved, became the place she could no longer stand to be in. Landing a job as Sheriff in Twin Bridges was exactly what she needed. When steer start turning up mutilated, the investigation leads her to Dakota, the beautiful and spirited veterinarian and the careful wall that Hadley had built around her heart was in jeopardy of being taken down, one brick at a time.

The Half-breed & Soiled Dove by Tina Kunkle. In 1866, spring arrived early for the small town of Spindle Top, Texas, and twenty-two year old Johanna O'Riley wasn't at all prepared for what it brought with it. One fateful morning, the tranquility and peacefulness was shattered by the loud sounds of gunshots and her Ma's horrific screams. In her blood soaked dress she laid her entire family to rest. The anger inside her grew with each and every shovel of dirt she threw on them. When Johanna finished, she stood on that hill top over-looking the three freshly dug graves and vowed to get revenge on the outlaws who took her family from her. She was willing to do anything to keep it, including dressing as a man to get it done, but the one thing she didn't count on, was the beautiful Isabella entering her life.

Meant to Be by Graysen Morgen. Brandt is about to walk down the aisle with her girlfriend, when an unexpected chain of events turns her world upside down, causing her to question the last three years of her life. A chance encounter sparks a mix of rage and excitement that she has never felt before. Summer is living life and following her dreams, all the while, harboring a huge secret that could ruin her career. She believes that some things are better kept in the dark, until she has her third run-in with a woman she had hoped to never see again, and gives into temptation. Brandt and Summer start believing everything happens for a reason as they learn the true meaning of meant to be.

Coming Home by Graysen Morgen. After tragedy derails TJ Abernathy's life, she packs up her three year old son and heads back to Pennsylvania to live with her grandmother on the family farm. TJ picks back up where she left off eight years earlier, tending to the fruit and nut tree orchard, while learning her grandmother's secret trade. Soon, TJ's high school sweetheart and the same girl who broke her heart, comes back into her life, threatening to steal it away once again. As the weeks turn into months and tragedy strikes again, TJ realizes coming home was the best thing she could've ever done.

Special Assignment by Austen Thorne. Secret Service Agent Parker Meeks has her hands full when she gets her new assignment, protecting a Congressman's teenage daughter, who has had threats made on her life and been whisked away to a Christian boarding school under an alias to finish out her senior year. Parker is fine with the assignment, until she finds out she has to go undercover as a Canon Priest. The last thing Parker expects to find is a beautiful, art history teacher, who is intrigued by her in more ways than one.

Miracle at Christmas by Sydney Canyon. A Modern Twist on the Classic Scrooge Story. Dylan is a power-hungry lawyer who pushed away everything good in her life to become the best defense attorney in the, often winning the worst cases and keeping anyone with enough money out of jail. She's visited on Christmas Eve by her deceased law partner, who threatens her with a life in hell like his own, if she doesn't change her path. During the course of the night, she is taken on a journey through her past, present, and future with three very different spirits.

Bella Vita by Sydney Canyon. Brady is the First Officer of the crew on the Bella Vita, a luxury charter yacht in the Caribbean. She enjoys the laidback island lifestyle, and is accustomed to high profile guests, but when a U.S. Senator charters the yacht as a gift to his beautiful twin daughters who have just graduated from college and a few of their friends, she literally has her hands full.

Brides (Bridal Series book 2) by Graysen Morgen. Britton Prescott is dating the love of her life, Daphne Attwood, after a few tumultuous events that happened to unravel at her sister's wedding reception, seven months earlier. She's happy with the way things are, but immense pressure from her family and friends to take the next step, nearly sends her back to the single life. The idea of a long engagement and simple wedding are thrown out the window, as both families take over, rushing Britton and Daphne to the altar in a matter of weeks.

Cypress Lake by Graysen Morgen. The small town of Cypress Lake is rocked when one murder after another happens. Dani Ricketts, the Chief Deputy for the Cypress Lake Sheriff's Office, realizes the murders are linked. She's surprised when the girl that broke her heart in high school has not only returned home, but she's also Dani's only suspect. Kristen Malone has come back to Cypress Lake to put the past behind her so that she can move on with her life. Seeing Dani Ricketts again throws her off-guard, nearly derailing her plans to finally rid herself and her family of Cypress Lake.

Crashing Waves by Graysen Morgen. After a tragic accident, Pro Surfer, Rory Eden, spends her days hiding in the surf and snowboard manufacturing company that she built from the ground up, while living her life as a shell of the person that she once was. Rory's world is turned upside when a young surfer pursues her, asking for the one thing she can't do. Adler Troy and Dr. Cason Macauley from Graysen Morgen's bestselling novel: *Falling Snow*, make an appearance in this romantic adventure about life, love, and letting go.

Bridesmaid of Honor (Bridal Series book 1) by Graysen Morgen. Britton Prescott's best friend is getting married and she's the maid of honor. As if that isn't enough to deal with, Britton's sister announces she's getting married in the same month and her maid of honor is her best friend Daphne, the same woman who has tormented Britton for years. Britton has to suck it up and play nice, instead of scratching her eyes out, because she and Daphne are in both weddings. Everyone is counting on them to behave like adults.

Falling Snow by Graysen Morgen. Dr. Cason Macauley, a high-speed trauma surgeon from Denver meets Adler Troy, a professional snowboarder and sparks fly. The last thing Cason wants is a relationship and Adler doesn't realize what's right in front of her until it's gone, but will it be too late?

Fate vs. Destiny by Graysen Morgen. Logan Greer devotes her life to investigating plane crashes for the National Transportation Safety Board. Brooke McCabe is an investigator with the Federal Aviation Association who literally flies by the seat of her pants. When Logan gets tangled in head games with both women will she choose fate or destiny?

Just Me by Graysen Morgen. Wild child Ian Wiley has to grow up and take the reins of the hundred year old family business when tragedy strikes. Cassidy Harland is a little surprised that she came within an inch of picking up a gorgeous stranger in a bar and is shocked to find out that stranger is the new head of her company.

Love Loss Revenge by Graysen Morgen. Rian Casey is an FBI Agent working the biggest case of her career and madly in love with her girlfriend. Her world is turned upside when tragedy strikes. Heartbroken, she tries to rebuild her life. When she discovers the truth behind what really happened that awful night she decides justice isn't good enough, and vows revenge on everyone involved.

Natural Instinct by Graysen Morgen. Chandler Scott is a Marine Biologist who keeps her private life private. Corey Joslen is intrigued by Chandler from the moment she meets her. Chandler is forced to finally open her life up to Corey. It backfires in Corey's face and sends her running. Will either woman learn to trust her natural instinct?

Secluded Heart by Graysen Morgen. Chase Leery is an overworked cardiac surgeon with a group of best friends that have an opinion and a reason for everything. When she meets a new artist named Remy Sheridan at her best friend's art gallery she is captivated by the reclusive woman. When Chase finds out why Remy is so sheltered will she put her career on the line to help her or is it too difficult to love someone with a secluded heart?

In Love, at War by Graysen Morgen. Charley Hayes is in the Army Air Force and stationed at Ford Island in Pearl Harbor. She is the commanding officer of her own female-only service squadron and doing the one thing she loves most, repairing airplanes. Life is good for Charley, until the day she finds herself falling in love while fighting for her life as her country is thrown haphazardly into World War II. Can she survive being in love and at war?

Fast Pitch by Graysen Morgen. Graham Cahill is a senior in college and the catcher and captain of the softball team. Despite being an all-star pitcher, Bailey Michaels is young and arrogant. Graham and Bailey are forced to get to know each other off the field in order to learn to work together on the field. Will the extra time pay off or will it drive a nail through the team?

Submerged by Graysen Morgen. Assistant District Attorney Layne Carmichael had no idea that the sexy woman she took home from a local bar for a one night stand would turn out to be someone she would be prosecuting months later. Scooter is a Naval Officer on a submarine who changes women like she changes uniforms. When she is accused of a heinous crime she is

283

shocked to see her latest conquest sitting across from her as the prosecuting attorney.

Vow of Solitude by Austen Thorne. Detective Jordan Denali is in a fight for her life against the ghosts from her past and a Serial Killer taunting her with his every move. She lives a life of solitude and plans to keep it that way. When Callie Marceau, a curious Medical Examiner, decides she wants in on the biggest case of her career, as well as, Jordan's life, Jordan is powerless to stop her.

Igniting Temptation by Sydney Canyon. Mackenzie Trotter is the Head of Pediatrics at the local hospital. Her life takes a rather unexpected turn when she meets a flirtatious, beautiful fire fighter. Both women soon discover it doesn't take much to ignite temptation.

One Night by Sydney Canyon. While on a business trip, Caylen Jarrett spends an amazing night with a beautiful stripper. Months later, she is shocked and confused when that same woman re-enters her life. The fact that this stranger could destroy her career doesn't bother her. C.J. is more terrified of the feelings this woman stirs in her. Could she have fallen in love in one night and not even known it?

Fine by Sydney Canyon. Collin Anderson hides behind a façade, pretending everything is fine. Her workaholic wife and best friend are both oblivious as she goes on an emotional journey, battling a potentially hereditary disease that her mother has been diagnosed with. The only person who knows what is really going on, is Collin's doctor. The same doctor, who is an acquaintance that she's always been attracted to, and who has a partner of her own.

Shadow's Eyes by Sydney Canyon. Tyler McCain is the owner of a large ranch that breeds and sells different types of horses. She isn't exactly thrilled when a Hollywood movie producer shows up wanting to film his latest movie on her property. Reegan Delsol is an up and coming actress who has everything going for her when she lands the lead role in a new film, but there one small problem that could blow the entire picture.

Light Reading: A Collection of Novellas by Sydney Canyon. Four of Sydney Canyon's novellas together in one book, including the bestsellers Shadow's Eyes and One Night.

Visit us at www.tri-pub.com

CPSIA information can be obtained at www.ICGtesting.com
Printed in the USA
LVOW07s1000210615

443285LV00001B/93/P